BROKEN COLORS

ALSO BY

MICHELE ZACKHEIM

Fiction
Violette's Embrace

Non-fiction
Einstein's Daughter: The Search for Lieserl

Michele Zackheim

BROKEN COLORS

Europa
editions

Europa Editions
116 East 16th Street
New York, N.Y. 10003
www.europaeditions.com
info@europaeditions.com

Library of Congress Cataloging in Publication Data is available
ISBN 978-1-933372-37-2

Zackheim, Michele
Broken Colors

Book design by Emanuele Ragnisco
www.mekkanografici.com

Printed in Canada

CONTENTS

BROKEN COLORS

For Jack Simon Zackheim

In beginning a picture,
he could never say how it would come out.

—ÉMILE ZOLA ON ÉDOUARD MANET

Sophie Marks never knew her parents. They both slid into their shallow graves at the end of the First World War, her mother working as a doctor in the Balkans, her father as a mapmaker, sent to Africa to chart an alien land. A battered and cracked sepia photograph was the only real likeness she had of them. They are holding Sophie when she is still wrapped in swaddling clothes. Her mother is tall and thin; at least she appears tall, standing next to the outdoor table under the apple tree. She has dark hair, cut in a sensible fashion, no frills. There is no evident sensuality. Staring straight on, into the camera lens, she is apparently cool and unafraid. On the other hand, Sophie's father is blurred, having turned his head ever so slightly. That could have been why Sophie's impression of him was always as a romantic, a dreamer, a vague man wandering along the hazy edges of her mother's rationality. "You can just see their personalities," Sophie's grandmother, Claire, declared. But Sophie used to wonder how people could make that claim. In a photograph, could you really see a person's self in his or her eyes? Could one detect wickedness in the eyes of villains? Later, with photographs of Hitler, she honestly could not say that she sensed evil in his heart from looking at his eyes.

It was before the Second World War, before the displacement, before the dark curtain was pulled across the sun. Sophie lived in England, far into the core of the country—the Midlands. Her surrogate parents were her father's parents. Her grandfather, who had always insisted Sophie call him by his first name, Eli, made a living as a potter, but his true vocation was painting. His canvases were portraits of anyone who would sit for him, from the village drunkard to the tea-shop lady to the local constable.

"You have to learn to read faces," he told Sophie over and over again. "People's faces are etched with their life stories. Then it's up to you, the painter, to translate their stories onto the canvas as a visual language."

Eli's painting technique had been developed and refined over his lifetime. He painted with a thick impasto, using a palette knife more often than a paintbrush—yet he allowed glimpses here and there of a delicately stained linen. Wide ranges of ochre and raw umber and burnt sienna were his primary grounds, along with the deep tones of Hooker's green, cerulean blue, Indian red. His signature gesture was to outline the portraits roughly in lampblack, creating a shadow that brought the faces in the portraits forward, as if they had something to say to the viewer. He imbued his work with deep-colored emotions that swirled from passion to despair, always leaving the viewer with a promise of redemption. Not only were his canvases pictures of people; his paintings also reflected his beloved wooded landscape. Indeed, Eli used to say, "My palette is borrowed from the people and this forest around me. Because it's on loan, I must respect it, utterly. Each time I make a painting, I try to honor the agreement."

Sophie grew up amidst his portraits and landscapes. Local people would walk up the road, passing the crumbling garden wall with the deep-pink, single-blossom hollyhocks peeping over it. They would be carrying a couple of chickens, the mail, a basket of eggs, a newspaper, on their way to Eli's studio to be immortalized in paint. This was nothing unusual to Sophie. The country people were self-sufficient, great moralists, and they minded their own business. Sitting for Eli was, in a way, how they paid their respects to him.

While a painting was in process, Eli would hang it somewhere in the house. Sophie not only lived with painted faces staring at her while she ate, or read in the sitting room, she on occasion slept with them.

"I'd be interested to know what you think of Mrs. Ramsben," her grandfather once said as he placed dear Mrs. Ramsben on the wall facing Sophie's bed. "When you open your eyes in the morning's light, you'll see her in the purest way possible. You must report to me your impressions." And come morning, Sophie woke and looked at Mrs. Ramsben with an open heart and unveiled eyes.

"She looks kind, Eli," Sophie reported.

"Good," he replied, "that's the look I wanted to capture. But sometimes," he cautioned, "a sitter isn't a particularly nice person. Sometimes your subject does indeed have a callous look, a hungry look, a look of disappointment at what has happened to her or his dreams. As an artist, you've a responsibility to be honest with your perceptions." With this advice Sophie learned not only to see a painting but to feel it. His teaching simply became a part of her person.

As soon as Sophie could hold a pencil, she was drawing; as soon as she understood paintbrushes, she was painting with watercolors. And as soon as she understood not to put brushes filled with paint in her mouth, she was painting with oils. Many an hour she sat and worked alongside her grandfather. He had taken an old drawing table and sawed off the legs to fit Sophie's height. Sometimes she would work from his models; other times he would set up a still life for her; sometimes she would look out the window and paint the garden. On occasion she would copy him. Eli did nothing to discourage her. Painting became second nature. "You have an artist's eye; it's good work, Sophie." Once, when she had painted a skyscape, he said, "You certainly have an eye for a Turner sky," and she giggled at his rhyme.

Eli was a man of medium height, neither fat nor thin, but knotted in the joints. He thought it humorous when he had trouble getting the kinks out. "My body reminds me of a bag of twigs and stones; smoothed by the rain and wind, rattling against each other, getting stuck, coming apart." He had an unusually large and handsome head, almost out of proportion to his body, and covered with thick, white, wild hair. His nose was narrow and long, and the older he got the longer it became, nearly touching his upper lip. Once he reached seventy, he had to shave off his mustache because it made the tip of his nose itch. He had a voice stirred with gravel; it could fluctuate from a lyrical note to a growl, and back again. Sophie loved to hear him sing arias from operas, lullabies, and, after 1923, catchy tunes from the radio. In the studio he would hum all day long and then complain that he did not know why his throat was so dry.

He always dressed in the same style of clothes: a tan workman's shirt without a collar, dark-brown corduroy trousers, and in the winter a brown tweed waistcoat with specks of green, and brown leather buttons. And at all times draped from one pocket of his trousers was a gold watch chain, attached to the burnished gold timepiece given to him by his father.

When Sophie was about five years old, her grandfather took a map of England and spread it out on his worktable. With a ruler, he drew an equal-sided box around the country, and although his table was potholed with old and dried paint, he managed to find the center of the drawn box. He wanted to prove to Sophie that where the lines intersected in the middle was where they lived. He showed her that they were halfway between the towns of Stoke-on-Trent and Stone, and but a few feet, her grandfather promised, from the center of the world. She later understood he was trying to show her how important she was to him; even though she had been orphaned, she had not been abandoned.

They lived within the patina of a Constable painting: terre verte, amber and sorrel browns, yellow ochre; always a stroke of sky, a translucent cobalt blue. Generations earlier, it had been an area where, from the knolls, one would see only bleak valleys with black coal smoke billowing, valleys scarred by huge ovens where bricks were made. When Sophie was little, there were still the same imposing nineteenth-century soot-blackened stone churches and buildings. "But listen, Sophie," her grandmother said, "I'll read you the other side of the mountain." And when Sophie was eight years old, by the light of a gas lamp, Claire, each night for many months, read *Anna of the Five Towns*. "Listen to the color," she would remind Sophie. "Listen to Arnold Bennett write about our home."

In front, on a little hill in the vast valley, was spread out the Indian-red architecture . . . tall chimneys and rounded ovens, schools, the new scarlet market . . . the crimson chapels, and rows of little red houses with amber chimney pots, and the gold angel of the Town Hall topping the whole. The sedate reddish browns and reds of the composition all netted in flowing scarves of smoke, harmonised exquisitely with the chill blues of the che-quered sky . . .

The region was the home of the Staffordshire ceramic factories, and the district where Josiah Spode and Josiah Wedgwood were born. In 1715 Wedgwood established a factory, having fine clay brought all the way from Cornwall and Devon. The soil in the Stoke-on-Trent area was more sandy and gravelly than one would expect; it was wonderful for gardens and rough terra-cotta pots, but not for fine pottery.

Their house, called Pottery Cottage ever since it was built in 1803, was balanced between two small, mottled-gray, rocky hills. Sophie's grandmother was a poet. She used to marvel why anyone would build a house of brick between the two jutting breasts of a woman. Eli would reply (each and every time), "Two breasts, my eye. A mule's ass with a bucket between its back legs, that's what it is!" Sophie always thought her grandfather correct, for the basement of that old house filled annually with water, causing great grief and a lot of work. Adding to the upkeep was the perennial problem of the ivy-choked chimneys, which forever had to be cleared; the dampness of the spot encouraged ivy to grow faster than the clover in the fields. Once a year, her grandfather would climb a shaky ladder onto the roof. With a tool he made from pieces of wire, he reamed out the soot.

But it was the birds Sophie would remember most. Especially the nightingale. She never knew a day when she did not hear its song. When she was small, she was convinced that the nightingale sang for only the three people in her family. Her grandmother often quoted a passage from Shakespeare when Sophie was being put to bed and they heard the nightingale. *Wilt thou be gone? It is not yet near day. / It was the nightingale, and not the lark / That pierc'd the fearful hollow of thine ear. / Nightly she sings on yon pomegranate tree. / Believe me, love, it was the nightingale.*

Claire adored caring for her chickens. Her family often challenged her by saying it was an obsession, but she did not mind, and blithely carried on. She always had at least a dozen Dorking hens, which had five toes instead of the normal four, and a few sweet-tempered Buff Orpingtons, most of whom were good layers of tawny-colored eggs. Claire had a number of customers from the nearby village and was quite serious about providing them with the best eggs in the district. Each summer she entered her eggs in the competition at the village fair. Sophie remembered standing before the egg display and seeing her grandmother's three raw eggs, poised firmly on a teal-blue ceramic dish made by Eli especially for the competition. Alongside the dishes of her contenders, her eggs shone and never failed to win one of the three prizes. Right before the war she was given a silver cup: **For Lifetime Achievement to Claire Marks, Best Eggs Category.** "Just look at that cup," she would crow. "It makes me want more chickens. You can never tell, Sophie, perhaps I make better eggs than poems!"

Sophie detested the entire chicken operation. The acrid smells. The constant mess. The ghastly mash her grandmother spent so much time making. And the feeding twice a day. Even though Sophie loathed the feeding more than anything, she was often asked to help out in the morning before going to school. "My dear," Claire would excuse herself, "I have a poem in my head." And Sophie would have to boil together bits of bread, potato peelings, and leftover vegetables, mix them with a baler of bran and three balers of meal, and stir it all up into a pulpy mess with her hands.

Then she would put on the dirty blue apron and the old black rubber boots by the back door and go out to the chicken house. Here she placed the metal troughs and then plopped the nauseating feed equally into each one. But Sophie did enjoy gathering the eggs. Reaching into a warm nest and cupping her hand around a found egg was quite gratifying. She never got over the excitement of uncovering a warmed gem and giving it to her grandmother, who always carried on as if it were the first time she had ever seen an egg.

Claire loved pleasing new customers. "I've never, Madam, tasted an egg like your egg," they declared. And she would answer, "Fain would I kiss my Sophie's cheek, which is as ivory and smooth as one of my eggs." This sent Sophie into a flush of embarrassment. But one thing she could say on her grandmother's behalf was that she kept separate aprons for her duties. Always hanging on the hook on the back door was the heavy blue factory apron for the chickens and the lighter-weight red-and-white checkered one for the house. Considering Claire's helter-skelter methods of housekeeping, this was an accomplishment.

Almost every night in front of the fire, Claire would read to Sophie. Sophie relished her grandmother's warmth and the aroma of lavender that was part of her clothing. They would cozy up under the softest afghan, Claire would put on her glasses, and off they would go. Once, Sophie, after hearing a story about an imaginary princess, asked, "Claire, do you ever hear voices inside your head—for instance, having this princess talk to you?"

Claire looked at her with a solemn face and Sophie thought she had said something foolish. "My dear child," Claire said, "of course I have people in my head! What a question! Every artist I know hears special voices; it's part of the profession. Are you trying to tell me that you have voices visiting you?" And Sophie nodded yes.

"Are they good voices or scary ones?"

"Mostly good voices, and sometimes they sing to me."

"Well, that's good to hear, dear," Claire said, patting Sophie's hand. "An artist you're certain to be."

People thought that being the only child of aging grandparents would make Sophie feel responsible for them. On the contrary, she felt she must be old as well, and that they were all three caring for one another. Sophie hung in the margins of her school class, watching her friends as if they were children of a rare and mysterious tribe. They all had such energy. It was hard for them to sit still. She could sit quietly for hours on end, happily entertaining herself by painting or drawing in her grandfather's studio or looking through his art books. When she did have a spurt of energetic activity, she knew instinctively that she should take it outside and run in the pastures across the road or swing as high as she dared from the chestnut tree.

Sophie grew so fast that for a dreadfully long while, her arms dangled almost to her knees. It was a painful time; her entire body ached. And so did her grandparents'. They were shrinking, moving in reverse. Their backs were no longer straight; her grandparents appeared to bend to the wind and stay there, complaining about their aching limbs, their stiff joints, changes in their skin. This would confuse her because her bones also ached and her joints felt as if they were rubbed together like stones in a sack and her skin was the shame of every waking moment. Instead of feeling that she was becoming a grown-up, she felt as if she were meeting her grandparents at the headwaters of the river and floating right along with them out to sea.

Sometimes Sophie could discern surprise in a new student's eyes when her grandparents were introduced as her parents. Neither Claire nor Eli ever made the correction. Sophie knew, although everyone was perfectly pleasant to her, that the others found her odd, disjointed, and aloof. And being the only left-handed student even further distanced her from her peers. "Force yourself to use your right hand," her teachers would warn her. "Otherwise you'll never learn good penmanship, and you'll certainly never be as good an artist as your grandfather."

She was intrigued by her grandparents' hands; she would find herself staring at them, then turn red, feeling she was being impolite. Her grandmother could sit for long hours at her rosewood writing table with the mysterious pigeon holes stuffed with scraps of paper. She would stare out the window and then mark long dashes of spidery words on the violet pages in her cornflower-blue exercise books. As Claire grew older, Sophie noticed that the veins on the top of her hands began to bulge like tiny pebbles moving ever so slowly along the bottom of a stream. Her fingers changed as well. They became slightly twisted, with the top third of each finger angled in a contrary direction. Eli's hands took longer to transform. They were so thickly covered with coarse, dark hair that for a long time Sophie could not see their age. Then she began to notice a deep magenta becoming visible through the hair—what she always thought of as his "fur." At first she supposed he had been using this color on a canvas and it had stained his hands. But it soon became apparent that his hands were changing into ancient tools, and he began to have a difficult time holding onto a paintbrush, or even his cup at teatime.

"Whom do I look like?" Sophie would ask her grandparents. They were too old for her to see herself reflected in their faces, although she tried. "Tell me again about my parents."

"Of course, Sophie, your father was handsome," Eli said.

"Well, my dear, he looked quite like you!" Claire replied, smiling at her husband.

"Your height," Claire continued, "has been passed to you by your mother, but your coloring is quite like your father's. He had dark, almost black hair, and sensitive brown eyes, with the same bronze specks as yours glittering around the edges. Also, he had a pleasant-shaped mouth. I used to tease him about his lips and say they looked like a lovely mauve tulip. He was about an inch shorter than Judith, enough for her to throw away her high-heeled shoes."

"And he had a physique like mine." Eli laughed and showed Sophie his popping arm muscles. "He was especially muscular, and looked more dapper in country clothes than in a suit and tie. But he was not a bully, even though he was so strong. He was the opposite; very quiet, gentle, and vague. You know, kind of dreamy, like you."

"Your mother was very pretty, like you as well, my dear," Claire said. "Thin and a bit gangly. She had fawn-colored, voluptuous hair, which she wore styled like the actress Mrs. Patrick Campbell. Sometimes your mother was glamorous. Sometimes simply pretty. And sometimes there were hints of dangerous storms that swept across her face. A nice woman. She was rather clever, but from another class."

Her name was Judith Rodney and her family was on the verge of the upper stratum—quite High Church, well educated, with many maids. Judith's father, Harrison Rodney, was a well-known surgeon in London, caring for the wealthy on Harley Street. He was always busy, spent his extra time at his club, and was rarely home. Judith's mother, Helen Rodney, was a society lady, prone to nipping Cointreau in the larder, having the vapors, and allowing her child to be raised by the nanny.

"Your mother's parents weren't particularly fond of her choice for a husband. After your parents died, we saw Judith's parents only once. They happened to be passing through and called on us. I think it may have been the only time you met them. But you were still a baby and wouldn't remember.

"But I remember," Claire continued. "How could I forget? They were the opposite of Judith, having quite no curiosity at all. We invited them to see Eli's work, which meant they had to walk down the dirt path to his studio. 'Oh, my dear Mrs. Marks,' Mrs. Rodney said, in a chirrupy voice, 'it's my shoes, you know. Can you believe I'd be so daft as to wear these in the country?' And Mr. Rodney said, 'Yes, my wife can be quite heedless sometimes.' He was trying to protect her. After a cursory, polite look at Eli's work, they barely sat long enough to have a cup of tea, balanced on the edges of their chairs. I thought surely one of them would fall flat on his or her polite face!

"It was a strange state of affairs. When you were two years old, they sent you a card at the Jewish New Year. That was it. The following year Mrs. Rodney died in an automobile accident. I read about it in one of the London newspapers. The reporter appeared to relish the grisly details; about how she had come from a fancy party—and that she had too much to drink—and that she was wearing a Prussian blue satin moiré dress with matching jacket and shoes with rhinestone buckles. All that was missing in the article were the vivid scarlet bloodstains."

Sophie's parents met at the National Gallery in March, 1914. Her artist father, Ethan, had gone there to draw. He was sketching in a gallery that held Velázquez's painting *The Rokeby Venus*. There were a number of people in the room but he was oblivious to them. All of a sudden he heard so many skirts making their swishing and swirling noises that he looked up. There in front of him was a woman with a meat ax in her hand. Everyone stood frozen, as if in a tableau. And then she twirled around and with an expert arm whacked the naked back of the exquisite Venus seven times before being wrestled to the ground by a gallery attendant, a police officer with an energetic billy club, and a female observer.

The ax-wielding woman's name was Mary Richardson. She was protesting the offensive and unfair treatment of the suffragette leader Mrs. Pankhurst. Mrs. Pankhurst had been arrested many times for civil disobedience, as well as for minor acts of destruction that were intended to draw attention to the feminist cause. Mary Richardson was trying to make a point, a shockingly radical one. She was trying to prove that the authorities would react more strongly to a destructive act against property than they would against preventable human suffering—such as child labor or the malicious treatment of women.

One of the women who helped wrestle Mary Richardson to the ground was Sophie's mother, Judith Rodney. She tended to Mary's billy-club injuries with her own torn petticoat.

"My son was horrified by the wanton destruction of a powerful piece of art. On top of which, he had never seen such a physical act of defiance by a woman. But despite his horror, I almost think he would have liked to fall in love with Mary Richardson! But Judith's act was also courageous." She laughed.

"Ethan didn't look back. He courted Judith and tempted her with a life quite unlike anything she had ever experienced. She fell just as hard. They were married in a civil ceremony in Trentham and lived here before going off to be part of that ridiculous war."

Sophie understood why her mother had been entranced. Her grandparents lived a truly bohemian life. Her grandfather's studio, which had once been a barn, always smelled of turpentine and oil paint. To Sophie, this smell was forever an aroma of comfort and safety. Eli used to swear that he could tell one color from another by its smell.

"Here, try this," he encouraged Sophie. And she would smell the lemon yellow he squeezed from the silver tube. "Does it smell like lemon, Sophie, or like sunshine? Go ahead, try."

"I don't smell lemon or sunshine," she complained. But he laughed because of the yellow paint on the tip of her nose. Then he had her smell the cerise that he claimed smelled like cherries, or the ultramarine that he claimed smelled like the sea, beyond the Channel, away from their home.

"Well, most pigments," he finally admitted, "smell the same because they've been mixed with linseed oil. But many of them do indeed have an original scent, such as Indian yellow. I know this color sounds like sunshine, or dry grasses in India, but it isn't. It was originally made by heating the urine of cows that were fed on mango leaves—isn't that something! Then there's Dutch pink, which can be made from sweet-smelling buckthorn berries. Lovely-sounding color, eh? But it can also be made from the bile of oxen!

"Don't forget, my dear, imagination will give you permission to move beyond the tip of your nose. All you have to do is try a bit harder."

And she did try. Her grandparents gave her permission to

move, with all her books and drawing materials, into her mind's eye.

"You have all the time in the world, so don't be afraid to explore," they encouraged.

But Eli was nervous about time. Being responsible for a young girl made him quite conscious of his approaching death. One day he took Sophie to visit a friend, Mr. Witherton, who made bricks for a living. Sophie was fascinated with Mr. Witherton's work area, which was behind the house in an enclosed yard. Red dust, a kind of Indian red with a dash of orange, was everywhere, including all over Mr. Witherton.

The wall was made of brick as well. "Go look closely," her grandfather said.

She was hesitant at first, afraid to go too close since she would be certain to get brick dust all over her pinafore. "Don't be timid, Sophie, it'll all come out in the wash. Go ahead."

"But, careful of them hollyhocks, Miss," Mr. Witherton warned. "They're me wife's favorites."

To get to the wall, Sophie walked over broken bricks, bits of wood used as spacers, and small piles of brick dust mixed with leaves and dirt. What she found was that each brick had a date on it and they were laid out in chronological order. She must have had a puzzled look on her face, for both men laughed.

"Go ahead and tell Sophie the story," Eli said to Mr. Witherton, who was leaning against the opposite wall and waved her over to lean with him.

"I'm afraid of time," Mr. Witherton told her, bending down to her height. "I've been told me fear's all daft, but I don't hold no confidence with these modern ideas."

Mr. Witherton's father was a brick maker, as was his father, and his father as well. Every day their job was to make one brick after another, all the same size, all the same weight, never ending.

"When I was twelve years old and finished with my schoolin'—sixty-six years ago 'twas! I got an idea into me head that if I counted the days, time would go more slowly, and that by buildin' meself into time, I'd be safe from time itself."

For more than a year, he worked to catch up to himself. Averaging twelve to fifteen extra bricks a day, he also made one to include that day's date. Altogether he figured he made four thousand six hundred eighty bricks to catch up with the lost time. Then he settled down to making one brick for each day, again with its date baked into it. For all those years, at the end of each week, he would add another row of seven bricks.

On their way home, Sophie asked her grandfather *why*? "Why, he told you," Eli said. "He told you that he wanted to keep himself safe."

"You mean safe from dying?" Sophie asked.

"Yes, that's the main part of it," he agreed.

"But why?"

"Some people," he said, "are so afraid of dying that they don't live while they're alive. Their fear of death overwhelms their desire for life."

The Marks house was made of the local brick, its roof covered with flat red-clay tiles, mostly turned green with moss. The rooms were as complicated as a rabbit warren, with low ceilings and odd steps leading into various areas with an assortment of angles and heights. One had to be careful not to hit one's head on the slanting beams. Rough-cut and turning black with age and soot, those beams sloped into and heaved out of the rooms, making one slightly seasick if one stared too long.

Claire's study was unique. The walls were painted a dense sea-green, casting watery moirés upon her as she sat and wrote. Sophie always felt as if she were diving into a pond when she entered the room. The other rooms were reds and ochres with thickly painted cabinets and doors. No one had ever bothered to strip the old paint, and the layers had accumulated over the years. "You could determine the history of the house," Eli claimed, "if you revealed each layer of paint, just like a tree."

There were at least two windows in each room, most of them French windows that were meant to open outward. But long ago Eli had reversed their hinges, thinking they looked better opening in—more inviting, as if to welcome nature into the house. The window frames were painted black, and were always in the process of peeling and needing to be painted yet again. In place of real rugs on the wide-planked floors, Eli had painted replicas of Indian blankets and Turkish carpets. Deep crimson reds, ochres, and burnt siennas, along with dashes of Naples yellow and black, would often confuse a new visitor for a moment.

Claire detested the smell of coal, although they were forced to use it to heat the house. During the winter, they tried to overwhelm its unpleasantness by masking the odor with logs of chestnut or oak. They burned these in the tin-hooded fireplaces in the kitchen and the sitting room. The fireplace in the sitting room was set into a deep brick alcove, allowing for two comfortable upholstered chairs, one on either side. As long as Sophie could remember, the two chairs had been covered with a knobby red fabric that "hid the dirt," as Claire claimed. Their backs were covered with dense green and maroon barge-mule blankets. There was also a raised hearth that could be used either as a footstool or as a place on which to keep tea warm. In the main part of the sitting room were two more upholstered chairs and a number of small tables loaded with books, newspapers, and two oil lamps with jade-green glass shades. There were handmade, colorful pillows in every chair, paintings hung one above another on the walls, and dried flowers in clay vases. On the oak table under the windows was a Prussian-blue ceramic jug with honey-yellow cowslips in summer, forsythia in spring, russet-orange oak leaves in autumn, and forest-green fir boughs in winter. There were photographs and picture postcards: pictures of the American desert and the flowering cacti; pictures of the Italian landscape; reproductions of favorite paintings, densely tacked up in any available open space.

Sophie thought the only problem with their house was that it was quite dirty.

"No, it's not dirty," Claire would protest. "It's simply messy. After all, my dear, we are artists, not philistines!"

By the time Sophie was fourteen, she had grown to her full height. Slender and tall as a new and flexible sapling, she had the same heavy hair as her mother, but it was almost black like her father's. Her face was long and narrow, with a small chin, and faint dimples on either side. Dark bronze-brown eyes, with heavy black eyebrows and enviable dark lashes, were her most prominent features. Most of her friends were light-complexioned, with blond hair and blue eyes. I'm more like a monkey, she used to think.

One day Claire insisted that Sophie bring her school friend Anne Vernons home for tea. Although Sophie understood that both her grandparents were anxious about her being alone so much, her chagrin was extreme. She was at a naturally peevish age. Nothing was right. Everyone around her had sharp angles, sticky barbs. She acquiesced only to please her grandparents.

Claire took pains with her appearance for the occasion. Rather than dressing up, she actually dressed down. It was a spring day and still chilly. In the morning, she had worn layers of clothes: a simple, ankle-length, thin grey wool dress, over which was a heavy blue work shirt of Eli's, over which was a long vest of violet wool. To top it all off, she had worn a muffler crocheted from garish wool collected from old sweaters and afghans she had unraveled. Along with thick tan cotton leggings, she wore practical brown leather boots that laced up to her ankles. To prepare for Anne's visit, she undressed down to the dress, adding a soft saffron-yellow shawl and shining her boots with beeswax. Her curly grey hair was pulled back, not into a bun, like that of other women in the area, but braided into a pigtail that hung down her back like that of the Chinese man painted on their blue-and-white vegetable platter. Her face was reminiscent of a fourteenth-century Simone Martini fresco: clearly Semitic, with curious dark-brown eyes and black eye-lashes and eyebrows, which contrasted stunningly with her grey hair. Born in Paris, Claire had a city way about her even when she was digging in the garden. She wrote her poetry in French, only bothering to translate it into English when she was being published in *The Potteries Poetry Review* or some other English-language journal.

As soon as Anne arrived, Sophie could tell she was nervous. Anne lived with her parents in an elegant manor at the edge of the village. To arrive at the front entrance of Anne's family's home, one walked a circular path of pure white pebbles that was bordered by sharply trimmed yew hedges—a dreamlike property of order and serenity.

In contrast, the Markses' entrance was cluttered with bro-ken terra-cotta flowerpots (kept "just in case"), fallen branch-es, upturned rocks from the previous winter's frost, and dead plants waiting to be cleared for new ones in the spring. And rather than there being a maid to take Anne's coat, Claire said, "Just throw it on the bench, dear."

That afternoon, Claire happened to be in one of her poetic moods and spoke in metaphorical and abstract sentences. These appeared to befuddle Anne, even though they made complete sense to Sophie. She was relieved that Claire was at least speaking in English and not her everyday French.

While showing Anne her workroom, Claire prattled on without a pause, making it difficult to know where one idea began and the other evaporated into the air. She quoted Tennyson, reminiscing about her own childhood while holding Anne's hand to her heart. *Queen rose of the rosebud garden of girls . . . There has fallen a splendid tear / From the passion-flower at the gate, / She is coming, my dove, my dear.*

They went into the sitting room for their tea. Claire and Anne sat at the small round table near the window, Claire chatting away. Sophie scurried around them, clearing off old newspapers, books, and foolscap from the windowsill and the table. She thought it a relief that they did not have to eat in the kitchen, convinced she would faint dead away from embarrassment about the disorder. As Claire regaled Anne with stories about her favorite poets, Sophie went to the kitchen and prepared the tray. When she reentered the room, Sophie saw Anne surreptitiously cleaning off her fork on her skirt under the table.

To Sophie's surprise, Anne declared that she adored her visit, and made it clear that she wanted to be asked back. "It's like being in another world," she told Sophie. "I like it much better than the stuffy one I live in."

When Sophie turned sixteen, Claire copied in her slanted, steel-tipped, deep-blue-ink handwriting a quotation from Keats and taped it to Sophie's bedroom wall, directly above the lamp: *I am convinced more and more day by day that fine writing is next to fine doing, the top thing in the world.* A few days later, Sophie came home to find that her grandfather had scratched out ~~writing~~ and printed above it *painting*, using a brush and cadmium-red paint.

At times, guided by Claire, Sophie tried to write poetry. But the words were colored—run through with references to physical forms that eventually had to be made with materials, not language. It was never really a choice. Sophie had always known she wanted to be a painter like her grandfather. The temptation to create a person's face, a person's essential being, wooed her to the canvas.

Claire was the one who gave it away. "You don't have to be a poet, dear," she said. "With your talent you can make poetry out of paint."

But Eli was cautionary. "Both of these choices are problematic. Choosing to be an artist, Sophie," he warned, "is choosing to mine deep caverns. It's like getting lost in the darkness and spending the rest of your life trying to find your way."

Over the years Sophie had observed her grandparents working on their art. She heard Eli's pacing in the middle of the night and then the screen door banging as he headed to his studio. Or upon waking to go to school, she would find Claire downstairs with a cup of tea and her writing book on her lap before the fire, having been up most of the night. Occasionally, Eli or Claire would be plunged into despair when the work was not going well. When that happened they would become inarticulate and seem like ghosts. Sophie would stay out of their way; she had learned early on that it had nothing to do with her.

"Don't worry, Sophie," they would say, "this restlessness is normal. Indeed, we perversely look forward to it because it means that new ideas are brewing, trying to find their way to the paper or the canvas." Sophie was fascinated by the tumultuous drama of it all.

At the end of Sophie's schooling, she decided that she should go up to London to study at the Slade School of Art. Having never left her grandparents before, she was a rather innocent nineteen-year-old, and terrified. But she did have the imagination to worry about the future; she was concerned that if she lived with such old people, she would die without having lived. Her grandparents encouraged her. Once she was on the train, and could no longer see her grandparents on the platform, she felt an odd sense of relief—a feeling that would have embarrassed her a mere hour before. Through the grit and swirling steam, as she watched the canals winding alongside the train's path and then snaking away to the horizon, she felt she was forever altering her life.

But within a couple of days of arriving in London, Sophie slid into depression, what she called a "mud hole." Everything was strange. There was no routine. She felt exposed, vulnerable. Her bed-sit in an artist's house was not only ugly, but fronted a noisy and dirty road. She was used to the stillness of the country, the comfort of the cottage that she had known since birth. Sleep became her solace and she craved it as if it were illicit.

It took two months of forcing herself to go to classes before she was awake enough to look around. Slowly she acclimated herself. In the painting department, there was only one other woman in their class of twenty-six. She was as shy as Sophie and worked as hard. Although they were friendly, the other woman did not have time to socialize; she worked at a local tea shop to pay her way.

Then Sophie fell in love. It was totally unplanned. She was not aware that men ever looked twice at her; certainly they never flirted. When she was a foal-legged adolescent, she assumed that boys paid attention to her only out of fascination with her physical ineptitude. Her grandparents used to soothe her feelings of homeliness by telling her that someday a gentleman would discover her true beauty. She knew she was a queer card; indeed, she had grown so used to being one that it never occurred to her seriously to try to be otherwise. But the idea of love danced attendance upon Sophie's imagination. "It"—the idea of love, that is—would cross the threshold of her consciousness while she was reading or daydreaming. Sophie was easy prey for the flailing of the heart, having been educated by her reading in Victorian swooning and mysterious romances—

E. M. Hull's *The Sheik* being one of her favorites. But this vague, somewhat intellectual understanding of the emotional cracks she could trip over did not stop her falling in love. She did not understand that love could be both the devil and an angel. In her naïveté she chose to recognize only the angel.

Her angel had blond ringlets. Sometimes when he sat with his back to the window, the light shining through his hair created a gossamer halo. His name was René and he was from a village in southern France; he was as comely and lithe as one of the bamboo stalks in the field next to Eli's studio. Sophie did not have a chance. They were the same height and when they danced they were nose to nose, lips to lips. He was intoxicating.

Sophie's work became voluptuous in its shapes, silkily sinuous in its lines, almost nauseating in its fleshy colors. She loved the studio oil-painting class above all others. The models were of every shape, every shade of skin tone, and both sexes. If the class was assigned quick drawings from the model, Sophie would plant herself in front of her easel on her stool and not move. But if the assignment was to paint one of the models taking a long pose, she would circle the room like a stalking cat, looking for the best angle from which to make the painting.

Years later, Sophie realized that many of her classes were a waste of money and time. Her art education had essentially been conducted in her daily exercises at home with Eli. In contrast to those of most students, her eye had already been trained to see the negative spaces, the most interesting forms, the best angle of the studio light. Yet she did not have the sophistication of some of the other students, having lived deep in the country and rarely traveled to visit a museum. But this also served her well. Her work had a freshness that set it apart from the others. When the first paintings in the class were completed, they were hung for a critique. Sophie felt that her painting was rough, too much like her grandfather's—perhaps an obvious copy of Pissarro's self-portrait that she had recently seen at the Tate. The professor, dressed in a moldy-looking black cape, stood in the middle of the studio, turning, looking at each painting one by one. Lighting his briar pipe, he spun around and pointed to her picture.

"This painting is the liveliest, the most original in the class," he said. He turned on his heel and left for the day. Sophie was flabbergasted.

When Sophie was thirteen, Claire had spoken to her about sex in her unique, poetic way. But Sophie had no idea that the act itself would be so astonishing. The second half of the year at the Slade was a time of making love and making paintings. Sophie spent almost every evening in one of the local pubs drinking beer and smoking endless cigarettes in a continual and delightful conversation with René and their friends. At last she felt herself being released from the fragility of her aging grandparents.

Her friends all spoke the same metaphoric language—splattered with references to painters and techniques, almost a secret language. Sophie was a serious listener, never taking up a remark made into the air, whether teasing or confrontational. But she was well liked and enjoyed the comradely late-night hanging about in René's favorite pub, the Plough, his home away from home. Like all her earnest student friends, like René, she was totally immersed in her work and her life.

Her grandparents needed her home for the summer. While she worked in the garden and helped with the house, they could have a brief respite from their daily chores. Saying good-bye to René at Victoria was theater at its most absurd. As the train was leaving the station, she did not want to let go of him; she clung like one of those sticky vines that swallow the life out of a young tree. Along with the traditional passion of youth, she was feeling torn from someone she had (without his even knowing) transformed into a member of her odd family.

Three hours later, swollen-eyed from crying, with her red cardboard suitcase in one hand and a roll of canvas in the other, she walked down the tree-lined road to the house. There was a scent of sap in the air and the unfurling leaves of the copper birch trees were blood red, announcing summer.

Her grandparents were waiting for her under the apple tree. As she drew closer, she could smell the apple blossoms and blooming roses, the last of the lilacs. Sitting in lounge chairs with floppy straw hats on their heads, glasses on their noses, and books in their laps, they were both dozing in the dappled sun.

Even though she had been tempted to throw herself into their arms, seeing them now, she did not want to alarm them. "Hello, there," Sophie sang, and they lazily opened their eyes. Then both their mouths, in unison, stretched into wide grins. She was amazed at how they were beginning to look alike.

Her grandfather was seventy-five and her grandmother was turning seventy-seven. Sophie's father had been their only child, born long after they had given up all hope for a baby. It was inevitable, then, that their son's early death bequeathed them a life of poignant sorrow. Consequently, they used art in an attempt to transform his death into a bearable state of being. They did have an inimitable way about them, appearing to be suspended in time—floating away, off the edge of everyday life.

Sophie had been away for almost five months. She was shocked to see them. They were truly elderly people. And when she embraced each of them, she smelled their age: an unexplainable smell, like a cupboard filled with old wool and camphor, a cupboard that had not been opened in a long while.

But it was Claire who commented out loud on a difference. "You've fined down, Sophie dear, become a woman."

Later in the evening, Claire had Sophie to herself.

"So, dear, who's the young man?"

"What young man?" Sophie answered, quick as a thought. "How did you know, Claire? How did you know?" Sophie tried not to break into a big self-satisfied smile, or even laugh out loud.

"Sophie, it's so obvious, you silly girl! You look like you've risen from a *bed of roses and a thousand fragrant posies*—but Marlowe wrote that, not I. You must tell me only what you want to tell me. I won't probe, I promise."

Sophie told her grandmother about René. About his family in France, whom she had never met, but wanted to. About his work as a painter. About his apprenticeship to a well-known artist. But she did not tell Claire about her private life. It was a piece of her that belonged wholly to her, no one else. Not even René.

The summer dragged, as it only can when one is away from a new love. But Sophie appreciated the consolation of her old school friend Anne. They would meet at Miss Tellwright's Teahouse and spend long late afternoons huddled over cooling cups of tea, talking—imagining romance. It was almost the same make-believe they had shared as schoolgirls . . . the big difference being that Sophie was no longer inexperienced. As with Claire, Sophie could not confide in Anne those most intimate parts; yet together in their youthfulness, they painted a future for Sophie.

"How I envy you," Anne moaned. "'Here I am stuck in these desolate plains of pits, bricks, and smoke.'"

And Sophie reminded her that the description was taken from one of their favorite books, *A Mummer's Wife* by George Moore.

"I know, I know," Anne declared, "but, darling, it's actually becoming the story of your life, not mine! Oh, how I long to be the heroine Kate Ede and be seduced by a devil-may-care revolutionary artist. But here I am, stuck in the phony aristocracy of these barren plains of England.

"Oh, Sophie, I want so for something dramatic to happen."

"But *your heroine* Kate," Sophie reminded her, "ends up in a hateful place."

"Yes," Anne laughed, "but I would just love to grasp the nettle and see what happens."

René and Sophie wrote each other long, achingly erotic letters, which she hid from her curious grandparents. She put them high up in her cupboard, knowing that Eli and Claire were both now anxious about climbing ladders and chairs. But she knew they knew the letters were there, for each time they knocked and came into her room, they would sweetly smile when they looked toward the cupboard.

Leaving her grandparents the second time was much too easy. Sophie was aware of the constant smile on her face, even though she tried hard to look sad. "Alas," Eli quoted from Ovid, "how difficult it is to prevent the countenance betraying our guilt," and he smiled.

"You're not to feel bad about returning to London," Claire good-naturedly assured her. "We're certainly old enough to care for ourselves!"

Sophie rented the same room in Bloomsbury that she had the previous term. Now the formerly unbearable, noisy road was poetic, lyrical.

Through that first night, she waited impatiently for René to return from his village. On the second evening, as she was rounding the corner after visiting the food shop across the road, she saw him. He appeared lost in thought and did not see her until she tapped him on the arm. Hugging and laughing, they headed immediately for her room and began to unbutton buttons before they had closed the door. It was ecstasy. It was the absolute abandonment of time.

In the morning they sat by the open window and drank coffee, saying little, simply basking in the sunlight and the warmth of being together again. Sophie felt that her life was really about to begin. Finally, René left for his job with the famous painter, backing out the door, holding on to her like a silkworm releasing its thread.

He disappeared. He never showed up for his apprenticeship with the painter. He told no one where he was going. After a week of searching and waiting, she wrote his family. Five days later she received a short note.

Mademoiselle Marks. Please be informed that René has married and is living here in the south of France. We request that there be no further communication from you. There was no signature.

Sophie tried to be attentive to her classes, but it was hard. She daymared through each one, painting dark, almost black canvases with indistinguishable figures floating in a stormy sky.

Her friends did not know what to say to her. With each other they were intimate with their confessions, but Sophie did not invite such closeness. They continued to include her on their jaunts to the tavern, and she did join them. But rather than even trying to participate in their conversations, she smoked cigarettes, drank wine, listened, and brooded.

Two months later Sophie realized she was pregnant. She wrote again, telling René her situation; there was no answer. She was lost in a haze of depression and desperation. She could tell no one. She had no choices. Even those at the art school would soon not be bohemian enough to avert their gazes from her ballooning belly. There was nothing for her to do but go home.

Telling her grandparents was easy. They clucked around her, not for a moment fazed. Indeed, Eli said he felt blessed to see another generation in his lifetime, while Claire began to teach herself to embroider so she could make the baby's first bib.

But Sophie wanted the pregnancy to go away, to leave her alone. She did not want to be a mother. She did not want to be reminded of René. There were no maternal feelings, but there was certainly rage.

"I can't do this," she declared to her grandmother a few days after returning. "I must have an abortion. I must."

"Sophie, dear," her grandmother crooned, "it's against the law. You know that."

"When, in heaven's name," Sophie yelled, "have you ever cared about the bloody law!"

First she tried drinking a small glass of gin, followed by four tablespoons of castor oil, six times a day. The second week she tried quinine tablets. The third week it was a douche of Sunlight soap and water in the morning and at night; then it was strapping fabric around her belly. She ran up and down the road until she was exhausted. She did jumping jacks. When she vomited, she thought she might be succeeding and tried harder. But it was not working.

Not until Claire caught Sophie sneaking a knitting needle out of the basket was there a serious confrontation.

"Put that back," Claire furiously ordered. "How dare you? Don't you know about the butchering, even death, that can happen if you put that needle into you? Are you insane?"

"Leave me alone," Sophie said, pointing the needle at her grandmother in a threatening way and shouting and crying at the same time. "You have no idea how I detest what's happening to me."

"No, I don't," Claire admitted, stepping back and sitting down hard on a chair, "but I have to admit to you that I don't know what to say, or what to do. The only abortionist I know about is the fishmonger, Mrs. Blake. Not only are her hands always filthy, but there are whispers in the village that she has botched more jobs than we'll ever know about.

"Now, please, Sophie, put that down. You're frightening me."

Sophie could see that she might not be able to kill the fetus, but she could certainly drive her grandmother into the grave. And this deeply terrified her.

"Oh, bloody hell," she yelled, throwing the knitting needle across the room and flinging herself out the door.

As time dragged by, Sophie became grudgingly accustomed to her situation. It was obvious that being pregnant did not bring about a great mothering instinct. She felt clumsy and leaden with ambivalence. Her grandparents tried to be helpful in their sympathetic manner, but she cut herself off emotionally. For months Sophie was terribly long-faced, befuddled, choked with anxiety about the unknown.

"You know, dear," Claire said one day, "a sorrowful face can be beautiful, but an unhappy face is quite distressing."

Sophie tried to be more cheerful.

For the entire time, Sophie waited to hear from René. It was not until she felt the first violent pains of labor that she realized he was truly gone. She gave birth to their son, André, on the fourteenth of June 1936. He was born in her old bedroom, with his father's letters still hidden on the top shelf of the cupboard, kept as symbols of hope by his mother. Although a midwife performed the delivery, Sophie's grandparents sat on either side of her head and cooed to her throughout the labor.

For the first year after André's birth Sophie was overwhelmed, and meandered through her mothering duties like a ghost. She sensed her grandparents' disappointment, but could not conjure enough energy to care. Time was blunted; there was no definition. Sophie nursed and was tender toward the baby, but felt as if she were floating, waiting—waiting for a crack of thunder, a bolt of lighting to bring her down to earth again. Severe physical pain finally brought her back to reality. It was a silly and careless accident. She fell off a ladder while cleaning the fetid fecal matter off the slippery tiled roof of the hen-house. She broke her leg so badly that the bone came through muscle and skin and she fainted from the pain. They had no telephone, so her grandfather hobbled down the rutted road to a nearby neighbor who came in his automobile and lifted her onto the back seat. By the time she had soldiered through the broken-leg ordeal, an operation to reset her bone, and then a plaster cast, three months had passed. Now it was clear to her that she had a child to look after, along with elderly grandparents. Making things even more tense, the threat of war was pushing against their island's shores.

André was a fussy infant. Intuiting his mother's unhappiness, he would start to cry, as if he were rolling a creaky old barrel that he could not stop down the road. Sophie was convinced she was being punished. Mothering was not coming naturally to her. If someone had asked, she would have declared that her grandfather was a better mother than she was. She accused herself of lacking the patience an infant required. She was bored. When she was nursing, she would look out the window and try to identify every shade of green she could see. Then, in her mind, she would name the various colors that would have to be mixed to achieve each of those greens.

But after Sophie's leg healed, André calmed down and so did Sophie. She began to enjoy him, began to see his personality emerge. Before she knew it had happened, she had fallen in love with her child. And the child knew it. He flourished. He was quite lovely, with a long, lean body and thick hair, dark like Sophie's and with her slight widow's peak. As he grew, they were all amazed at how self-contained he was. He would imaginatively play by himself for long periods of time, was early to speak, and had an impish sense of humor that entertained the three grown-ups in his house. One day in the kitchen, André was playing with a little boy who lived down the road. The little boy came to Sophie and said, "André took my ball."

Sophie turned to André. "Did you take his ball?"

And André answered, "No, Mama, not yet!"

When André was almost three, the government formed emergency committees that would run England's cities in wartime. There was no escaping the anxiety racing through the air.

All the same, life for the Markses was quiet. Their energies were centered on André and his well-being. Her grandparents never prodded Sophie about René; they never spoke about him at all. And having no father did not bother André; after all, he had a dedicated great-grandfather. What Sophie did not admit was that André's face looked just like his father's, although her grandparents thought he looked the image of Sophie. But they had never seen René, not even a snapshot. When René and Sophie had been lovers in London, other students often commented that they looked like brother and sister, even though René had blond hair. Both of them were tall and thin, and they loped down the street, rather than walking like most people. There was a fragment of her memory that was uncomfortably jiggled when she saw André from a certain angle. But she kept her toe against that emotional door until finally, after a couple of years, the memory faded into fiction.

Before the war she tended to André and helped around the house and with the chickens. When she had time she painted clock faces and pottery in Eli's studio. She found it pleasant to sit and listen to a symphony on the radio while painting simple flowers and birds.

Eli taught her how to throw a pot. She was challenged: throwing on the wheel, the wheel's constant hum; staying focused on the movement of the wet and slippery clay in her hands. "You have to be careful with clay," Eli said. "It seeks a way back to the earth, longing to rest in the ground."

Their pottery was selling faster than they could make it, even with the threat of war.

Then there was the art of the narrow canal boats. The Midland Canal System meandered through their area. It had been constructed in the eighteenth century to move heavy bulk materials, such as coal, as well as manufactured materials and the fragile local pottery. A new fleet of boats, built of oak and elm, had been launched earlier that year and needed painting—not a simple, one-color coat of paint, but a coat of colorful decorations. These boats had always been known for their ornate lettering, delightfully rendered flowers, famous castles, lively animals, and abstract decorative elements. Painting the boats was part of the local tradition, and there was keen competition among artists to get the jobs. Eli was not particularly interested, but felt he should show interest because the boats were such an important feature of the area. He was given a boat to paint. Five mornings a week he and Sophie left André behind with Claire and the two of them cycled to the boatyard in Stone. The canal was quiet. The only real noise came from two great white swans who occasionally fought over an invisible problem. Then they would rise in the air with a thunderous clapping of their wings and land a few yards down the canal, floating on as if nothing had happened.

It was lovely working outdoors and they both enjoyed the size of their joint "canvas." Roses framed the access hatch in the foredeck, painted in clusters with bright-green leaves and highlights of deep reddish-brown shadows. Red roses were traditionally painted with a black background and a brown center, while white roses had a pink background with a red center.

Although there was a recipe for the images, artists did take liberties. Eli especially liked painting hidden faces; the idea came to him after he saw faces concealed in Persian miniatures in a book at the library.

But Sophie was worried because she had not been doing her own work.

"Don't worry that you're not painting," Eli tried to reassure her. "Life has to be lived before serious paintings can be made. You have to build your own layers of history. Losing René, being blessed with André, threatened by war; you'll soon have valuable, although painful, experiences to paint about. Of this I can assure you."

"But I have all those unfinished canvases from the Slade. They plague me," she grumbled.

"Not to worry, dear, you won't abandon them. You'll go back to them, don't you fret. But be aware that they may not hold the same meaning for you."

Months went by with the country preparing for war. And then on the third of September, 1939, Britain and France declared war on Germany, and Sophie's, André's, and her grandparents' lives changed forever.

"This is the end of the world," Eli declared. "Human beings can't take another war like the last one. Since we obviously haven't learned," his voice lowered to a growl, "we will be punished."

In November, 1939, Sophie was recruited to draw for the Propaganda Department in nearby Stoke-on-Trent. She had no choice but to leave André with her grandparents.

Sophie was both worried and relieved to get away from her family. She often felt suffocated in the intimacy of their tight, small household. Sometimes she felt as if there were cotton between her imagination and her skull. Their daily life was rote. There was no time for her own work. No time for dreaming. Certainly no time for romance. Sophie had to help make money. The floundering economy left no choice.

She let a room in Miss Maudlin's house in Fenton, settling halfway between her obligations: only a mile and a half south of home, which gave her the satisfaction of being able to get there quickly, and only a mile and a half north of the war office.

Sophie's job was to draw pictures for the army's propaganda machine. Brave, square-jawed men, hefting heavy weapons without a grimace; muscular women, pretty, open faced, determined, operating machines in munitions factories. She drew in black and white, using charcoal and ink, sometimes employing one of the secretaries and her husband as models, but more times than not using only her imagination. Although the sameness of the assignments became quite tedious, it was an honorable way to contribute to the war effort. Sophie earned a salary of thirty shillings for a forty-eight-hour week, plus another eight pence an hour for overtime, which she did as much as possible.

While Sophie lived in Fenton, she worried about the chickens. But Claire carried on, adjusting her feeding and cleaning duties to her growing fragility. On one occasion, feeling frustrated, she confided, "Besides you and Eli and André, I don't know what work is more important to me now, my chickens or my poems!"

About once every ten days, when Sophie could get leave from her duties, she bicycled home to help Claire clean out the henhouse and check on everyone's well-being. She found it ironic; just as she had been bequeathed to her grandparents by her parents, now another child had been given into their care. They never complained, although they were so much older, so frail. But after two months it was obvious this arrangement was not going to work. André was running around like a mouse in a cage and her grandparents were visibly exhausted.

Sophie heard about a childless Jewish couple who had fled Berlin and were seeking to establish themselves as British subjects. They had left Germany with no money, but had their passports, steamer tickets, and two suitcases, both filled with books. Through a village magistrate, she met with Mr. and Mrs. Samuels and liked them immediately. They were academics, he a professor of European history, she of English literature. She spoke English, but not too well; she sounded like a primer. However, she read the language flawlessly, and spent hours reading to André, which made them all quite content. The couple was attached to each other by an invisible thread, appearing to move to a rhythm of their own composition.

For the first week Mr. and Mrs. Samuels dressed in the same dark-brown and tan tweed suits. Each of them wore a plain white shirt and sensible shoes, which they quite carefully tended to. Claire realized that they had only the clothing on their backs and one pair of shoes each. She gave them each a change of clothing, placing it on their beds and refusing to discuss it when they came to say "thank you."

Once André was situated, Sophie's grandparents gave up on the world. Claire and Eli made it clear that they simply wanted to be quiet, to be removed from a chaotic world that they knew only too well. More and more often their conversations were filled with memories and secrets, causing them both to smile enigmatically. Since Eli's sight was fleeing, Claire read to him: Shakespeare, Hugo, Eliot, George Sand, even Mark Twain. "We're reading everything we had forgotten," they declared, "and at our age, we've forgotten everything!" Every once in a while, a flicker of rage at the state of civilization was ignited and they carried on as in the old days. But soon, the chaos of their diminishing world made them weary again, and they would slide back down into their aging selves.

By January, 1940, bacon, butter, and sugar had been rationed, and everyone began to cut back and be far more careful about meals. As if they were planning a class lesson, Mr. and Mrs. Samuels designed an elaborate vegetable garden. Having always lived in Berlin, they had no idea about gardening, so they educated themselves through jaunts to the local library and discussions with members of the garden club. As soon as it became warm enough they were vigorously digging, with an instructional book propped against a fence post, their soft hands bound with rags.

Despite all the apprehension created by the war, Sophie's family was managing. André was kept busy, Sophie was swamped with work, her grandparents were seemingly content, and Mr. and Mrs. Samuels were actually enjoying their newfound occupation and encouraging André to help. The radio, though, brought them constant, dispiriting bad news. Invasions, bombings, starvation, death—all were being reported from a frightened and besieged Europe. In May, Germany invaded Norway and Denmark, both countries to which the Samuelses' family and friends had previously fled. Before this, every couple of weeks, the Samuelses had received letters from the Continent. These abruptly stopped and the couple hid their distress behind a mask of politeness.

German bombers began to appear over the Midlands. Their gray bellies pregnant with bombs, they rattled over the rooftops, ravenous, looking for a nest for their eggs. At first the members of the household watched with a morbid fascination, not quite believing their eyes. Then, with deepening dread, they became conscious of the reality they were facing.

By autumn, the bombs began to fall; the main targets were the Michelin Factory, Shelton Steel, and the railroad. Every time there was an air-raid warning, Sophie would fetch her bicycle and begin to ride home; no matter that the rules said she had to be in a shelter. If she heard or saw that the bombs were falling in another area, she would turn around and go back to work. After a while she was able to sense if the Germans were going to attack or go on to another target.

"You must send André to rural Staffordshire," Eli advised. "It's simply no longer safe here and the lad's having a rough time."

Sophie could see he was right. With this new anxiety in the air, André felt everyone's apprehension. He was becoming nervous, clinging to his mother as soon as she arrived home, refusing to sleep in his own bed, hysterical when she had to return to work. Like many war-afflicted children, he began to seem more like a ghost than a real child.

"Just look at him," Eli insisted. "He has eyes of the distant past."

The dread was gnawing away at everyone, but Sophie could not make up her mind to send him away. She simply could not. Her family, including the Samuelses, tried even harder to accommodate the child.

By the following spring, the raids had intensified. Then on the ninth of April, an onslaught began that sent Sophie racing home with the worst clump of fear in her throat she had ever experienced. As she rounded the curve toward the rutted road to their house, she heard the whirr of doom. Sophie rode straight into it, still moving forward, before she was lifted off the ground and violently tossed into the volcano.

In that one day, the Germans dropped 650 high-explosive bombs and 170 incendiaries; 1,121 people were killed. Sophie's family, following the air-raid warden's instructions, had fled to the basement for shelter.

It was a direct hit. It could not have been more precisely aimed.

The dead included Mr. and Mrs. Samuels, Sophie's grand-parents, and Sophie's son. Their beloved home became their tomb. If there were remains left to bury, they were not apparent. They evaporated with the intensity of the explosion. All they left behind were their names. Many years later those names would be chiseled into one side of the dark granite war memorial in the middle of the village green.

I meant to write about death,
only life came breaking in as usual.

—Virginia Woolf

The stars disappeared. The moon faded into the dense black night. The birds ceased singing. Sophie was in the hospital for many weeks. Besides having suffered a concussion, her body was riddled with tiny fragments of earth, along with shrapnel and minuscule scraps of history. Her fingertips burned with reminiscence. Her heart had filled with leaden memories, sinking her into an eternal night. She lived in a darkened container. Even if the sun was shining, she could not see it.

Sophie did whatever she was asked. But her real self was somewhere else, distinctly separate from her body. She knew that the people she loved were dead. She had only a sliver of memory of the actual catastrophe. Once her physical body was functioning, the doctors and the newly instituted National Health Service moved her to a sanitarium in the village of Field in Staffordshire. For eighteen months she lived with other shell-shocked citizens, many of them soldiers who were part of the overflow from military hospitals.

For the first few months she did battle with the voices in her head. They were trying to decide if she should live or not. Totally detached from what came out of her mouth, the demons carried on their conversation. Every now and again, one of them, the one with the lyrical female voice, would slip out onto her shoulder and whisper encouragement in her ear. But it was not good enough. Sophie would try to pull the menacing black sky down and bury herself. The doctors diagnosed shell shock. She had no name for it; she did not even have the interest to inquire.

The sanitarium was divided into three sections. The military was in the main part, being treated in bright white rooms with large, multipaned windows. The noncombatant male population was housed in the dark wing facing north and the women in the wing facing south. Sophie could only assume that they were kept separate for senseless and bureaucratic military reasons, for they were all alike. It was a community of zombies, dead-hearted, blunted people, wandering the halls and gardens, wondering why they were in the world at all.

Every day there were activities intended to encourage the patients to come out of their cracked shells: sewing, knitting, drawing; peeling potatoes and carrots. But when the patients were not wandering, they simply sat and stared out the windows into nowhere.

Slowly, the fog that was smothering Sophie began to give way. A wisp here, a wisp there, a bit of light here, a sliver of light there.

One afternoon she smelled turpentine and thought how odd it was that someone was painting. A heavy, dark door inside her opened and she clearly remembered her grandfather. Her entire body began to shake like a dog coming from a swim in the river. She was freezing cold, her teeth chattering. She tried to climb out the window to get to her grandfather, to the sunshine, but was pulled to the ground by two nurses. Taken back to her ward, Sophie was administered a sedative.

In the evening, as the medication wore off, she noticed a nurse, dressed all in white, sitting by her side. "Welcome back, Miss Marks," the nurse said with an open smile. "Would you like to talk a wee bit? It'll be good for your soul."

Sophie wanted to talk, but could not. "Take your time, Miss, it'll come. Look at me and tell me what you see."

I cannot even see my dreams, much less a human being, Sophie thought. "I can see you, but you're thin, like a piece of tissue paper," Sophie shouted.

"Ssh, Miss, you don't have to yell. What do you mean, not being able to see the whole me? I'm a pretty big woman; hard for me to hide, I promise you that!"

"What did you say?" Sophie yelled. "I'm not hearing you."

Sophie had not been hearing well since the bomb fell. She could hear a word, then a space of silence, then another word, then a space of silence, allowing her to string together just enough of a sentence to make sense. Now, listening to the appealing voice, she was suddenly able to hear two paired words. And as the nurse continued, the words began to wash over Sophie as if she were being baptized into the religion of language.

"Well, my dear, just take a look at you! You have a blush of pink on your cheeks. Now the doctor will be happy to hear about this.

"My name's Nurse Watson," she said, patting Sophie's hand.

That evening there was a concert for the patients and Nurse Watson helped Sophie to the sitting room. It was a string quartet, evacuated from London and playing for any hospital that wanted it. There was a cello, two violins, and a viola. The cello was wheeled in (resting on a crisp white dining-room tablecloth) in a rusty green wheelbarrow with a caddy-wampus wooden wheel. Sophie could hear the noise of the uneven wheel, and, disconcerting as that was, it made her feel better to be able to hear it at all. But as for the first Bach piece, the Concerto in E, she listened hard but could not hear a note.

She turned to Nurse Watson with panic on her face.

"Close your eyes, dear," Nurse Watson whispered, cupping her hand around Sophie's ear. "Close your eyes and feel the music floating by your face."

The next afternoon, smelling the turpentine again, Sophie felt her body moving toward the odor. She had no control over her feet; they seemed to be rolling along well-oiled tracks, moving her automatically toward the familiar.

Nurse Watson opened the door for her. There, sitting at an easel, was a soldier with his back to them. He was dressed in a well-pressed khaki uniform. His hat, crop, and leather gloves were neatly placed beside him on the floor. Sophie was struck by his painting. It was an accomplished portrait of a dead man, painted in grays and browns. The body was roughly painted, probably unfinished. But the head was almost like a photograph, intricately painted in exquisite detail. It was a monstrous depiction. The man's head was thrown back, looking up vacantly at a winter's sky. One of his eyeballs was dangling from its socket on an expensive-looking silver chain with diamonds set into the silver. It was so visceral that Sophie could almost smell the rotting body. The soldier turned to look at who was standing behind him. One half of his face was there. The other half, the right side, had been scooped out, leaving a horrifying mottled red shell.

"Good afternoon, Major Roderick," Nurse Watson greeted him in a chirping voice. "How are we today?" The soldier turned back to the canvas without saying a word, without even shrugging. And Sophie went back to the ward, got into bed, and pulled the blanket over her head.

For the next week, she was drawn to the familiar scent of turpentine. She would get as far as the door, then return to her bed and her blanket and often, the sweet vacancy of medication. But after that first time, the soldier never turned around.

It did not matter, for Sophie could visualize him as plain as could be.

One afternoon, Nurse Watson, who had taken a particular liking to Sophie, gently guided her to the studio. This time, though, there was an easel and an empty canvas and paints set out next to the soldier. He was sitting in his usual chair, working on the same painting.

"Come and have a seat," Nurse Watson encouraged.

Sophie could not resist.

Without thinking, she began to paint again. Her choices of brushes and colors were quite limited. The kindly nurse had found a beginner's school kit for her. But for the first few days it did not matter. Sophie simply could not let the painting alone. The subject matter was not hard to find; she merely looked out the window and began. A fruit tree, a bench beneath it, some distant hills, a stroke of sky, a whiff of cloud.

The soldier never said a word, never looked at her; he was working and reworking the same painting. She grew used to his presence, and then became oblivious of him.

Sophie was divided in two. One part of her was painting a vapid, although somewhat sweet, landscape. The other, the part that was not painting, was as dense and cold as a stone. Each time she began to let one side bleed into the other she would shiver and flee to her bed.

One day she started using her fingers because she had already worn the cheaply made brushes down to a stubble. That night, when she went to her bed, she refused to clean her hands, finding comfort in the messiness of colors left on her fingers, along with the sweet smell of paint reminding her of an innocent time in her life.

But her painting became darker and darker, more muddy, opaque. Each day she reworked the canvas, until the image no longer existed. When the last glimmer of light was gone from the painting, she took the palette knife and began to hack at it.

"No, don't do that!" the soldier said, jumping up from his chair and trying to grab her hand.

"Stay away from me," Sophie screeched, and lunged at the hole in his face with the palette knife.

Before she knew it, she was wrestled to the ground by two orderlies and dragged off to a cell-like room with walls made of white cotton ticking.

Something had snapped and Sophie was tossed back into a roiling sea of memories and horror.

Time moved along. The inner demon grew larger until it absolutely filled her body and her mind. For days, Sophie screamed, then she muttered, then she became mute.

It took another two weeks for Sophie to return to a semblance of reality. Now she was conscious that she had lost everything precious in her life. Indeed, she did not even have a picture of her childhood home, nor her treasured love letters from René, her paintings from the Slade, her grandfather's paintings, Claire's poems. Nothing. Not even a photograph of André. She began to weep. The crying rose in fury, the ferocity gathering the orderlies around her cot. "Let her alone," she heard Nurse Watson direct. Finally, with a heaving shudder, her sorrow broke on a distant shore.

That night, for the first time in more than a year, Sophie slept with only one sleeping tablet.

The next morning she asked to be taken to the painting room. There was the soldier standing by the window and looking out at the hills. When she entered he turned and smiled. The vacant part of his face had been covered with a mask, made of simple beige cotton, tied behind his head at his neck and above his ears. Sophie nodded hello and went to her chair. But she knew she owed him more than a nod.

"Sir," she said, wanting to look him straight in the face without flinching, "I want to apologize for my rudeness. Please forgive me?"

He looked at her straight on. "It's not necessary, Miss, I understand."

Sophie realized that someone had placed a canvas that was larger and better-stretched on her easel. There were more tubes of color and better brushes.

"Given that it's obvious you're a real painter," he said to her out of the corner of his mouth, "I thought it would be better to begin again with serious materials."

"I'm most grateful," she answered, and did not know what to say next. He flustered her. She could see that he had been quite a handsome man.

He smiled his lopsided smile and went to his easel, where he was working on the same painting. Sophie stared at her empty canvas, not knowing what she wanted to paint. Paradoxically, she felt emptied, even though both the doctor and Nurse Watson told her not to worry, that she had "opened to the world again."

"Excuse me," she said to the soldier, "but I prefer to paint portraits rather than landscapes. May I paint you?"

He looked at her, horrified. "Of course not," he replied, obviously cross, and began to leave the room.

"No, wait," she pleaded. "I'm sorry if I've offended you. Please. Let me explain."

The soldier leaned against the door jamb.

"I want to paint your profile, the side of your face that hasn't been altered."

"Ah, a contemporary Renaissance painter," he responded sarcastically. "I thought you were a *real* painter."

"I am. At least I think I am," she responded. "Just give me a chance. Three or four sittings, that's all I need. I promise."

Suddenly, painting his picture had become an all-consuming

necessity. She had absolutely no idea why; she simply had to do it. And he agreed.

She sat him in front of the window, the distorted side of his face invisible. He looked ghostly, softened in the silvery late-winter light. With charcoal, Sophie began to sketch his portrait directly onto the canvas. It felt good to make a sweeping line, using the thin side of the charcoal, then pressing it ever so slightly to thicken the line, then releasing the tension to go back to a finer line. Using the side of her hand to create shadows, she used her fingers to emphasize the edges, forming the head, giving it a natural weight.

"Take a break, if you would like."

"Thank you," he said as he turned toward her. It was almost as if Sophie had put the right side of his face back together while she was painting the left. Each time he showed her his missing face, she felt he detected her surprise, but he kept it to himself.

They hardly spoke. When they did, it was pleasantries, nothing more. Because he spoke out of the side of his mouth, his accent was difficult to place. Somewhere in England? Scotland? She could not tell.

After finishing in the evening, she would cover the canvas with a piece of cotton sheeting, as she had always done, to keep the paint from drying too much. For each sitting she liked to be able to place her brush upon a particular color, break the thin skin of oil that had formed during the night, and begin painting with the wet paint that was underneath.

She felt the portrait building, being constructed. Daub by daub. Stroke by stroke. Each movement was an ache of desire to come alive again.

The evenings had become warmer and Sophie was beginning to enjoy the change in seasons. She started to take walks. The grounds were lovely, especially because they were out of the flight pattern of the thundering warplanes. Indeed, she remembered with sickening remorse, it was this remote area to which Eli had begged her to send André. But one could, if only for a brief moment, forget about the war, about the suffering, about the vacancy in one's heart. In a flat area of the grounds, mirrored lines of silver birch trees had been planted in exact, precise rows. She enjoyed glimpsing them from different perspectives. Sometimes they looked like a forbidding tree prison, bars of iron-like bark showing up against the blue sky visible between the rows. Sometimes they looked like people, possibly soldiers, all dressed in winter colors, at attention looking up. And sometimes the trees reminded her of a giant open-weave woolen blanket that had been flung over a clothesline.

Sophie never saw Major Roderick on the grounds. Actually, she almost never saw anyone. But she knew there were people milling about in the woods, in the thickets, down by the river, and thought this "people-blindness" had to do with choice. No one wanted to see anyone else. No one wanted to talk to anyone else. They were all too busy trying to keep together what pieces were still there, find which pieces were missing, find replacements.

One late afternoon she was surprised to come upon Nurse Watson sitting on a bench beside the river. Her legs were stretched straight out and crossed at the ankles, her face raised toward the sun. "Have a seat, dear," she invited, patting the bench beside her. And Sophie sat, stretched her legs out, crossed her ankles, and put her face up to the sun. For the longest time they were silent. Then Nurse Watson, still with her eyes closed, facing the sun, said, "I think I'll stay here tonight and not bother to go home to Gratwich. Too lonely for the likes of me."

"But why would you want to stay here?" Sophie asked, also with her eyes closed, still facing the sun. She was really asking herself why Nurse Watson would want to stay there among that sometimes silent, sometimes screeching, ragtag group of weird people.

"My husband's fifty-six years old and works as a street sweeper for the village. He has to work the midnight shift tonight," she said, with the first hint of sadness in her voice that Sophie had ever heard.

This made Sophie sit up. Nurse Watson certainly did not appear the type to have a husband who was a street sweeper. Nurse Watson did not move. Still with her eyes closed she said, "He was a conchy—you know, a conscientious objector in the Great War; he served his time in that inhuman prison, Wormwood Scrubs. When he was not locked up in solitary confinement, he was making shoes for soldiers. Now, being too old to be drafted, he's been assigned to community service because he refuses to back away from his philosophy. It's almost as if our local draft board finds pleasure in not letting him rest. You do know, don't you, that all of the cleaning staff in the sanitarium are C.O.s?"

"No, I didn't know," Sophie said. "But now I can understand why there's such a feeling of kindness throughout the hospital."

Sophie had come to the part of the painting of the soldier where she had to make a decision. She was pleased with the portrait, thinking she might have captured his elegance, along with a skewed look of loathing for the future. The viewer would have to imagine what the other side of his face was feeling.

"May I see?" he asked, frightening her, since she was far away.

"Of course." And he came around and stood beside her.

"It's sublime," and he sounded as if he sincerely meant it. "I don't mean I'm sublime," he laughed, "but you have certainly captured the best side of me, to be sure."

She was amused, pleased that he liked it. "But I'm upset

about the background," she complained. "I can't see what it needs."

"I think it needs something to be happening," he suggested.

Unable to sleep that night, she tossed and twisted, anxious about the canvas. Afraid of disturbing the other women on the ward, she rose, put on her dressing gown and slippers, and walked down the hall, through the heavy oak swinging doors with the shiny brass plates, into the forbidden, **STAY OUT! MILITARY AREA** section, turning right toward her new studio. She did not see anyone. The entire building was as still as the spring night. Quietly turning the studio's doorknob, she stepped into the room. A small light was on and the soldier was sitting at a table reading.

"Oh, excuse me," she whispered. "I'm so sorry; I didn't know you were here. I'll leave," she said, and turned to the door.

"No, no, it's all right, it's all right," he whispered back, at the same time tying on his mask. "Please come in. You can work. I'll not disturb you. Here, I'll turn on your lamp."

Sophie smiled at him, and without saying more, she sat down, forgetting to put on an apron. She began to work with charcoal, trying to clarify the background, trying to keep her hand light. She drew in a window and through the window a road, the perspective purposely taking the eye to the horizon.

No, she thought, this isn't enough. I need a narrative in the background, the soldier's story, or at the very least, a history of this time. She looked over at him and caught him looking at her.

"I think I know what I need," she whispered, "but I don't know how to ask you."

The soldier rose from his chair, picked it up, then quietly set it down next to her.

"I think I need to tell a story in the background. You know, like Lippi's *Portrait of a Man and Woman at a Casement*?" He nodded his assent.

"But you mean my story, don't you?"

She nodded. Then, without being conscious of what she was doing, she gently pulled his mask up and removed it from his head. With her right forefinger, she tenderly traced the scar tissue. He did not move. He must have been disturbed by her action, but at the same time there was an amused look on his partial face. With her finger she continued to wander over the map of his war. Then he took her hand and, turning her palm up, kissed it gently. She felt forgotten stirrings.

He quietly took her hand away from his lips and, while still holding it, slowly brought it to her breast. With his fingers still holding her hand, he began to feather small circles upon her gown, coming closer and closer to the tip. When he finally touched her nipple, they were suffused with silent passion and slithered to the floor, entering a private world.

Later, sitting in the same chairs as before, they looked sheepishly at each other and smiled.

"Now," he said, pointing at her canvas, "you have the beginning of a story."

The next morning Sophie awoke to an uneasy rustle in the ward. "What has happened?" she asked an orderly. He shook his head. "Please, tell me," she insisted.

"See Nurse Watson," he advised.

And she told her.

"I'm so sorry, darling, but your soldier friend has hanged himself. He left you this." Nurse Watson handed her a package wrapped in brown paper with string. In the upper right-hand corner was written in blue ink: *This package is to be given to Sophie Marks. Otherwise kindly deliver to my home: Major Hugh Roderick, Cardine Manor, Garshall Green, Staffordshire.*

Sophie's hands were shaking so much, she could not untie it. "Here, sit down and I'll do it for you."

The soldier had given her his painting. But he had razored out the horrible, dangling eye. Behind this hole, so it would be seen on the face of the painting, he had taped a delicate pencil self-portrait, unscathed by war, full of hope for the future.

Her reaction was of absolute terror. It was her fault. She had reminded him of what he had lost, had broken the spell he wove around himself. She opened her mouth to scream but no sound came forth. All she was aware of were vivid images of the soldier leaning over her nude body. The images seemed to roll out of her mouth, like a continuous strip of celluloid, frame after frame, in slow motion. All she could see to do was to flee from the nightmare.

Sophie tried climbing out the window even though it was closed and she was high off the ground. Strong arms encircled her and she felt a sharp prick of a needle. Blessed sleep. Blessed escape.

It was as if she had known. It was as if she had known that somewhere in the vastness of the horror she had already lived through, this would happen. Although she appeared to be drugged, her mind was racing. Sophie was convinced that because he had brought her back to life, she had enabled him to end his. She was afraid to say this out loud. It was presumptuous; it was vain; it made her blush with shame. But as soon as she could speak to Nurse Watson, the words of mortification tumbled out of her mouth in a torrent of self-abasement.

"My fault. I only bring death. My fault."

Then came the self-accusations: if only she had sent André away, as her grandfather had pleaded with her to do; if only she had stayed the night with the soldier; if only she had spoken to him more; if only she had not been so afraid of everything. The inner voices of condemnation were rising from the still-smoldering fires of the wayward bomb.

The psychiatrist was sent. For three days Sophie clung to the lip of sanity. But she wanted out of the world. Through the haze of medication, she could not see hope. Nothing was in front of her but a vast landscape with no definition, barren of life, with no promise in the offing.

Four days had gone by when she overheard the psychiatrist speaking to Nurse Watson. "If there's no change by this afternoon I'll order the shock treatments. I'm worried about her. I'm worried that she'll slip further into this comatose state and it'll be more difficult to bring her round."

"Could you wait until tomorrow?" Nurse Watson asked. "I think that if I have some time with her, I can bring her back. At least I feel the need to give it a go."

The psychiatrist did not like her interfering in his domain. But the pressure to patch together the soldiers on his wards made him cool to the feelings of noncombatants. He had been directed by the Home Office to get the soldiers well enough to return to the war effort. Reluctantly, he agreed to Nurse Watson's suggestion.

Nurse Watson withheld three-quarters of Sophie's medication and settled with her knitting beside Sophie's bed. She could soon tell that the medication had worn off because Sophie was becoming agitated. Nurse Watson said, "Now listen, dear. Listen carefully. You don't want to be electrically shocked back to reality. You really don't. I can promise you this. Now, can you hear me?"

Sophie opened her eyes and looked at the nurse. "Good," Nurse Watson encouraged, "now I'm going to read you the beginning of *Silas Marner*. Listen carefully to every word. As I read to you, think only about the world you are seeing."

And she began. "In the days when spinning wheels hummed busily in the farmhouses—"

*

It took another eight days for Sophie to be fully awake without the paralyzing anxiety that had almost drowned her. She became more and more aware of the ghostlike creatures who wandered the halls in ill-fitting robes, their slippers shuffling, their hair matted on the back of their heads from lying in bed most of the time, escaping into sleep. I'm one of them, she realized.

On the morning of the ninth day, Nurse Watson appeared from behind the white gauze curtain around Sophie's bed. "I heard voices," she said, "and thought you had a visitor."

"Sorry," Sophie replied, "no, no one's here. I must have been talking to myself. I'm mad, aren't I?"

"Well, let's try to work this out before you go off calling yourself names," Nurse Watson said. "Do you know who you're speaking with? Can you see this person?"

Sophie pulled the sheet up and covered her mouth. She mumbled, "It's a woman of my age. She sits on my shoulder and whispers in my ear."

"Is she there all the time?" Nurse Watson questioned.

"No, only when I tell myself to die."

"Oh, what a relief!" Nurse Watson boomed. "You're fortunate. Name her," she said.

"What do you mean, name her?" Sophie asked. "It shows how insane I am even to be seeing her!"

"You're wrong, dear," Nurse Watson rebutted. "She's living in your psyche to keep you sane through these hard times. You need to honor her. She's a good and healthy friend, someone to talk to in times of stress. She's probably been with you all your life. You have to acknowledge her by giving her a name. What's the first name that comes into your mind?"

"Stella?" Sophie whispered.

"Stella she is. From now on, dear, whenever you're in a bother, don't you worry a bit, she'll help you."

One morning, Nurse Watson said, "I think you should look at your soldier's painting. It'll do you good to remember him as he saw himself before the war. Do you agree, dear?" And Sophie agreed.

Propping the portrait on the nightstand next to Sophie's bed, Nurse Watson patted Sophie on the head, smiled, and left.

What a beautiful man. What a wonderful painting, Sophie thought. She studied the portrait for a long while, allowing, even encouraging herself to enjoy his life in the painting, rather than grieving his death.

Now she needed to dream. Taking her time, moving as if she were a machine, she dressed and went out the French doors onto the lawn. It was almost summer again, and the world was being painted with color. Yellow crocus and daffodils, a few red tulips scattered here and there, and voluptuous buds on the magnolia trees were welcoming the ailing souls of the sanitarium. She rested by the side of the River Blithe and realized she was hearing birds for the first time in years. During the war, Sophie was convinced that all of England's birds had followed the German planes over the horizon to somewhere else in the world. Now they had returned, bursting with melody and ready to settle, to resume.

Sophie sat and remembered the soldier the first time she had seen him; she remembered the fear she felt upon seeing part of his face missing. She realized he had made the mask for her, to protect her feelings as much as his own. He must certainly have been able to see that she was a ghost, understanding that the only way for her to come alive again was to feel desire. Sitting there by the moving water, Sophie remembered that last evening, and longing filled her body. The welcoming smell of oil paints, the good smell of his hair. His hands.

For the next two weeks she worked on the portrait of Major Roderick. In the background, as in Lippi's painting, through the oak-framed window behind his head, she painted the part of his life that she knew: the steel-gray bomb fragment blasting through a deep-blood-red, old-fashioned rosebush, which impaled his eye on a thorn and sent it to the moon; his painting his own self-portrait while dressed in the khaki uniform and hat, with his dark leather gloves and crop neatly by his side. And last, the ultramarine evening sky with glimmers of gold, mere indicators of the stars and the endlessness of possibility. She knew the definition of "ultramarine" was "beyond the sea." It was the perfect color.

While standing back and looking at the painting, Sophie realized that something was missing. The color was wrong. It was too vivid, too new. She wanted the muted incandescence of the soldier's history to be buried in the very fiber of the portrait. The only way she could think to do this was to varnish the painting, but she already knew there was no varnish to be found. Besides, she did not like the idea of faking history, of antiquing the painting. And then, almost as if she had held out her hands in supplication, an angel dropped the idea into her palms. *Cover the painting with wax and bury it in the earth.*

Sophie began to collect candle stubs. This meant she had to speak to people. No more hiding. No more looking only at the ground. She had a mission and the mission helped her feel more a part of the world.

One of the cooks found her a dented and misshapen kettle in which she could melt the wax. Nurse Watson found an old putty knife. Slowly, the wax was melted on one of the kitchen's stoves. She then applied it to the surfaces of both her painting of the soldier and his self-portrait. While the wax was still warm, she placed a clean piece of canvas over each surface and applied more wax. Once the wax had set up, she turned them over and repeated the process. The paintings were now inserted between wax and canvas, reminding her of toasted cheese sandwiches. Wrapping them in brown paper, she tied them with string and put them under her bed. Sophie was beginning the burial process.

Sophie's ghosts had a complicated task. To slither around the corner of her memory they had to be quite resourceful. They tried to trick her, to catch her off guard, to trip her while she was daydreaming. She worked hard at ignoring them.

Nurse Watson was obviously pleased with Sophie's recovery. "I feel as if I've been a bit successful here, dear. But you need to be careful. What you've gone through doesn't simply fade away. It'll be a constant battle for you for quite a while," she said, patting Sophie's arm, "perhaps your entire life. The only advice I can give you is to be careful about drinking alcohol, force yourself to eat, and take brisk walks to get your blood moving to your head. And the most important thing is to talk to yourself, to your imaginary friend, when you're frightened."

"They will surely send me away again, if I do that!" Sophie said.

"Well, mumble then, dear, or carry on a conversation in your head. You seem to do that already, don't you?" And she looked at Sophie with a twinkle in her eye. "I know you do because sometimes I see clouds, sometimes storms, sometimes even sunshine moving across your face."

When Sophie had been moved to the sanitarium, the ambulance orderly had given her a bundle. Because she did not know where she was (much less who she was), the bundle was put in the sanitarium's cupboard with a tag affixed with her name. Toward the end of her stay, Nurse Watson handed it back to her.

"Now, dear, I want you to open this in front of me." Nurse Watson was patting the bundle, tidying the corners. "I don't know what's in it. But, just in case, I want to be here with you."

The bundle, a scrap of faded sepia sacking, was tied with a knotted piece of string. Sophie could not get it open. Her hands began to tremble.

"Here, dear girl, let me." Nurse Watson took the scissors that were hanging on her belt and cut the string.

The bundle smelled funny, like old leaves that had turned to compost. The tan sacking was not familiar. But when Nurse Watson shook out the russet-red dress, with the tiny ivory buttons that ran down the front, the dust of leaves and the gravel of Sophie's family's road fell on to the table.

"It's my dress," Sophie said, bewildered.

And the day came back to Sophie, glaring fragmentally at her as if she were looking through a splintered piece of glass. The last thing she had been able to remember was bicycling toward the explosion. The doctor, even Nurse Watson, had tried to lead her past the edge of the cataclysm, knowing that the act of remembering would be the significant step in healing. But Sophie deliberately flew around the catastrophe in ever-broadening, then ever-shrinking circles, like the spirals in her astronomy lessons at school. When she would get close to recognizing what had happened, her fingertips would begin to burn. Then, within a moment, an imaginary wall would appear before her, and she would be forced to step back. What she had not been conscious of was that over the past eighteen months she had continually been chipping away at that wall. Now a light was finally being shone upon the concealed memory.

Sophie remembered.

After being thrown from her bicycle and hitting her head, she had come to almost instantly on the gravel road leading to the house. In front of her were raging fires, many different fires, traveling toward each other at such a speed that she did not know which way to turn. She began furiously to circle the fires, screeching for André. But all she heard in response was the roar of fire and the popping sounds that must have been exploding tins of turpentine.

It was torrid, far too hot for her to get close. There was no water even to begin to put out the fires. She ran toward the flames, listening, looking, screaming—imagining André calling for her, imagining his terrified face; her grandmother sitting at her desk, looking at her with stark emptiness; her grandfather looking at her straight on, desperately trying to tell her something. And she imagined the Samuelses looking at the fire in abject disbelief. After all they had been through, they were going to die in an agonizing red blaze in a cool green pastoral glen in the welcoming heart of their savior, England.

As neighbors rushed to help, Sophie refused to be moved from the area. She resisted their hands, their clutching arms, their screaming mouths. "Leave her alone," she heard a man's voice say. "She'll play a straight bat and collapse."

But it took longer than anyone thought. She was in a frenzy. "Get closer," she screamed at those dark, dancing neighbors. "They're in the cellar! Get closer! They're safe under the ground!" And she began to claw at the earth, as close to the fire as she could bear. "They're under here," she pleaded. "Please, I know they're under here. Please help me. Please." Then a prick in the arm. And then nothingness.

Eighteen months after the bomb, sitting on her bed with Nurse Watson standing before her, Sophie could see that the dress was spotted with dirt, stained with tears. She wondered if the prick of the needle, and yanking back her arm, had caused the rip in the right sleeve.

"But, Sophie, there's something in the pocket," Nurse Watson exclaimed. "Shall we have a look-see?"

And kindly, well-meaning Nurse Watson pulled out a scrap

of paper. Worn and frayed and covered with stains, it was the only surviving fragment of her youth. Claire, on one of Sophie's days off, had given it to her. "Here, dear," she had said, "here's my recipe for Country Fish Pie. If you make it tonight it will keep for a couple of meals in the icebox and you won't have to worry about cooking":

Take a large piece of smoked haddock. Bring to a boil in frying pan with butter (if you can find some!), milk & water just to cover. Simmer for 2 minutes and OFF! Save stock. It should just cook through enough so you can take the skin off. Boil 3 or 4 eggs—the more the better! Boil potatoes but take off before they are cooked through & cool. Easier to slice. Grease pie dish with butter and flake fish and slice eggs. Add parsley if you have some. Make a sauce with the fish stock and add milk to richen it. Make a lot of sauce! Pour over fish and eggs and then slice potatoes thickly—a lot of butter on top and put in oven to brown. P.S. Add lemon juice to sauce to taste.

After Sophie held it for a moment, Nurse Watson tenderly, reverently, placed it in an envelope and tied it with a faded blue ribbon.

There were deep-in-the-night battles about what was true and what was not. Her memories were too radical, too intense, too filled with self-loathing for being the lone survivor. Her fingertips still burned. She would wake in the morning and be forced to wrestle with the truth. So Sophie talked. She talked and talked, to anyone who would listen. She talked to blank eyes, to eyes filled with terror, to eyes that seriously tried to listen. She talked herself back to her original, quiet Sophie.

"We'll make an appointment with the doctor," Nurse Watson said. "I feel it's time for you to leave this place."

It took another ten days for the psychiatrist to see Sophie—more than enough time to make her quite nervous about the interview. She was afraid he would in some way trip her up, reducing her to tears to keep her there.

"Whatever you do, darling," Nurse Watson warned, "don't let him see a single tear or he'll queer your pitch. For him, the sign of health is stoicism. He's an odd duck, I admit, but we have to put up with him, as he's the only one here with authority. Oh, and dear, be sure to call him 'sir.' He needs to be recognized."

His office was the nicest room in the building, with oak paneling and four stately tall windows along the south wall. The top panes of all the windows had stained-glass pastoral scenes: a brown-and-white hunting setter with a deep-green pheasant in its mouth; a peasant woman gathering water in a wooden bucket at a stream; a brown wolf, almost hidden in a copse; a gentleman dressed in a red tartan jacket with a shotgun resting in the crook of his arm. None of these images was comforting to Sophie. Leather high-backed wing chairs and a sofa with a cashmere afghan of rich forest green were arranged pleasantly in front of a cozy fire. A perfect setting for weeping and the wringing of hands, Sophie thought, and gripped her hands behind her back.

"Have a seat," the doctor said, inviting her to the sofa, which she ignored. She sat instead in one of the chairs, her hands folded on her lap.

He sat opposite. "Well, young lady, how are we today?" he asked while lighting a match and bringing it to his briar pipe. As she began to say something, he took two noisy puffs, trying to get the pipe going.

Looking at him benevolently, she answered, "Fine, thank you, sir."

"So you want to go home? And whom will you go home to? Do you have family?"

Sophie dug her fingernails into her palms. "No, sir, I don't. They were all killed."

"Oh, yes, of course. Sorry, I forgot. Well, well, let's have a look at your report."

As she sat there trying to be both still and attentive, he quickly glanced at her file, got up, went to his desk, and signed a piece of paper.

"You're probably not ready to leave, Miss Marks, but we're in desperate need of beds. I'm going to give you tablets, so be sure to take them as I've instructed.

"Now, you must promise me that if you have trouble sleeping or find yourself slipping back into melancholy, go immediately to your local surgeon. You've had us to depend upon for a long time. Now you're being tossed back into the world; try to keep your feet upon the ground. Remember, my dear, one's life is a maze from the beginning. You simply have to learn to live within it as comfortably as possible. All right, there you go, Miss." And he handed her the release papers.

"You'll be fine, darling," Nurse Watson crooned, patting her arm while they waited by the side of the road. "Just be sure to get yourself painting again; it's good for your soul, I can assure you."

With only the two paintings rewrapped in an old sheet, and a used and tattered green army knapsack with her belongings, Sophie was given a ride back to her village in a Red Cross truck. They came to Garshall Green and Sophie saw Major Roderick's home; it was run down and looking eerily empty. But soon, they drove through a splendid, tree-dappled region along the river. Then, as they turned a corner, the world went upside down. She was driving through a nightmare. There were dark olive-green and army-brown burned-out trucks with dented hoods and empty windshields lining the road, along with vague smells of gasoline and motor oil. Huge bomb craters pocked the hills. The landscape was gray and black. The woods and fields on either side looked as if Satan had had a tantrum.

After being let down at Trentham, on the village green, she decided to go directly to her family home.

She should have known better.

The ruts in the road made the trip slow. It was an hour before she turned to go down the track toward the house. But she lost all sense of direction, standing still for a moment in the middle of the road. Then she turned like one of her grand-father's pots on a wheel. That is it, she understood; the holly hedgerows had gone berserk. Not only had they not been trimmed for years, but there were bald spots where the war had landed. They were growing helter-skelter, their limbs reaching toward the sunlight; it was impossible to see their original forms. Nothing was as it had been before—although she did glimpse the old apple tree, now a mere two-foot-high sapling growing out of what was left of the original trunk, and struggling to form leaves. She closed her eyes and concentrat-ed, trying to smell apples, but all that wafted through the air were damp remnants of fire. There was no old table; there were no rickety wood chairs; no brick garden path lined with old lilac bushes; no bridal-white rhododendrons growing under the kitchen windows; no pink climbing roses wandering along the fence leading to Eli's studio. Everything was erased.

Now the forest was encroaching upon the fields. Each year Eli had gone out with an ax, cut down the invading saplings, and thinned the wooded areas. Otherwise, as was happening now, the untended saplings would reforest the fields, taking them all back to their natural state. Along with the new trees were wastes of gorse, old-man's beard, and a variety of plants and field flow-ers whose names she had lost. It pleased her, though, that she could still identify the peculiar aroma of bracken.

But there was no way for her to miss the enormous, gaping hole. Not only did it bring back the image of the devastating bomb, but it also reminded her of the hollowed-out crater in the soldier's face. This hole, though, was filled with rubble, rocks from the foundation, bricks from the house, pieces of rusty pipe, objects she could not identify. She was too upset to search for memories, afraid she would see things that were too close to human. Struck with vertigo, she vomited into the bushes. Her family was now part of this earth, part of these weeds. She had no idea what she was going to do. With a bitter taste in her mouth and an aura of hopelessness around her, Sophie realized that she had to make a choice: stay here and rebuild, or plant herself in exile. Whatever she decided to do, she understood that, to survive, she would have to distance herself from the confusions of the world, so grossly illustrated by the crater.

To do this, she would have to live on the farthest margins of her memory.

Using her hands and a flat rock and a stick for turning up stones, she dug a hole about six inches deep by twelve inches long by twelve inches wide beside the reviving ghost of the apple tree. The painting she had done of the soldier and the painting he had given her, all sealed with hospital candle wax, fit perfectly. She had already removed the soldier's pencil self-portrait from the hole in the canvas. The wax would not preserve the paper; this she knew for certain.

Covering the paintings and tamping the earth down with her hands, Sophie sat for a moment, legs crossed. She was remembering not the soldier, but Robert Browning: *That shall be tomorrow / Not to-night; I must bury sorrow / Out of sight.*

She placed rocks around the perimeter, turned, and left. Walking back the way she had come, she seemed to go faster in the opposite direction. She was relieved to glimpse the tip of the village's bomb-damaged steeple.

It was spring, 1944. Nurse Watson had advised her to go to the bank to see about any money that might be there in her name. Sophie remembered Mr. Albright, the bank manager. He was a grizzled old man—always had been—who wore spats and a high white starched collar and habitually hung his derby on an outmoded brass gas sconce next to his door. He was still there.

"Of course I remember you, Miss Marks. I was wondering what had happened to you. I'm so sorry about your tragedy. Don't really know what to say," he said, looking down at his shoes as if they were entirely new to him. "You're a fortunate young lady," he went on, waving his hand to invite her to take a seat. "Not many people have been left with any money. Indeed, there's not much of anything left, thanks to this awful war. Your grandfather, as soon as you were born, established an annuity, along with making you the owner of the house, the property, the pottery works, and the trustee of your grandmother's book rights. But, as you know, there is nothing left—just the property itself, plus a pittance of a monthly allowance. Of course, you can sell the property, but I strongly encourage you to wait. It's too soon. No one knows what's going to happen next."

Mr. Albright finally looked up and continued. "What may be a surprise to you is that a small amount of money was left to you by Mr. Rodney, your mother's father. Did you know this?"

"Well, no—I am surprised. I had no idea."

Mr. Albright looked directly at Sophie and smiled. "This is a part of my job that I enjoy. Surprises! Good ones at that."

"Is he still alive?" Sophie asked. "Why do I only know about it now?"

"No, he's no longer alive," Mr. Albright said. "He's been gone for a long time, way before the war. But the money was left for you when you were about five, with the stipulation that you could begin receiving a yearly annuity when you turned thirty."

"But why didn't my grandparents tell me? I don't understand."

"Can't answer you that, Miss. They knew about it. Perhaps Mr. and Mrs. Marks wanted you to learn to work first. Not live in cotton wool until later. I really don't know."

She had to admit to herself that he was probably right. Her grandparents had often spoken about the problem of living too comfortably. They had warned her that it was hard to make serious art out of silk and gold.

"Even between the two trusts," he said, "you're not going to be terribly comfortable. But at least it's something." And he stood and bowed.

Having such a small amount of money did not give her an answer, although she had assumed it would give her a clue. But, remembering Nurse Watson's advice, she decided to take her time. For the next year, while waiting out the end of the war, she lived in a rented room above Mrs. Reed's bakery and did clerical work for a branch of her old propaganda office. She did not get in contact with anyone she knew, even avoiding her old friend Anne. She neither painted nor drew, choosing instead, in her spare time, to sit in the library and read. Truth be told, she sat in the library and looked out the window and pretended to read. And there were others like her swallowing time in the reading room. The shell-shocked, the wounded, the cripples. Simply by their presence, they provided safety for one another without saying a word.

Sophie honestly could not say where the year went. Later, a unique smell, such as that of moldy books or of a blooming apple tree, could remind her of that lost time. She continued to take the prescribed tablets, afraid of what would happen if she stopped. Mostly she felt that her body was a fragile vessel filled with air. Living in the gray vagueness of mourning, Sophie moved through the days as if in a bank of fog. She was unable to think terribly clearly, simply performing by rote and a sense of self-preservation. Even with the cruel violence that had been hurled down upon their poor bodies, the death of her grandparents was not catastrophic. They had both lived full and apparently happy lives. It was André. It was his memory, and the shame about her ambivalence toward him, that made her heart ache with longing and regret. If only she had something left from him. She could not conjure his face in her memory. She was terrified even to try to remind herself. She knew that painting his portrait would be therapeutic, but the idea of actually recreating him on canvas was unbearable.

The war was coming to an end. Week by week, the Germans were being defeated. When Sophie heard at the end of April that Mussolini had been killed by partisans, she knew it was over. Her supervisor at the propaganda office asked if she would like to transfer to London and continue working as the government turned its efforts in another direction. She refused the offer; she hoped to be finished forever with the tedium of bureaucracy.

Then on a Tuesday evening, the eighth of May, the church bells rang celebrating the end. A bittersweet victory. Sophie was swept along with hundreds of people moving gaily toward the center of town. Families, strangers, and friends were singing and hugging and dancing on the green. Out of nowhere appeared an endless supply of gooseberry, dandelion, and rhubarb wine. Even dearly rationed food appeared abundantly on long tables placed hurriedly on sawhorses. The blackout curtains were dramatically torn down and there were dazzling candles everywhere. Not a door nor a window was closed. The villagers sang until they were hoarse and danced until they were dizzy with exhaustion. For that short time, everyone's mourning was placed in a basket and put away in the cupboard. After being pursued by laughing men who wanted to hug her, dance with her, kiss her, Sophie retreated to the edges. She was frightened by the attention, yet heartened by their gaiety.

"Sophie? Sophie Marks?" she heard someone yell. And there was Anne Vernons pushing her way through the crowd to reach her.

No, I can't do this, Sophie thought, and turned, slipping away around the corner.

The next day Sophie walked out to the property. She had not been there since the day she returned from the hospital. The fields had run riot with new vegetation. She looked for the apple tree, her beacon of orientation, and saw that it had grown another year bigger in the recuperating earth.

Sophie had to battle her way through the tall brush that was obviously enjoying its freedom to spread, though it smelled dank and moldering. The crater had filled with grass, weeds, and puddles of dark water. Although she could still see that it was a crater, it no longer looked ominous; indeed, it looked almost natural. Hands clasped behind her back, she circled it, trampling down the weeds, making a path, disturbing the ground enough to bring out a couple of harmless snakes and a large old frog, which made her smile.

Walking farther back onto the property, she came upon her grandfather's studio. Although it had not been hit directly, the firestorm had burned it almost to the ground. What was left was a section of the brick chimney and a number of pottery shards scattered about. A touch of color caught her eye and she leaned down. It was from one of the vases they had paint-ed: a small and delicate deep-purple flower, almost puce, with a piece of a green leaf. She could not remember if it was she or her grandfather who had painted it. It did not matter. At least she had something. Sophie wrapped it in a handkerchief and put it in her pocket.

Now that the war was over, the world appeared infinite and enigmatic and without borders. There was no one to nurse Sophie or show her the way. England was too full of memories, and her home, Pottery Cottage, was a mass grave. She could not live her life upon her family's bones. And even if she wanted to live there again, she did not have the energy, or the money, to rebuild.

More than ever, she had closed herself off to people, winding Ariadne's thread around her life, creating a maze, making it tricky for people to know her. Even her landlady, Mrs. Reed, whose bakery she had to pass through at least twice a day to go to and from her room, was a stranger. Simple "good mornings" and "good evenings" had been the extent of most of their conversations over that past year.

But a few days after the armistice, Mrs. Reed, who always smelled deliciously of yeast and sweetness, asked Sophie about her plans. She had not been conscious of even having an inkling of a plan, but out of her mouth tumbled her desire. "I've decided to go to Paris," she said.

"Paris," Mrs. Reed answered, wiping her flour-covered hands on her apron. "Why, that's like the other side of the world. Are you certain, dearie? You know, don't you, that no one there ever speaks English on purpose?"

"It was my grandmother's place of birth, and French was our household language," Sophie told her. "I'll be all right. Anyway, I need to do something. I can't spend the rest of my life here in the Midlands."

"And why not, may I ask you?" Mrs. Reed insisted, putting her fists on her wide hips. "What's wrong with our Midlands?"

"Oh, Mrs. Reed, I'm sorry; I didn't mean to be rude. There's nothing wrong with the Midlands. I just need a change."

When Sophie left, she was so distraught that as she climbed the narrow serpentine stairs, she hit her forehead on the overhang yet again.

"Watch the lintel, dearie," Mrs. Reed called out.

Sophie made herself a cup of tea and sat by the window. She could see out over the tile rooftops toward the west and a sky that moved from dark gray to a burst of hazy pink-and-yellow color. Every few minutes there would be a tinkling of the bakery's bell as the front door opened and another customer entered to buy pastries for her tea. Sophie's surprise decision felt right, but moving would not be easy. She did not have many possessions, but she did have a load of heavy burdens.

With an apple, I will astonish Paris.

—PAUL CÉZANNE

Yes. Paris. It was chaos. The lines at the passport office extended forever. Finally, *Sophie Marks, pleasure traveler* was written in brown ink on her legal papers. Immediately after checking into a cheap hotel in the sixth arrondissement, she went to bed. Sophie had had to pluck up every ounce of daring to get across the Channel. She needed to recover. Purposely, she reduced herself to one tablet a day. And then none at all. Lightness appeared before her eyes. The darkest shadows went into hiding.

Even though Sophie had entered France as a tourist, she was now a refugee. She searched for rental signs. Although not conscious of it, Sophie was also searching for André and René. Indeed, one day, coming through a passage, she looked up and saw a crowd of people standing on a corner waiting to cross the street. Her stomach made a leap. Was that René in the blue shirt with the small boy by his side? No, of course not. But it rattled her. For a moment, she was not sure whom she was missing most.

Apartments were scarce. With the war over, soldiers, displaced persons, people who had been living out the duration of the fighting in the countryside, everyone was coming home. Finding a place to live was an almost ridiculous task. Finally, after three weeks, she happened to be walking by a small, whitewashed stone apartment building on the cobblestoned and winding rue Bonaparte, at the exact moment when the concierge was putting the For Rent sign in the window.

Sophie had arrived in Paris with one battered brown card-board suitcase she had found empty and abandoned under the bed at Mrs. Reed's. It was packed with two floral-print summer dresses, the pottery shard, the pencil portrait of the soldier, and Claire's recipe for fish pie. She also had her old army knapsack filled with the art supplies she had been given by the soldier.

The flat was bleakly furnished. A mattress was the challenge. She refused to buy a used one. The idea of sleeping upon someone else's dreams was impossible to consider. After much rummaging about, she had been able to buy stray remnants of cotton batting and loosely lashed this together with strips of cotton sheeting and sewed a cover to go over the lot. It was lumpy, but it worked.

Sophie roamed the streets of Paris, trying to get lost on purpose. She forced herself to become acquainted with the city. When she found her way home to the rue Bonaparte, she always felt a sense of triumph.

One day Sophie came across a devastated site where there were pieces of marble, many the size of a loaf of bread. They must have once been cornices of a building or a windowsill or an ornament over a door, all blown off their original homes by explosions. In the midst of that gray wasteland, there was a tall man with longish, curly dark hair and glasses. He was sifting through the debris. As Sophie began to ask him if they were allowed to take the marble away, she was interrupted, from her left, by another man whom she had not seen.

"Need some help, mademoiselle?" he asked with a flirt in his voice.

This man was a tad shorter than Sophie, with a muscular body, reminding her of a coal miner in the Midlands. Well dressed, especially for that time, he had a sense of safety and privilege about him. Yet his face did not fit his clothing; he had a round head with German-style cropped blond hair and a pugnacious nose and a thin, almost mean, mouth. He was wearing the tortoise-shell, round-framed glasses that French intellectuals had adopted for their badge. A man of many faces, he was too complicated to catalogue.

"Can I help you?" he asked again.

"No, well, yes, but you'll get dirty," she said, and he simply shrugged.

"Not a problem," he answered. "This isn't my entire wardrobe," he said, as if she should have known better.

His was not an educated French; the accent sounded as if he had come from the countryside. But Sophie really had no idea, coming from the rarefied world of her grandmother's kitchen table.

"I would like to take that home," she said, pointing to a heavy-looking piece of white marble.

"What will you do with it? It's only a piece of rubble."

Meanwhile, the other man, the one with the dark hair, had lifted a few pieces of scrap wood into a wheelbarrow and was wobbling his way to the sidewalk, where he turned the corner and disappeared. There she was, standing alone in the midst of wreckage, anxiously talking to a stranger.

"I plan to use it to mix with gesso," she finally said. "I'm a painter."

"What do you mean? You paint the rubble?"

"No." She had to laugh. "I'll beat the edges of the marble to dust and add it to gesso to create a luminosity on the canvas."

"Odd," he said, shaking his head as if to say, I don't understand, but it doesn't matter. He turned around and beckoned to someone. Before Sophie could protest, another man appeared, lifted the marble, put it on his shoulder, and walked over to a car.

She began an affair with the close-cropped blond man. His name was Jean.

A pattern was quickly established. His driver would meet Sophie in front of her apartment building and drive to Montmartre. Because Jean's street was much too steep and narrow for automobiles, the driver would drop her at the bottom of the hill.

Jean's apartment was uncomfortably elegant, richly decorated, and entirely new. It felt like a stage set. This made her curious. But her curiosity was unsatisfied. Jean lived in a vacuum. No mail left on the desk. No photographs. No clues.

Sophie was hungry for him and everything he offered. He would fill her with superb black-market food and wine in clandestine restaurants. She entered an oblivion of carnal feelings, the wine allowing her relief from her nightmares, the passion allowing her to be tethered to her body.

There was not much talk. When Sophie questioned him, he would exhale only a trifling bit of information that she intuitively knew was a lie. Sometimes he would tell a story she had heard before, but with a different slant. When she caught him in a discrepancy, he would merely shrug his shoulders and smile. And truthfully, Sophie really did not care if he was lying or not. It made no difference. The situation suited her. There was nothing more she wanted. After each evening together, no matter what time it was, he would send her back to the rue Bonaparte with the driver.

One evening, as Sophie was beginning to walk up the hill, she saw Jean farther up the road with two men. The men looked coarse. One was dark, perhaps Algerian, and the other glaringly white, more like someone from Sweden. They were dressed in rough clothing: work trousers, collarless shirts, black fedoras, and sabots.

When Jean saw her coming, he motioned to the two men to move around the corner, and went along with them. She stood there like a dumb ox.

"Look here, Mademoiselle," his driver said, appearing at her side and startling her. "I think I should take you home. He'll be busy the rest of the evening and you'll have to wait in the car. Come along now."

"No, I'll wait around the corner at the café," she told him. "I'm hungry."

He simply shrugged and Sophie walked on.

Entering the café was like walking into an icebox. Cold stares, icy shoulders; she had never had an experience like that. After waiting a good ten minutes, with no one paying her any mind, she rose and approached the proprietor, who was positioned like a soldier at the cash register.

"What's going on?" she demanded in a newly found voice of indignation. "Why am I being ignored?"

"It's him," the proprietor snarled, tossing his full head of white hair at the street.

"You mean Jean?" she asked.

"Mademoiselle," he emphatically responded, "his name is not Jean. His name is Paul Ribard and he's a collaborator—a thief, and a murderer." And the proprietor pretended to slash his own throat with his thumb. "You do not know this? What's wrong with you?"

Sophie had to sit down. "What are you saying?" she whispered, as he leaned toward her to hear better.

"He should be hanged," the proprietor announced, standing tall and placing his hands around his own neck. "And I'm sure he will be soon. Be careful, Mademoiselle; don't get caught in his net."

Something in the way Sophie reacted must have convinced the proprietor that she did not know about Jean, now Paul Ribard. "Here, I'll get you a brandy," he said, and he signaled to the bar. She realized that everyone in the café was watching her.

"But," she asked, sweeping her eyes around the room,

"how do these people know about me? I've never seen any of them before."

"Mademoiselle, this is a neighborhood café, we all know everything about everyone. Especially about collaborators and their friends!"

Sophie was stuck. She knew the proprietor was correct.

"Aren't you afraid to tell me these things?" she asked, inviting him to sit down.

"After what Paris has been through," he declared, "I am no longer afraid of anything. Unless you're one of them, and I don't think you are—I see a Jew in your eyes. Be careful, Mademoiselle."

All she could do was nod in agreement and drink down the brandy. She was stunned by her own stupidity, her naïveté, her unbridled hunger for comfort.

The proprietor kindly patted her hand. "You don't need to know more, Mademoiselle. I can see that you now know enough. Let me suggest that you get out of here. Does he know where you live?" And she nodded.

"My God, my God," he said, shaking his great mop of hair. "You must be very careful.

"Come with me," he ordered, standing and taking her hand. "I'll show you a private way out. Fortunately, I have a feeling that *Comrade* Ribard will not be around much longer. There's been a lot of activity today outside the building. I think something serious is going on."

The next day, still shaken, Sophie warily skulked onto the street. Suddenly a shadow transformed into a man. The driver gripped her wrist like an iron bracelet. "Mademoiselle, come with me."

"No," she cried out, terribly afraid. "Let me go."

"Please, Mademoiselle," he warned between his teeth, "don't make a scene. You don't know who you're tangling with. You don't want to cross him, or—"

"Tell him I'm ill. Tell him I'll get in touch with him when I'm feeling better."

"No, it's not going to do. He wants to see you now."

"Look," Sophie pleaded, "you've been very nice to me. Why are you doing this? I promise you that if you don't let me go, I will begin to shriek—I will call for the police—I will—"

The driver wilted. He let go of her wrist. "All right, Mademoiselle. I'll tell him I looked for you, but your concierge said you had left. You must be very careful. He'll be looking for you. I suggest you go to the country."

Of course she did not go to the country. Such an idea! But it took Sophie a couple of weeks of slinking around her neighborhood, hugging the walls, trying to be invisible, before she got over the anxiety of being unearthed by Paul Ribard. She remembered being warned by Nurse Watson at the sanitarium that she had to be careful of being lured by the union of comfort and the want of emotional attachment. "One slice of you may want this," the nurse had said, "because it's the easiest way to wander through a life. But beware of bogus ease. It will embrace you warmly and then suffocate you to death."

Sophie was painting again. She needed to hone her skills; like a musician, like any artist, she needed to practice. She was easing her grandfather's style out of her technique of painting—his colors, his dark lines, his people's faces imbued with their rural lives—all giving way to her own style. Her colors were becoming muted, the edges gentler, as if her hand was moving in slow motion; she was reminded of the blurred photograph of her father.

Torn between the conventional, almost stoic Renaissance form she had used for the soldier and the emotional approach of Soutine, which was more her grandfather's style, Sophie eventually, after worrying experimentation, wove the genres together. She began to hire models. Like her grandfather, Sophie was interested not in pretty people, but in people with the world in their eyes. After the war they were certainly easy enough to find: in soup kitchens, sleeping in doorways, sweeping the streets. It was not difficult to hire subjects with the promise of a few francs, a carafe of red wine, and a pot of hot soup on the stove.

She was moved to paint the moisture that was pooling at the corners of an old woman's hungry mouth. She painted the expressive fear in a man's eyes, using a modeled black, with highlights of zinc white; she painted the benevolence that a charwoman was revealing toward an unfair world, not using black at all, but instead a burnt sienna to tone down the emotion. They spoke to her while she painted. Their stories, their opinions, their dreams—all helped Sophie construct their portraits. She did not mind their moving out of their poses; this showed her more about them, allowing her to capture intimate angles of their emotional characters.

Sophie no longer thought about the calamity of Paul Ribard, nor was she any longer aware of a desire to dig René out of the ashes of Paris. But André's head still appeared on the shoulders of little boys. Her guilt about not heeding Eli— not sending André to safety—weighed upon her at times to such an extent that she was rendered wretched with heart pain.

Sophie worried that she was better at seeing herself from the inside out rather than the outside in. She had always envied the women in ornate Italian sixteenth-century paintings who were both luminous and voluptuous, available to inquisitive eyes with such haughtiness, such assurance. Much to her chagrin, she was a bit taller than average and rail thin. And because she was alone so much, when she spoke she heard her voice as tall and thin as well. It sounded to her as she imagined a giraffe would sound: squawking and high up, with clouds girdling the neck.

Some people thought Sophie quite poised, but it was really an almost unbearable shyness. She was not a beauty by any means. She had a plain face with dark eyebrows that were a little too full. Her nose was a tad too long, although her mouth was quite pleasantly shaped. What made her so distinctive were her stunning, almond-shaped eyes with their long, thick black eyelashes. As she grew older, her eyes became darker, almost black. Her face was supple; when in repose it appeared to be too long, drawn too low. However, when she was animated, it firmed and looked shorter than it really was. It was a mysterious face—part Semitic, part gentrified English.

If Sophie lived cheaply there would be enough money to last for a little while. But it was obvious that she had to get serious about making a living. Sophie wandered along the Seine, thinking, trolling for ideas. She was certain that she wanted to paint for a living. But how? She knew that she appeared masked; no one was really able to tell if she was hiding behind secrets or a painful shyness. She understood that people thought her detached, even cold; most likely working in a shop was out of the question.

Sophie realized she could join other artists on the quay. She set up her easel on the sidewalk near the book vendors on the quai de Conti. Drawing portraits of American soldiers and a smattering of tourists appeared to her to be a perfectly honorable way to make money.

The first day at work, Sophie could barely look at the people passing by; she felt that she was a hunter, looking for prey. But she was determined. Having dressed in black, fixed her hair in a long braid, and applied kohl around her eyes, she tried to appear mysterious, somewhat bohemian.

She watched the other artists. Tourists simply arrived on their stools, sat quietly for thirty minutes or so, and then reached into their pockets for money. She understood that she had to feign being French to give the encounter a "foreign" flavor; she knew that a touch of theater was necessary.

Pretending to be lost in her work, she began an imaginary portrait of her grandmother. Claire's face emerged out of the conté crayon and before Sophie knew it, a small group of people had gathered around.

"May I?" a soldier asked, and sat on the stool—and Sophie could hear Claire laughing in her memory.

It was awkward to look him in the eye. She remembered Eli telling her that if she was to be a serious painter of portraits, she must study how people used their eyes to express emotion. "If you're uncomfortable," he said, "it means that they're telling you something you don't want to know." She knew he was right. However, Sophie was terrified that she might read the truth about the whole world if she looked too closely.

When she leaned back for a moment, she noticed the same tall dark-haired man who had been at the marble site with the wheelbarrow. They smiled at each other with shy recognition. But then she ignored him, too involved in work to flirt.

The soldier paid Sophie his francs. Too embarrassed to count them, she put them immediately in her pocket. She walked over to the stone wall to have a cigarette, already having learned that that was what the artists did when they did not want to be bothered—an unspoken recess. The tall man was nearby, drawing in a black, paperbound sketchbook that he had placed atop the wall, using it as a table. Out of the corner of her eye, she watched. The sketches were of abstract forms and sinuous nude women. She though him quite handsome, and his drawings accomplished. She went back to her stool and a bulky woman sat opposite her, waiting to be drawn.

To be an artist is to believe in life.

—HENRY MOORE

Luca Bondi, the man standing beside Sophie, felt that war created a profound form of loneliness and longing. People, scattered, unable to root themselves again, searched for stability, for love. He had been in Paris almost a year and had been working diligently in his studio, too determined to take the time to create a community for himself. Paris was his dream. In Paris he would become a serious and well-known artist. But he was lonely.

Luca was a tall, gangly man. Although his ears were a trifle large, they were hidden by his thick black curly hair. He had a broad forehead with a prominent nose, distinctive in its Roman bearing. One's eyes were always drawn to his mouth because it was firm and sensuous at the same time. His eyes hid behind the reflection from his glasses. But when he took them off to read, one could see that they were nice eyes—brown with black circles drawn around the iris.

It was a soggy day in September, with little sun, and a dense gray blanket of hot air sitting glumly over Paris. Luca was excited to see the mysterious woman again. Very few women artists drew on the streets. He thought Sophie intriguingly angular, as if her joints were connected by thin wires like a marionette. But it was her face that captured him. She looked as if she had just wandered out of the Arabian desert, thrown back a veil, and was seeing the world for the first time. He was so moved by the look of wonder in her eyes that he imagined she must have been traveling for centuries.

He watched as she drew an artificially redheaded and copiously perspiring woman, concluding that the woman must not be French because she stood out so grossly among the thin citizens. He marveled at how Sophie drew her true to life—multiple chins and all.

"It's finished, Madame," Sophie said in English with a French accent, and sat back for the woman to have a look.

"Bloody hell," the woman exclaimed in English. "You've made me fat and ugly. How dare you." And she snatched up the drawing and tore it in half, and then in half again. Sophie was stunned. As the woman dropped it at her feet, she declared, "You're not an artist. You're a fraud, sent by the devil."

"No," erupted the group that had gathered around.

"Madame," Sophie said, beginning to stand. "You owe me ten francs."

"I will not pay a penny," the woman firmly replied, and turned to leave.

"Money her," Luca demanded in broken English.

"Make me!" the lady challenged.

"No speak that way," Luca said, purposely standing in her way.

"Get out of my way," she snarled.

"A policeman . . ." Luca countered, and headed toward the boulevard.

By the time he returned with the policeman, Sophie and the crowd had all evaporated into the muggy late-summer air.

Sophie's studio on the rue Bonaparte was the alchemical lab of her imagination. If she was not drawing on the quay, she traditionally began the day as a nomad, wandering from the painting wall to the worktable, straightening the tubes of paint, having a cup of coffee, a cigarette, staring out the window. Before long, a door in her imagination would inevitably open and she could invite in the winds of possibility. Sophie would pick up her brush and dip into a color. Then, placing the brush upon the canvas and making that first sensuous and hopeful stroke, she was off, lost in her task.

Even though Sophie was forced to use an easel on the quay, she never liked working on one; their wobbly tripod legs drove her to distraction. In her studio, when she began a new painting, she tacked a piece of cloth directly onto the wall. Then she primed the surface with gesso or rabbit glue, or a mixture of both, transforming it into an acceptable painting surface.

When there was too much light in the room, the colors on both the canvas and the palette would become so refracted that she was not able to distinguish their nuances. That was when she put on the kettle to take a break, waiting for the light to soften. As soon as the sun passed over the roof, she would work again. Evenings arrived without warning. It was at a particular moment, that moment when Sophie unconsciously reached over to flick on a light switch, that everything changed. Colors changed, forms changed, lights changed. The engagement of the working day had ended.

Next to the painting area was a bookcase made of bricks and planks of wood. On the top shelf was a variety of brown leather sketchbooks. Sophie was never without one, either in her pocket or in her bag. Eli used to tease her and say that a pencil was growing out of her hand like the tree in the Hans Christian Andersen fable. Sometimes, to pique her sensitivity, she would close her eyes and draw into the darkness. That private visual vocabulary always appeared as a surprise, a gift of inner sight.

Sophie worked on the quay until late autumn. She wondered what had happened to the man who had tried to help her; she hoped she would see him again. But he never appeared. It soon became too cold for her to hold a piece of conté crayon, and certainly too cold for anyone to want to sit. When she counted the contents of her savings bank (a hole she had cut in the underside of the mattress), she saw that she had enough to get through the winter.

Winter isolated Sophie. She spent long hours closeted within her imagination. She understood that to accomplish good work she had to be honest, even if she had to scrape her own bones, listen to their excruciating sounds, and feel the unbearable pain. Sophie remembered Eli saying, "If you're not honest with your work—if you're being merely decorative—then the world will know. People intuit honest work. They know when they're being tricked by clever metaphors in pictures, by dishonesty in the artist. You have to trust that your audience wants to learn, that it longs to feel something while looking at art. It's your responsibility to fulfill this task. If you don't try to keep to this purpose, then you should be doing something else."

One day Sophie went to buy a bottle of black ink at the Laubreaux Art & Framing Shop. Tacked up on the wall was an announcement for a juried competition that was sponsored by the shop. She submitted three paintings. "Will people come, do you think?" she asked the owner, Monsieur Laubreaux.

"But, of course," he proclaimed. "Many artists in Paris buy supplies from me. I'll post an announcement in the window, that's all I can afford to do. But I'll serve wine at the opening, and you know what that means!"

All three of her paintings were accepted. The canvas of the old charwoman with a faded red head scarf, sitting on a stool and peeling a potato into a bright green bowl while she told Sophie the story of how, a century before, her family had been gentry. The canvas of Madame, her concierge, keeping a discreet distance behind her grimy lace curtains, but with her head turned and one piercing blue eye seen through the lace. And the canvas of the gnarled old ragman, holding a cigarette while resting his crossed wrists upon his brown corduroy lap. He wore a crucifix around his neck and was squinting one eye from the constant smoke. He hardly spoke, but hummed popular tunes. Besides student exhibitions at the Slade years before, this was to be her first real exhibition.

On a frigid winter's evening, Sophie went to the Marais to the opening of an exhibition of work by Tomas, a Czech artist; he was known for his gruesome depictions of the bad times they had all been through. Each canvas was painted with large, violent gestures of ivory, black, and occasional touches of a variety of browns. Sophie longed for a spot of color.

She noticed a man coming in her direction. Sophie's heart skipped. It was the man from the obstinate-woman fiasco and the marble site. His thick, dark hair set off an animated face. Silver wire-rimmed glasses had slipped a bit down his nose as he moved slowly through the coagulated cigarette smoke from one painting to the next. He must have just had a haircut for he looked quite trimmed. In order to study a painting better, he swayed his body back like a thin and vulnerable limb of a tree, his feet rooted to the floor. When he turned to move on to the next painting, he caught her eye and smiled.

"Do you like?" he asked, his long arms sweeping the room.

She shrugged.

He appeared surprised by her aloofness. But in reality, her stomach was going in circles. After the muddle she had made of the Paul Ribard affair, she worried that she could not handle diversions and was afraid she certainly could not handle the complexities of a flirtation. So instead of introducing herself, she simply smiled and walked into the crowd of people, out the other side, and through the door.

*

Luca was flummoxed. He had looked forward to the evening, longing for heat and the opportunity to meet new people, especially women. When he saw Sophie, he sensed the possibility of an adventure. Of course he remembered her. At the rubble site he had watched her, even though he pretended to be busy. He imagined she had fallen through the rays of the sun to find him. But then she was approached by a well-dressed stranger and before he could make a gesture toward her, she was getting into the stranger's sleek black car. It was hopeless. Luca could not compete. Then when he reconnected with her on the quay, he felt he was being given another chance. But again she slipped away and he assumed that, if she had been interested, she would not have left. Luca had a short romance with an artists' model, but still could not get Sophie out of his imagination.

Sophie went to the opening at Monsieur Laubreaux's gallery and flattened herself against the wall, trying to observe the observers, trying not to be observed.

"Hello, Sophie, it's been a long time." And there before her was Anne Vernons, her old childhood friend. Anne looked almost the same. Long blond hair, a pale, coral-colored, open and simple face. Except now she had bright, sensuous ruby-red lips. Sophie paused a moment, trying to hold herself back, still rattled by memories of England. But she could not resist the joy of seeing Anne again, and they embraced.

"Your work's wonderful, darling," Anne said, "and I hope you don't mind my saying but it reminds me of your grandfather."

Sophie's enthusiasm froze.

"Oh, Sophie." Anne caught on very quickly. "Oh, darling, I'm sorry! Please don't run away like you did at the armistice celebration."

They both tried to rein in conflicting feelings. "Please," Sophie said, "please don't mention those years."

"Of course not, darling, I promise."

Anne would be in Paris for only a few more days, trying to puzzle her way out of a semi-arranged engagement. The young man was from the upper class and the son of family friends. A trip to Paris had been her mother's bribe. "Go, have a nice time, darling." But her mother was hoping that Anne would see the ravages of war, feel frightened and alone and vulnerable, and flee back to the safety of their village in the Midlands and her fiancé. Mothers never learn.

Four paintings were sold from the exhibition; one was Sophie's painting of the ragman. Monsieur Laubreaux was happy. Sophie received two reviews, one good, one bad, and made the mistake of reading both. She could not remember what the good review said, not a word. However, she never forgot a phrase from the bad review: "Marks is too self-involved. Her portraits are not of suffering people, but of a suffering Sophie Marks."

The weather was improving, as was everyone's temper. Although Paris was a deeply exhausted city, it was beginning its long journey back to normality. Its citizens were planting. Instead of the usual prewar assortment of flower seeds in window boxes and ceramic pots, vegetables were being planted in every conceivable container: spent howitzer shell casings, cut-off gasoline cans. Aesthetics did not matter. The possibility of fresh food drove Sophie to the roof, where she built plant boxes.

For eight days, blessed by persistent sunshine, Sophie pedaled her bicycle out of Paris toward the countryside, looking for good dirt. She had to ride quite a way. The roadside ditches were still filled with wartime rubble and questionable debris. Finally, the ditches reverted to their normal soft earth, easy to dig. Using a bucket, she filled her basket, a wooden ammo crate she had wired onto the handlebars, and two oversized rucksacks, lashed onto the seat and balanced on either side of the back fender; a third rucksack she wore on her back. Sophie steadied, wobbled, and wove her way back to Paris.

On the ninth day of dirt gathering, just as she turned onto the rue Bonaparte, she almost ran down Luca. Truly, he gave her quite a fright. But then again, her heart landed in her mouth and she could not help but be happy.

"Do you remember me?" he asked.

"Yes, of course," Sophie said.

"Can I help you?" he asked.

"Yes, of course," she said.

They climbed to the top floor, each lugging a bag of dirt.

"Is the turpentine smell coming from your studio? May I see what you're working on? May I—"

"Not now," Sophie firmly said. "Another time."

For a moment, though, standing with him on the roof, looking out over the city, she had to admit that she felt more than a whisper of hope in the air. "It's magnificent," he said in French with an Italian accent. And Sophie answered yes, in French with an English accent.

They laughed at the confusion of accents, both realizing they were refugees.

"If you will allow me, Sophie Marks."

"How do you know my name?"

"Why, I saw your exhibition. Congratulations. I like the work very much."

"Oh, now I see. Thank you," she said, and put out her hand.

"Luca Bondi," he answered, putting out his.

Their friendship began with earnest discussions about the merits of certain vegetables: which ones they liked the most, which ones were the dearest on the escalating black market, and which ones were worth growing for their nutrition. They agreed it would be best to leave out all the whitish vegetables, sacrificing endive for kale, radishes for beets. And they laughed together and it felt awfully good.

"Since I have to plant more root vegetables," Sophie realized, "this will mean deeper planting beds. We need more soil." And both were relieved to keep the mission going.

For the next few days, Luca met Sophie and they rode out of the city to gather more soil. They also bartered for seeds with farmers and saved them in twisted pieces of newspaper with handwritten labels attached with a piece of string. In the end they collected most everything Sophie needed, including a head of garlic and four onions, all of which were sprouting new buds.

There were few cows or horses left near Paris; they had been slaughtered for food or revenge. But there were stashes of manure hidden by farmers, and this treasure was almost as precious as cigarettes and wine. Sophie and Luca traded cigarettes for all the manure they could carry, and cycled back to Paris, grinning with their bounty. Knowing how they smelled, they were delighted by the startled stares of people on the streets. In one day they mixed in the manure and planted the seeds. And then, as if by Providence, it rained.

Never once did Luca speak about his feelings for Sophie— nor Sophie's for Luca. At that point, she was protesting to herself, she was too engaged in creating her garden to plant her heart anywhere else. Then, all of a sudden, it was over. As soon as they finished planting, Luca disappeared.

Sophie missed him. She waited, but it was soon obvious that he was not coming. The encounter, and then the disappearance, was too close to what had happened with René. She was angry at herself for even dreaming of love. She went back the way she had come, alone.

What loneliness is more lonely than distrust?

—GEORGE ELIOT

Luca returned the following May. He drew alongside Sophie on his bicycle as she was walking at the edge of the Jardin du Luxembourg. Sheepishly, stumbling over his words, his thin body twisting like a pipe cleaner, he greeted her. Sophie was also confused and felt like a tittering young schoolgirl.

"I have to apologize to you," he said.

"No, it's all right—truly it is. There's no need to—"

"But I must tell you. I had to go back because my mother died."

"Oh, I'm terribly sorry. Oh—"

"No, no, it's all right, really it is."

"Why did you come back?" Sophie asked.

"I came back to find you."

Sophie found Luca's intensity enthralling. He had dramatic dusty-gray circles under his eyes, reminding her of the famous death photograph of Marcel Proust. She felt as if she were looking through his shadow to the other side. They agreed to have coffee.

When the war began, Luca felt that Cain had manacled himself to wheels and hauled Europe through the gates of hell. There was no escape. It was 1943. His best friend, Carlo Zanotti, had slipped away from their village of Monterosa to join a band of partisans. Although Luca agonized about going with him, he could not leave his parents. Since he was the only child, they depended on him. His father had been ill and was forced to retire early from his university position. Hovering over her husband, his mother needed Luca to deal with the heavy work in the house, and to bestow the hope of youth. So Luca stayed home and spent his spare time drawing and doing small iron-forging jobs in the village. It felt as if the family was waiting for war to find them. But, secretly, Luca got ready. From the day that Carlo left, Luca wore a leather pouch around his neck with his papers and a ruby that his mother had given him when he turned eighteen.

People who survived the bombing, Sophie understood, did not always survive the war. Their scars could be invisible—at least until someone said or did something to bump against the injury. Then these disfigurements could open up, causing pain to rise to the surface in frightening spasms. Before Luca returned, it had begun to dawn on Sophie that he might have serious war experiences, perhaps like her own.

"I can't believe," he said, taking her hand in both of his, "that I've found you again. You're still as lovely as I remembered."

Sophie knew it was not really a question of whether she wanted to continue on with Luca, but how she was going to do it. He fascinated her with his persistence, his tall, willowy good looks, his rose-colored confidence. After all that had happened in her life, she really had not thought she would allow herself to fall in love again.

They talked until evening about selected parts of their lives—it was too early to reveal secrets. He suggested they have dinner at his favorite café. It was in an ancient stone cellar where empty green raffia-covered wine bottles corked with candles tried to light the way. Sophie and Luca groped a path, tripping over chairs and feet until they found a table. It was noisy and smoky and vibrant with life.

They ordered the only item on the menu, *ragoût de lapin*, really an awful stew of rabbit and potatoes and gray green beans, along with a carafe of red wine. But it did not matter; except for the few people who could afford the black market, everyone else in Paris was suffering the same kind of meals. After they finished the first carafe of wine, Luca's tone of voice changed from light and chatty to dark.

"The war," he began.

Sophie interrupted. "I really don't want to hear about the war."

"Yes, you're right, another time."

Luca was relieved. He was afraid to tell his story; he was afraid his words could become bullets and murder the possibility of hope. He sat back, understanding that they were both going to keep some secrets. It was too early in peacetime to face the truth. So they talked about art. And they both could see that they shared a passion for it. From the textures of the surfaces to the alchemy of the paints to the psychology of the painting—they were fascinated by it all.

It was late and they were still in the same bustling café. People were dressed in the drab, overwashed colors of war. When Sophie squinted, all she could see were browns and grays, with splotches of mahogany and orange-vermilion henna on the heads of many of the women, along with the ugly turbans made necessary by the want of soap and fashionable by Simone de Beauvoir.

Luca crossed his gangly arms on the table, hands clutching his elbows. His long neck was swanning toward Sophie in a most becoming manner. As he reached for his wine, she noticed how dirty his fingernails were and how scratched and bruised his hands, the hands of a sculptor. Sophie liked that.

She liked the intensity of his hands—the expressive, sure way he used them to make a point. They were strong, useful hands. He waited until she looked up, held her eyes, took a drink. Sophie thought he was posturing, trying to look romantic; perhaps he wanted a quick affair? She was not sure. But she felt stirrings of desire. Not just to make love, but to be held in his arms and soothed—to chase away memory.

It was the decisive moment of their relationship. She decided not to flee.

"You can see, Sophie," Luca almost sang, "that we're in love. Probably have been since we planted your carrots!"

Sophie resisted. But she knew he was right; she had known it as soon as she saw him that afternoon. A future with Luca; was it inevitable? No, it simply could not be. "I have to live alone, Luca," Sophie said. "I'm not capable of living with anyone. Something is broken within me."

He was clearly taken aback. "What do you mean, Sophie? How can you say such a thing after today?" Taking her hand, he gently pulled her to him and they kissed. And she felt his softness—she smelled his skin—she sensed the idea of being cherished.

He was whispering, quite light-headed by now. "You do know, Sophie, that we've been dancing around each other. I want to be with you. I feel you agree—don't you? And I know this sounds preposterous, but I want to marry you."

"Please," she said, moved by his declaration, but miffed at his assumption. "You've had too much wine. Marriage, absolutely impossible. Luca, I'm not an easy person to live with. When I'm working I don't want to be bothered. I close myself away. I truly enjoy being alone. And I don't want children." Sophie lit another cigarette, and even in the dim light, she could watch emotions glide across his face.

"But women can be both artists and mothers," he said defensively.

"No, they can't, Luca. It's impossible. You'd be in the studio and I'd be at the kitchen table with a paintbrush in one hand and a baby in the other. All of us would suffer; you, the baby, me, *and* the painting."

"But if you're my wife—" He began to raise his voice and she could see the people around them listening, while trying to look as if they were not. "I'll be bound by honor to care for you and a child, too!"

Sophie's heart turned cold. "This is not going to work," she said, and she rose and began to leave.

"No! You're not to leave!" he growled, and she was so embarrassed that she sat down; seeking privacy, she turned her back to the closest table.

"Listen. Listen to what I have to say." His tone was hard; his words were sculpted, chiseled to sharp edges, precise. He looked Sophie straight in the eyes, forcing her to look away. "Oh, forget it. I don't even know why we're having this conversation." He threw his words into the air. "We've never even been to bed together. Come, I'll show you my studio."

"Absolutely not," Sophie shot back. "Don't you dare order me around like that." Luca began to laugh. It was a sweet laugh, a serious and real laugh that made her want to laugh right back. She liked the absurdity of their encounter; it reminded her of her grandparents and how they had flirted with each other. Her cheeks used to burn with embarrassment, but their laughter actually made her feel beloved, too, as if she was part of the vibrating air swirling around them. Now it seemed ludicrous to turn away.

As they walked, hand in hand, Sophie felt herself stepping off into an unknown land. Soon they entered Luca's studio and he switched on the light. The room was enormous, with slanted skylights facing north. Under the windows was an old dining table with carved, curlicue legs, two unmatched wood-en chairs, a stained coffee cup, and a half-eaten baguette. On the floor, to the left, was a pallet of straw, unmade, with grim-looking sheets.

Sophie was staggered by the strong, almost overwhelming smell of wood: more like a lumber mill than a forest—an unlikely aroma to find in a Paris studio. Then she looked more closely.

It was at that moment Sophie fell in love with Luca. His work was stunning. He had mortised together pieces of wood to create large blocks into each of which was carved a person. There were twenty-two people in all—all finely sculpted, smooth to the touch. They were dressed in country clothes, all carved into the wood. Some of their arms were linked; some were holding each other's hands; some were standing alone, lost in thought. A couple of elderly peasants were leaning against the wall watching the others. The people were life-size, five to six feet tall, and viewers, like Sophie, could walk among them, becoming part of the installation. Luca had encouraged the wood to life. Sophie could not resist running her hands over their bodies.

"This is amazing. You've created an entire world of your own."

"Not exactly a world," he replied, "but a village, my own imaginary village. After all," he shrugged, "the world has not proved to be Eden. So I've chosen to make my own world, both here," he said pointing to his head, "in my imagination, and here," placing his hand on his chest, "here in my heart."

Without speaking, Sophie placed her hand over his heart, too.

When Sophie woke, it was still dark and Luca was asleep, flat on his back, with a slight frown on his face. He was nude, except for the grimy sheet wrapped around one ankle. She liked his body. It was not as bony as she had imagined, but lithe. As she explored his body with her eyes, he began to smile, watching Sophie in his imagination. Passion was not asleep at four in the morning.

With the sun coming through a window, Sophie woke to the silent people watching them. "Do you have nightmares?" she asked, shivering at their looming bodies beside the bed.

Luca laughed. "Yes, actually it's not good for me to sleep with them. Sometimes I wake in the night and the outside light's being refracted by their surfaces and I think they're the roving gang of hooligans who took away my father. Sometimes, when the light is softer toward morning, they're comforting to me, protecting me."

"Your father?" she asked.

"Yes, he was taken away, beaten, returned to my mother, and killed two months later by the Germans.

"But I don't want to talk about that," Luca pushed on. "The sculpture won't be here much longer. I have an exhibition coming up at that new gallery near the Louvre.

"And I've decided," he said, "that if it doesn't sell, I'll eventually figure out a way to ship them home. Exactly where in England is your home, Sophie?" he asked, turning to face her on the pillow. What nice eyes he had. She could not detect even a tinge of malice.

"I don't have one," Sophie said to his kind face.

Over coffee Luca told her selected pieces about his family. His mother had been a French teacher; his father, a professor of European history. The Bondis did not have much of a family— no aunts, no uncles, but a few distant second cousins. Sometimes Luca felt they had all sprouted out of the earth from seeds dropped by migrating birds. "I talk to you about my family," Luca said, "but you haven't said a word about yours. Who are you? Did you arrive here on the wind?"

Sophie knew she would soon have to offer up a story to Luca. But which one? The entire truth? Utterly impossible. She finally told him a partial story. Her parents' deaths. Being raised by Claire and Eli. Pottery Cottage. Her work during the war. Luca was fascinated. But she erased her pregnancy: the catastrophe.

"And then what happened to your grandparents?" he asked. "Are they still alive?"

"Oh, no," Sophie said. "They both died."

*Love is a canvas furnished by nature
and embroidered by imagination.*

—VOLTAIRE

Falling in love with you," Luca said, "makes me want to take you home to Italy. Between the two of us working, we'll create enough excitement to make up for leaving Paris." Sophie felt perennially rootless, so it was an enticing offer. By this time she would follow him anywhere.

Luca, a gregarious person, needed Sophie to help him understand his inner world, and she certainly needed him to keep a door open to the outside. But of course there would be problems. Luca was vociferously opinionated and highly sensitive to political situations. And he was an ardent humanist. He could barely kill a fly. As a result, his studio was a veritable kingdom for rodents. He did not mind their tenancy but Sophie could not bear either their odors or their quick appearances on the bed. She believed in killing the rodents. Also, Sophie kept an arm's-length attitude about how the political world functioned; she believed governments were simply groups of hungry individuals, out for power for themselves, not for helping others.

"You think about governments as my mother thought about religion," he told her. But even with all the terror the world had experienced, still, somewhere tucked away, Sophie believed that, if she was kind to the world, the world would be kind to her.

They were in Sophie's apartment; Luca was sprawled on the floor, she on the bed. The windows were open to a soft breeze sending up faint noises from the street four stories below. It was a Sunday afternoon in late September, one of the most dazzling autumns Paris had ever seen. Chopin's Nocturne in B-flat Minor was playing on the radio and a road map of Europe was spread out on the floor between them.

"I'm excited, Luca. My family never traveled farther south than Bourges. Except for the desert in America, my grandfather adored the idea of Italy more than any place he could imagine. As far back as I can remember he had sepia postcards from Rome and the surrounding countryside tacked onto a wall in his studio.

"And," she said laughing, "I remember one of the postcards was of Michelangelo's *David*. I was fascinated since it was the first time I'd seen a nude man. Needless to say I was embarrassed when he caught me staring, but he had the good instinct not to tease me."

It was more difficult for Sophie to give up her studio than for Luca to give up his. After all, he was going home. And she was reluctant to admit that sometimes his certainty and excitement could be irritating. Now she was becoming nervous about moving into yet another alien land. She was leaving her home in Paris—the home she had created out of her own ability to transform the debris of war into bohemian comfort. The closer they got to leaving, the more her studio became a refuge. There, in that safe place, Sophie had been able to persist with her work. But her passion for Luca succeeded in driving away most of the anxieties. She could not keep him away from her daydreams, even when she was painting.

"I know this is difficult for you, Sophie, moving away from your world, your studio. Is there anything I can do to make it easier?"

"No, I'll be all right," she laughed. "I'll simply make you my world."

And Luca felt a dark moment of foreboding.

Luca's exhibition received reams of favorable publicity and Sophie felt that he deserved every sentence of it. The show was spectacular. He had painted the floor of the gallery white and installed the sculptures to give the impression, despite their size and weight, that they were floating on clouds. "You gave me the idea," he told Sophie. "You always appear to me to be gliding on top of the sky."

And Sophie did feel as if she was walking on glittering, pearly-blue air. Never having expected to love again, she was awed by her feelings, fascinated with the warmth that moved through her body when she saw him walking toward her. However, she also knew that loving him was dangerous—that she was taking a huge emotional chance. She had made it clear to him that she did not want a family. But that was not quite true; she did want Luca.

Before meeting Sophie again, Luca had made a promise to himself; if the exhibition did not go well, he would quit and move to Siena. There he would go to work with an iron forger, his childhood friend, Carlo's father. But now the success of the show gave him the courage to imagine the rest of his life as a sculptor. Since it had been impossible in Paris to set up a forge, he had been working with wood—not his favorite medium. By returning to Italy, he would be able to go back to working in metal.

Luca bought a 1938 army-issue truck. It was hilarious to look at, but at the same time it made them feel as if they owned the jewels of a maharani. Poor Madame, the concierge. Sophie was her best tenant, and she was leaving.

"Mademoiselle Marks," she asked dramatically with tears in her eyes, "would you like my nephew to help you load the truck?"

The purported nephew, a child of Madame's brother, arrived on the assigned day. However, he appeared to be a bit too old to be her nephew. Short, with gray, greasy hair, he had wattles dangling from his chin and neck, and his hands were bony and gnarled, surely arthritic. With blurred speech and wine-soaked breath, he stood at attention in front of the building, waiting for his orders. Luca and Sophie looked at each other, shrugged, and proceeded to load and tie down the crates. The nephew decided that his job was to hold open, and then close, the front door of the building.

It was an afternoon of slapstick comedy, ending with Sophie paying the nephew for nothing, and Madame forcing them to take a small package filled with uncooked sausages and a bottle of cheap wine.

It was not until after four in the afternoon that they drove away. "Luca, thanks for being such a good sport," Sophie shouted over the fearfully loud roar of the motor, as he steered their new life down the boulevards, leaving Paris. They drove until they reached the countryside.

"What are we going to do with the sausages?" Luca asked. "Perhaps we should stop in the next village and give them away. We won't be cooking them, that's for sure. Actually, I'm beginning to smell them already." Sophie looked over at him and winked. As he geared down to a slower speed, she cranked open the window and flung them toward a field where they flew like a knotted rope. Luca and Sophie did manage to drink the wine. After a couple of acrid sips, it tasted just fine.

They happily crawled through Europe, taking almost twelve days to reach their destination. The roads were appalling, many shredded by the war, some hardly existing at all. At night they stopped at farms that had handwritten signs out front, welcoming visitors for a small amount of money. Luca and Sophie made love on everything from a real bed in a private room to a pallet on the floor in a barn.

*

Once they entered Italy, Luca could not sit still. "Look, look," he said, pointing, and Sophie held on as he swerved in his excitement. Every time they saw a medieval hilltop village in the distance, Luca had something to say about it; he was a vessel of art history. "But my village of Monterosa is different," he promised. "It's the most beautiful in all Italy."

Sophie thought them all beautiful.

"There it is," Luca exclaimed, pointing to a hilltop village, "there's Monterosa. Isn't it lovely?"

They drove up a winding road, past silvery olive trees and row upon row of vineyards. "Look below," he said, pointing. And through the trees Sophie glimpsed the wheat fields, almost chartreuse in their intensity of growth. The air smelled like nothing she had ever experienced. She felt embraced by the aroma of lightness, of sweet linden trees, of blooming roses.

As Luca pulled up, a mottled cat scurried in front of them, while a scruffy white dog took its time meandering across the road. "We can't drive to the house. We'll have to leave the truck here; it's too narrow and the overhanging balconies are too low." The village had no straight lines. Everything in it was constructed of a mixture of rosy-beige sandstone and deep-red bricks. Luca's house clung to the side of a sharply winding way.

The Bondi house was empty of life, but everywhere they turned was a memento of history. For instance, leaning inside the front door were generations of Bondi walking sticks. Some were simple, gnarly tree limbs polished with use, while others were ornate, with sculpted knobs of lions and bears. "Why didn't you pack things away when you were here?" Sophie asked.

"I just never got around to it," Luca told her. "There was so much legal work to do, and I was anxious to get back to Paris."

He grinned and embraced her. And Sophie fell, without another moment of resistance, into his world.

The friendly neighbors helped Luca and Sophie move the contents of the truck up the hill by hand. By the time they finished, Sophie had met everyone in the village. Then, onto the cobblestones of the piazza were carried long tables covered with starched white tablecloths, held down at the corners with stones. The new arrivals were invited to sit in the middle of the center table. Large platters of food and jugs of wine magically emerged from behind doors up and down the road. "Better a near neighbor than a distant cousin, they say here," Luca said, and winked.

One early morning, soon after Luca and Sophie arrived, they were taking a ride in the countryside, cycling on the road leading to the next village; they were looking for a house to rent. Not only was Luca's family home too stuffed with memories, but there was no studio space. As they were going around a hairpin turn, banking into the wind, Luca yelled, "Sophie, watch out!"

By a hair's breadth, Sophie swerved to avoid hitting a cart being pulled by two swaying, nonchalant white oxen with bobbing red tassels on their flat foreheads, meant to warn away vexing flies. A farmer, a very old man, was standing tall on the cart and singing in a dazzling baritone voice the final aria, "E lucean le stelle," from *Tosca*. He was singing to the oxen and the glorious landscape, no doubt about it.

The cart was piled with crates of hens cackling away, not paying any attention to the farmer's grand song. And the farmer did not seem to be aware of what had almost happened, nor did he miss a note.

"Luca, you planned this, didn't you?" Sophie teased. "Who in the world would ever have imagined that such music could come from a farmer on a back road in the middle of nowhere?"

While Luca was laughing, something caught his eye. "I wonder where this path goes," he said, pointing between two apricot trees. "I don't remember it. But I've been away for so long that everything has grown and confused my memories. Let's have a look."

They turned their bicycles and headed down a rough path, winding between enormous boulders and scraggly shrub oaks. Rushing water sounded nearby. After riding a few more yards they had to get off their bicycles to cross carefully over the last vestiges of a bridge. They walked along a shady track, lined with very old cypress trees, rutted with the history of carts, and saw an old stone farmhouse. "Luca, it's empty!"

But just in case, Luca hollered, "Good morning. Is anyone home?" Only his echo answered.

Propping their bicycles against a stone wall, they gingerly approached. The yard was strewn with old and rusty farm implements. Ploughs with missing teeth, dried and cracked oxen harnesses, broken shovels, bent rakes, rusty hoes, mattocks missing their handles—all were abandoned.

The house had two stories. The ground floor was a barn with its double doors hanging from their hinges at peculiar angles. It was empty. No tools, no stalls, certainly no animals. "It's interesting," Sophie whispered, taking Luca's hand. "Everything inside's so tidy and everything outside's such a jumble."

"You don't have to whisper," Luca said, laughing, bringing her hand to his lips. "There's no one here."

But there was an odd stillness to the house; even Luca had to admit this. Without saying anything they turned to go up the stairs. The stairway was traditional, built on the outside of the building and constructed with stone steps. They passed under an arched entrance onto a stone floor. The door was locked.

"Look," Luca said, pointing. "The window's unhooked. I'll

climb in." And before she could argue, he had gone through. "The key's on this side; hold on there, I'll unlock the door."

The door swung open and they both turned to look at the room. Spiderwebs and ancient leaves had blown through the window; a faded pink-and-blue print of Our Lady of the Rosary was leaning on a shelf. A stone fireplace was built into the wall. Alongside it was a brick bread oven with solid black metal doors, decorated with engraved flowers and birds on either side gazing at one another. Otherwise, the room was empty. Looking out the back windows they could see the remains of a large garden of lilacs and roses and rows of grapes and olive trees.

"I can imagine working here," Sophie said to Luca. "I wonder who owns it. Do you think we can rent it?"

Luca sold his family house and they prepared to purchase the property from the local bank. He called his old friend Carlo Zanotti, now an attorney in Rome, to make an appointment. They took the train, and, for the first time, Sophie saw the city of her grandfather's dreams.

Luca greeted Carlo in French, obviously sensitive to Sophie's situation. But it was an easy shift. Before the war, Carlo had lived in France trying to write mysteries like the Futurist Luciano Folgore. But by the time he was ready with a book to publish, the Fascists had curtailed the mystery genre and then banned it outright, saying it was unpatriotic.

Carlo had a traditional Etruscan face: short forehead, straight-across black eyebrows that accented dark eyes, veiled by enviable black eyelashes. He had thick, curly, almost black hair and was short and thin. Sophie liked him immediately.

In his office, after filling out the preliminary paperwork, Luca asked about the history of the house. "I really don't remember the family very well," he said, "except for an occasional polite nod on the road."

Snapping his fingers, Carlo summoned his secretary. "Three coffees please, Signorina. And grappa. Come, let's sit on the veranda," he invited. "Our business is finished."

Dappled sunlight sieved through an arbor covered with grapevines. After drinking his grappa in one quick motion, Carlo said, "The entire family that lived in that house was killed by the Fascists. No one knows why it was that particular family but there are suspicions—mainly that they were harboring partisans."

"But that's awful," Luca said.

"True," Carlo agreed, "it's a tragic story."

"I don't know if we can live there, Luca," Sophie said. "It's the same as living in a grave."

"Sophie," Luca replied, "all of Europe is a grave."

Once the final papers were signed, Luca and Sophie moved in like turtles. It was an artistic whim: the first thing they did was to paint the trunks of the two apricot trees at the entrance cerulean blue. The neighbors grew used to the colorful trees, but occasionally Luca and Sophie would hear the squeal of tires as a stranger drove by.

There was a sound they heard, though, that was hauntingly romantic; every time that musical sound danced through the air, they were compelled to stop and listen. It was a nightingale. "We had a nightingale at Pottery Cottage, as well," Sophie told Luca. "Hearing one here is a lovely omen for me."

For more than a year, while camping out in their new house, Sophie and Luca worked at the renovation. They loved the hard work, they loved being together. At the end of the project, just as her grandfather had done at Pottery Cottage, Sophie painted replicas of small scatter rugs on the upstairs floors using oil paints mixed with varnish.

They did their studios last. Sophie's was on the ground

floor, formerly the shelter for animals. Although Luca had dreamt of an enormous studio, for now he would work in the small barn to the south of the house. It was good that they had the courtyard between them. His strident drills and grinders, along with the American jazz he played on the record player, could be irritating. She needed to hear the silence of her paintbrush gliding over the canvas.

Sophie teased Luca about creating a career, saying that his collection of galleries reminded her of a set of wooden building blocks. "You've carefully placed one gallery next to another, on top of another, beside another, until you've constructed a hierarchy of importance and need." They laughed together over this, but she felt a twinge of anxiety. Sophie worried that Luca's desire for recognition went far beyond hers and that he would go too far and leave her behind.

"Don't worry, Sophie," Luca said, "I recognize the unspoken competition between us."

And Sophie had to laugh at his disarming honesty.

"I have an idea for an opportunity for you," Luca promised. And the opportunity arrived when his new gallery director in London, Leland Ross, visited them. Sophie liked him. He came from a wealthy family, high up in the Midlands, even farther north than Sophie's home. She gathered that he was considered well connected in the blossoming postwar world of art. He had come to Monterosa with a photographer to document Luca's new work.

The entire time he was with them he wore an incredible zoot suit: a black jacket that came below his knees with very wide lapels, along with black trousers that were baggy about the knees, slimming down to his ankles and dragging on the ground. He wore a red string tie and white socks. Sophie and Luca loved his outfit; it was a wonderfully shocking addition to Monterosa.

Sophie worried that he said he liked her painting because he was trying to be nice to Luca. Leland promised to write when he had thought more about how to handle her work. It made her nervous, knowing that she had placed so much hope on him.

"I'm sure he'll take you on," Luca said. "Your work is so good, so unusual, that he would be stupid not to."

"It doesn't matter," Sophie said. "It's making the work that's important."

"You're lying, Sophie. You care about your career as much as I do. Stop being so annoyingly dishonest! You make me angry—"

Two weeks passed. *Dear Sophie, yes, I would like to represent your work. I can promise that you'll have an exhibition every other year in my gallery, as long as it suits the two of us.* This last sentence he underlined with a flourish; Leland was a flamboyantly dramatic gentleman.

Sophie had to admit she was relieved. The arrangement suited her. To celebrate, Luca bought her a microscope. "Your nose is always so close to the ground," he said, "you may as well see what you've been missing!"

"I want to paint your portrait," Sophie announced, thinking Luca would find it interesting. But he kept putting off his sittings. "Wait until the winter," he suggested. "Then we'll have time to be quiet. Why don't you paint someone else?"

"That I do all the time," she answered with amusement. "But I have a special style of painting that I only use for the men I love."

"Oh, be serious, Sophie, this can't be true."

"It is. But you've never seen the one I did. I buried it in England."

"You *buried* it? What do you mean, you buried it in England? Where in England?"

"Next to the apple tree, at Pottery Cottage."

"Who?" Luca asked.

"I'll tell you about him another time," she promised.

Luca shook his head and changed the subject.

It was just as well; Luca would not have been able to sit still. It was 1950, and it was the hottest summer on record. It was unbearable even to think, much less paint. Even though the house was made of stone, and they kept the green shutters closed against the sun, it was still not cool enough in the day to work. Instead, they spent most of a month sitting in the dwindling stream, reading and sketching. "It's odd, Luca, but it's so hot I can't smell the flowers," Sophie said.

Finally, the winds arrived from the sea in little gasps, like the mewing of kittens, then more strongly, like the fluttering wings of doves. For the first time in the region's history, when the rainstorm finally began, the church bells from the surrounding villages tolled with joy in harmony with the rolling thunder.

Soon after the heat wave, in an experimental mood, Sophie did a painting of abstract figures grouped around a tree. The piece pleased her and she thought that perhaps she had made a breakthrough toward a new style of painting. Luca was invited to look. "What do you think?" she asked.

Luca studied it for a few moments.

"I don't like saying this to you, Sophie, but—" he said, and he leaned against the wall, while she became more and more irritated. "Well, it's the truth," he protested, as if speaking to himself. "It looks like one of my sculptures."

She stood back and looked. "Oh, bloody hell," she said in English. "You're absolutely right! God! I'm such a chameleon."

Back to painting portraits. "Here I am," she told Luca. "Back to my grandfather. Back to living in the countryside. Back to looking for people to paint in my village." Sophie never thought this would please her so much.

"Oh, my dear Luca, I can never thank you enough for loving me—for putting up with me."

Luca was pleased that Sophie was becoming a successful painter in her own right. He was proud of her work; he believed it was imbued with a great depth of honesty. Over the next few years her gallery not only sold her work well but also scheduled exhibitions in other cities. Of course, her engagement with her work made it easier for him to pursue collectors and plan exhibitions with vigor. He would laugh at himself for how easily she stirred up his dander with her reluctance to map out a plan for her career. She simply let it happen. She did not attend her openings. She did not do interviews. She did not invite people for studio visits. She let Luca do all that.

I don't think there's anything more surreal or abstract than reality.

—GIORGIO MORANDI

One cold winter day they decided to go to Rome. First they needed to buy art supplies and then Luca would go to meet with his gallery director. Sophie visited with Carlo, who had become a good friend. They met for lunch around the corner from his office.

After they finished eating, Sophie looked at Carlo and said, "Do you have any idea what I'm doing that so upsets Luca? You've known him all your life. Maybe you could give me some advice."

"But everything seems fine," he answered.

"No, everything is not fine," Sophie said. "Indeed, sometimes it's quite difficult. I feel as if I don't know him . . . as if he's leading another life away from me. I don't know what to do," she said, and she tried not to cry.

Carlo did not know what to do either. He knew too much. If he lied, and offered Sophie platitudes, she would see right through him, making the situation worse. If he talked honestly with her, he would have to betray Luca's request for silence. He decided to take a chance.

"Sophie, you must understand that Luca asked me never to speak to you about our experience in the war, although he never made me promise. But I'm going to take the risk and tell you the truth. You know how much I love mysteries?"

Sophie nodded, afraid to look at him.

"Well, the end of a mystery story must have a resolution— otherwise the reader is unhappily hanging on to a cloud. So I'll try to give you the whole story—maybe it will create a new beginning.

"Roving Fascist informers were looking for human bounty. One evening they arrived at our village of Monterosa and pounded at the Bondi door. It was awful. Luca's father rushed to hide behind a cupboard wall, and Luca was sick to his stomach with dread and shame. His father, so erudite, so kind, was hiding like a common thief behind the linens. His mother was in the kitchen, pretending it was an ordinary day.

"Mr. Bondi insisted that Luca escape. And Luca reluctantly slithered away through the shadows of the village. He felt like a traitor, betraying his family: no better than the Fascists.

"Traveling only at night, Luca felt his way, trying to keep clear of steep ravines, slowly moving over the mountains. He knew he would not find the partisans; they would find him. But he longed to go back; he was convinced that by abandoning his parents, he had caused their deaths.

"The farther he climbed, the denser the groves of birch and fir trees. It was the beginning of winter and already too cold to smell the pine needles. He bought cheese from shepherds and bread from remote farmhouses. None of the mountain people cared who he was; they were poor and worked hard and had no time for Mussolini and his politics, much less a wandering stranger.

"One night, after many days of traveling, he made a fire against a rock formation. He was roasting a potato, lost in reverie, when the shadow of a man crossed his vision. As Luca dropped the potato a hand clamped down on his shoulder. Luca tried to wrestle free. 'Stop,' our leader said, in a fierce whisper. 'We're comrades.'

"Looking around, Luca saw the shadows of many people. He must have been very confused because our faces were covered in soot and we all had fear in our eyes. And, even though it was cold, I know that we appeared to have risen from a sound summer sleep. Our eyes were puffy and red and there were pouches beneath them, reminding me of when we were children and had slept in a hot room. When Luca saw me he smiled and stepped forward so we could embrace.

"'Not here,' the commander growled, and moved between us.

"We led Luca even deeper into the mountains and he was clearly amazed at what he saw. A city of caves. Doors made of woven willow twigs. Beds made of crushed leaves covered with tarpaulins. Tables and benches made of tree limbs strapped together with leather thongs. Forty-two people: thirty-one men, eleven women. And a dry cave stocked with arms and ammunition. A seemingly safe and fairy-tale island, created within a chaotic world.

"It was the quietest place either of us had ever been. People whispered and walked as softly as if they were animals in a forest. The leader was called Lo Sconosciuto—the Stranger. He was small, and slim as a young tree. Completely bald. Later, when Luca and I tried to recall his face, it was a blur. There was nothing distinctive, nothing to remember, as if he had made himself nondescript on purpose. Except for his hands. They were far too big, out of proportion to his body. Those hands were imbued with all his physical power. We all knew to be careful.

"My job was to teach Luca how to listen for footsteps on snow, on rotting leaves, on rocks; for the sound of horses; for enemy trucks; for jeeps. Another man taught Luca how to shoot a gun, lob a grenade, aim a flamethrower. Luca's aim was alarmingly off, and this was the source of many jokes. That was until Lo Sconosciuto warned, 'If this man doesn't learn to shoot, he must leave.' Luca learned to shoot.

"As it grew colder, we were issued captured German wool

army coats with thick leather belts, over which we slung a holster and a pistol and a clip for a grenade. We were fitted with sturdy boots, wool socks, itchy pea-green woolen trousers, and peaked caps that never sat comfortably on our heads.

"We were together in the mountains for two years, both of us plagued with fear—experiencing enough fighting and grief to last a lifetime. For me, the grisly skirmishes have become all jumbled together in one large horror. I think you understand; I don't need to go into details. But there was one event, what Lo Sconosciuto coolly called an 'incident.'

"It was toward the end. That particular morning broke with a gray sky and no promise of the sun. No matter how many layers of clothing we wore, we could not get warm. Luca was sent on patrol, along with three other men. They had been instructed to plant dynamite next to a bridge. It was a small bridge, not terribly important; the Germans would have it rebuilt in a week. But the operation was meant to slow things down and remind the enemy that it was not infallible. It went lethally wrong. Luca and his comrades were ambushed as they were laying the line from the bridge to the partially buried dynamite. I heard shots from their direction and remember grabbing my stomach, feeling ill. The Germans had uncovered the plot— obviously through a collaborator—and had waited. Then they opened fire and hit the dynamite straight on. It exploded with two of our comrades still trying to connect the wire. Both were killed.

"The next day we captured six German infantrymen, one officer, and one very old man, all suspected of participating in the bridge incident.

"'We don't have a choice,' Lo Sconosciuto said. 'Their group will come looking for them. They have to be shot.'

"The eight people were lined up before a stand of trees and told to turn and look the other way. Without hesitation, Lo Sconosciuto ordered eight partisans, including Luca, but not me, to fire. The volley of bullets folded them over in unison. They were all dead. I could see that Luca was trembling and sweating; I was worried that he would faint.

"'They must be buried immediately in the forest' was the next order. We dragged them into the forest and began to dig in the rocky earth. I could see that Luca was stunned. He had never done this before—cold-blooded killing straight on.

"It took all morning. Once the graves were finished, Luca and I were ordered to bury the old man. I grasped his arms and Luca held his legs. As we swung him into the hole, his cap fell off. Luca said, '*Oh, Dio mio!* It's the man who used to bring wood for our stove.'"

She yelled only in her dreams.
—ELSA MORANTE

This is a true Shangri-La," Sophie said one evening, almost two years after her meeting with Carlo. It was the end of May, and she and Luca were sitting beneath their favorite tree. The tree, a cherry, was remarkable. Standing twenty feet high, it was laden with fruit. They could reach up and pick cherries while sitting in their chairs, while the birds feasted from above.

Sophie had honored Carlo's request and not said anything to Luca. She felt that she had no right to reproach him, nor remind him, considering her own silent memories.

"The birds are making such a racket," Luca protested. "I can't hear the music."

Sophie could see that he was not teasing. He was nervous. His work was not going well. He had hurt his right arm lifting a heavy piece of steel.

I have the same old complaint, Luca thought. And I cannot find a way to get past it. What is wrong with me? And then, out poured the venom. "We're living smothering lives," he said, "and it's making me uncomfortable."

Whenever Luca dove into that black-hearted mood, Sophie became anxious. It was as if he could ruin their life together with one wrong, misdirected hit of his hammer on a piece of stone.

"Damn it, Sophie, you've gone away again," Luca thundered. "Can't we even talk about what's wrong with all this without your disappearing into another world?" And without a moment's hesitation, he picked up his wineglass and smashed it against the trunk of the noble cherry tree.

Sophie had seen this before. She knew it was just a momentary fury and she was not physically afraid. But her fingers began to burn and she felt air rushing through her mind. "What do you want from me? Luca, what's wrong with all this?" And she swept her arm toward the horizon, avoiding the wine-splattered cherry tree.

"Nothing's wrong with all this," he said sarcastically as he mimed her sweep. "What's wrong is here," he said and he pointed to his heart. "Something's missing. This, this idyllic life we lead, isn't enough."

Sophie had heard it before. "I want more," Luca insisted. "I'm not interested in just working. I'm not interested in visiting our friends and playing with their children. I want to know why you won't have a child. I want to know why you won't marry me. I want to know why you won't talk about your family. Your not telling me means you don't trust me. So how in the hell can I live with a woman who doesn't trust me?"

"And how in the hell," she screamed, "can I live with someone who has been keeping something crucial from me? I hear you in your sleep," she said with rancor in her voice. "I hear you grinding through nightmares and I know what you're hiding. Carlo told me."

"What are you talking about?" he sneered. "Have you gone mad? What does Carlo have to do with this? I've had enough. Either something changes here or this is all over, this life, what you call your Shangri-La!"

He turned, grabbed his bicycle, and pedaled away. Sophie waited for the sound of him changing his mind and pedaling back. But the night became silent. Even the crickets' melody had ceased.

True, her years with Luca had had many moments of love. But

the fire-red anger was increasing and the distance between battles was shortening. He was traveling more and more, especially to Paris. She sensed an icy-blue coldness settling between them. That night's eruption had more serious anger attached to it than ever before.

Even though it was already dark, and there was only a lemon-pale half moon, Sophie got her bicycle and rode to the village. With no idea what she was going to say, she was propelled by apprehension. It took about twenty minutes to reach Baci's, the only bar. Luca's bicycle was leaning against the outside wall.

Inside it was truly gloomy and smelled of old sweat. There were two oil lamps at each end of the bar, and five tables with a few chairs. On each table there were plates piled with roasted and salted chickpeas, designed to make the patrons want to drink more. The floor was covered with sawdust for their spit. But here and there they had missed and those shiny spots of egg-white-like phlegm waited for an errant boot to slide and stumble. Sophie was transfixed by the squalor; she had not expected it to be so bad. Luca was sitting with a man at the table in the far corner. She recognized him as one Luca's political friends and remembered his first name, Paolo, but not his last. Luca leaned over and cupped a flame for his friend's cigarette. Then they both looked up, sensing that someone was about to enter. Sophie slipped back into the shadows.

She headed toward home. But now the moon was concealed behind a rainstorm. It was so dark, and the wind was whipping about so much, that she had to walk rather than ride. Far away there were flashes of lightning cautioning her to hurry. After a few minutes, without warning, Sophie tripped; her knees simply folded and thrust her forward onto the side of the road as the bicycle fell over. Both knees and the palms of her hands were bleeding and embedded with gravel. The pain was not so bad as the near-panic she felt. She tried to stand, but her trousers were tangled in the spokes. Sophie simply sat in the mess and wept in frustration.

"What happened?" Sophie had not heard Luca approach. He braked his bicycle. "Are you all right? I almost drove over you!" She waved him away and untangled herself. They walked back in silence.

While Luca made coffee, they sat at the kitchen table. "What were you doing on the road?" he asked.

"I was going to find you but changed my mind."

"Sophie, we've got to talk. There's something you're not telling me. It feels like we're sitting on top of Mount Etna, waiting for a volcanic catastrophe. This anxiety is intolerable. It's pushing me away."

"But why didn't you talk to me, Luca? Dammit, I'm so tired of being the batty one!"

"You're right, Sophie. I should have told you. I apologize. This is all terribly confusing. We've been sliding in and out of each other's shadows for so long now—I don't know whose is whose.

"And I'm so ashamed of myself. I'm sorry, Sophie. Without my being aware, year after year our secrets have piled up to be such a mess."

Leaning her elbows on the table, Sophie did try to begin. She knew she was being forced to the edge, balancing on a sliver of history; she had known this for quite some time. There really was nothing left to do but to tell him the truth, not hide anything, take the consequences.

"I'm an uncounted casualty of the war. You know that, Luca."

"We're all casualties, Sophie. You're not special."

"For Christ's sake! Luca, what are you saying? You're confusing me. I didn't ask for what happened. I didn't—"

"Oh, do be quiet, Sophie! You don't know what you're talking about."

"Damn it, Luca. Don't talk to me like that! If you have something to teach me, then do it. Don't be so bloody condescending."

For a few moments it looked as if their world could come apart. Both of them were trying to control their spinning thoughts. It was Sophie who took the next step.

"So, what exactly do you mean? I don't understand."

"It's about courage, Sophie, not about being victimized. We've all seen and experienced horror. It takes courage to go beyond the miseries that plague mankind. It takes courage to keep going in this imperfect world. Even though I've miserably failed, I have tried to be mindful about what that nightmare has done to me. But you wallow in your tragedies. You don't fight back. It's too bad you're not a religious Catholic—you could crawl on your knees to the confessional."

"You don't understand," Sophie insisted.

But she knew he was right.

At last, sitting at the kitchen table, her hand wrapped around a cup of coffee, cigarettes lit, forgotten, new ones lit, Sophie began to cry. And through the tears, she told him. She told him more about her childhood and her grandparents. She told him about René. About loving him and then his disappearance.

Luca was afraid to move. Afraid to stir the air surrounding them. Here comes the truth, he thought. Can I bear it?

With more tears, a running nose, and fingers burning with anxiety, she poured it all out. She told him about the bombing and the time she spent in the hospital. She told him about the soldier and his last generous gesture of making love to her. Of finding lost feelings. Of his suicide. She told him about the buried paintings. Then she abruptly stopped. "I can't go on," she said, "I really can't."

"I can tell there's more," Luca said, and leaned toward her, as if he was going to take her hand.

"No. Don't—touch—me," she said, and his compassion opened the gates to even more vast, dark lakes of tears.

Sophie was weeping so intensely that she was having trouble catching her breath.

Luca sat quietly.

She tried to calm herself. Finally, she said, "Yes, there's more." And in a droning, controlled voice, she told him about André. All about him. His birth. About how she did not want a child. How she had begged her grandmother to help her find an abortionist. About how difficult it was for her to be close to André. About how she finally fell in love with him.

And then Sophie held up her hands. "See these red fingers?" she said. "The tips of them burn with memories of the fire."

And she whispered André's death.

"My God, I never even imagined this! Oh, Sophie, how awful this must be for you," Luca said, and he came around the table and took her in his arms. And Sophie wept into his understanding.

"Here," he encouraged after a few minutes, "have a sip of this cognac." And like a baby bird, Sophie opened her mouth to receive his offering.

Luca was stunned. When they first met, he thought Sophie's reticence quite attractive, even seductive. Now that he had heard the truth, he began to understand how complicated everything was. Sophie telling her secrets drove Luca to love her even more.

Without saying another word, they went upstairs to bed. He held her hands. "Perhaps now your fingertips will never burn again." Neither could sleep, but holding hands, they pretended. At long last, as dawn was approaching, they dropped into an exhausted oblivion.

Luca made a determined effort to be kind, and Sophie tried to be more attentive. There was further conversation about her grandparents and her home and childhood, but nothing about André.

"Can we talk about André?" he would ask now and then.

"I'll try," Sophie would promise, but nothing more came out of her mouth.

However, Sophie had not been so quiet as she appeared. After mulling it over, she had made up her mind to paint a portrait. When she mentioned it to Luca, he said, "Sophie, I really don't want to sit for my portrait now. Can't it wait until another time?"

"It isn't a portrait of you, Luca."

"What are you talking about?" he asked.

She could see trouble roiling in his eyes. My, how self-absorbed men are, she thought.

"I'm getting ready to paint a picture of André."

He slid into another mood. "Oh, of course. How nice. It will be fine," he said soothingly. "Once you place that first line down on the canvas, it will all come back to you." He did not want to say too much; he was afraid he would break the spell of hope in their house.

It was the middle of the night and Sophie could not sleep. She went downstairs to her studio and settled in the old chair from Paris that was covered with a bright red Spanish shawl with pink and orange tassels. In one hand she held a cigarette, in the other a glass of amber calvados. Before her was a newly gessoed canvas.

As the first light of morning arrived, she sensed Luca watching her. "How lovely you are," he said softly. "I don't think you have any idea." And he tripped over his own feet. "Sorry, Sophie, I was worried when I woke and you were gone." When she turned to look straight at him, he realized how frightened she was.

"Oh, Luca, I can't do this—I can't remember his face!"

Although he tried to soothe her distress, Luca only made it worse. "I think, dear," Sophie said, "it's best to leave me alone."

It was the eighth afternoon, and raining, and almost as dark as a moonless night. Sophie came into the kitchen where Luca was preparing a pasta sauce that seemed to be primarily garlic.

"Umm, smells good," she said, walking up behind him and putting her arms around him. "Do you have time to come and look?"

Sophie took his hand and led him through the smell of garlic into the smell of turpentine. He was not quite sure what he was looking at. On a large piece of tacked-up paper was a collage. There was a nose in the middle, an eye on the left, a mouth under the nose, an ear on the left, and an eyebrow on the right. All were roughly sketched in raw umber on pieces of torn oatmeal paper. The collage looked as if a crazy person had been at it.

"Are you all right, Sophie? What is all this?"

She laughed with amazement. "Don't you see what I've done?" When he did not reply Sophie continued. "Finally this morning, after days of sitting here and trying to recall André's face, I realized I could remember fragments. His eyes were dark with short but dense lashes, so I painted his eye. His nose was like his father's, still infantile but beginning to form a slight bump. His ears were like mine. His mouth was the easiest to remember; indeed, I remembered it first. I can see him now, clear as a summer day, sitting under the apple tree with a slant of sunlight glancing off his dark hair."

*

Just one line on the canvas, she encouraged herself. Eli had always told her that to place the first mark down on the canvas was to create the necessary operatic mood for working.

Eli was right. His description of the "operatic mood" glided into Sophie and led her back to work. She dipped the sable brush in the turpentine, feathered a dab of raw umber on its tip, and made her first mark on the canvas. From then on she was in the music. Sophie drew André's intricate profile, molding his image in time to an amazing interior symphony. Since working in oil was slow, after the initial sketch she was able only to put down the beginnings of the flesh tones, with a sweep of highlighting. That would have to dry before the next layer could be added.

When she stepped back from the canvas, even though André's profile was before her, she averted her eyes and chose not to see. Sophie walked out, closed the door, and strolled across the courtyard to Luca's studio. He could tell by the look on her face that "it" had happened.

"You found André, didn't you?" he said, watching as she cleared the debris and sat down on his only chair. She lit a cigarette. "Stay here, I'm going to have a look," he said, and she did not protest.

He was gone an awfully long time, making her anxious. Finally, he returned. "Sophie, even though you've just begun, it's already an exquisite painting. I don't really know what to say, except that you painted him alive and puckish, as if he's ready to run out the door and get into trouble."

For the next month Sophie avoided the painting. She used the excuse of needing to finish some portraits.

One afternoon, in the midst of the pressure for an upcoming exhibition, with raw umber on her paintbrush, Sophie returned to André's canvas. André was painted in extreme profile looking out at the world through a window. When Luca returned, she said, "I wasn't even aware what I was doing. Once I got started I couldn't stop. Come look."

"I'm stunned," Luca responded. "I've never seen this painting technique. You're a much more accomplished painter than I've ever acknowledged."

"Oh, for heaven's sake, Luca, we've never worked in the same mediums, why do you have to use that tone of voice?"

"It looks," Luca continued, ignoring the remark, "it looks like a Lippi."

"Yes," Sophie replied, willing to let his rancor float away, "like his portrait of the young man draped with white—"

"—and the blood-red hat!" Luca remembered, and they laughed.

Luca thought the portrait was luminous. Sophie had painted with pigmented transparent glazes, thin layer upon thin layer, until André emerged as if he were ready to walk through the window and out into the fields.

There were three narrative scenes to the left of André. The top one was of René and Sophie, sitting on a bench in a painting studio and holding hands. The second was of Sophie running toward a large tree covered with apples, a blazing fire behind it. All you could see was her back, but Luca knew it was Sophie because of the thinness of the figure and her long dark hair. The third was a large hole in the ground. She was sitting on the edge, dressed in black. Her legs were dangling over the brink, her feet lost in the shadows of the abyss.

"What's the meaning of that one?" he asked.

"My grandfather once told me that in Hindu lore, the feet are the seat of understanding. I suppose this means that I don't understand much of anything—that I'm dangling over nowhere."

That evening they sat down to a quiet supper with a celebratory bottle of wine. Something inexplicable had happened;

some pocketed faded dream had slipped through a hole and traveled beyond the night, far out into the universe.

"I can't explain how I feel," Sophie said. And Luca did not push.

A few weeks later Luca woke to find her gone. He looked out the window and saw her sitting beside a newly dug hole in the garden. She was holding André's portrait, waxed and prepared for burial. As Luca watched, she set the portrait into the shallow grave, gently spreading the soil over it until it was completely covered. She stood for a few moments. Then, Luca was shocked to see, almost violently she scraped the soil away from the grave and pulled André free.

When Sophie came back into the house, Luca was making coffee.

"You saw what I was doing?" she asked him. He nodded.

"But I don't understand," he said.

"André doesn't belong here," Sophie said. "He needs to be buried with my grandparents in his own soil, at Pottery Cottage. I'll wait."

Luca served coffee. "How about a grappa?" he asked, and Sophie smiled.

Behind the house, facing east, was a piece of land Sophie called the painting garden. It was there that she had been planting her wax-covered portraits of the villagers. Within a few weeks, the natural elements would begin to act upon the chemical properties of the oil pigments, altering the colors just enough to make them curious. Sophie knew that the changes would be subtle, almost indescribable—certainly not blatant. They befuddled even educated viewers, and they never failed to sell. People asked what colors she had combined to make this or that. She did not tell. She simply shrugged her shoulders and smiled a practiced Mona Lisa smile.

But after finishing André's portrait, the burial process unraveled. Sophie had begun to have nightmares about the paintings. Even during the day she saw them as people who were once happy enough and now were dreadfully unhappy, stashed away in the dirt. She did not feel she had a choice. Sophie dug up the crop.

"It's wrong," she told Luca. "My portraits of André and the soldier are too important to me to dilute their meaning by planting the others in the same way. I have to ask myself: what's the philosophy behind burying my other portraits? And I have to answer honestly, there is none at all."

Luca could not argue. Indeed, he felt proud of her for taking such a big chance. She had been selling so well, this technique being unique. Now she would have to create another technique to capture that mysterious surface in a new way. He knew she would.

Their garden was a miraculous sight. From the back door they had a view of the now voluptuous patches of roses and lilac bushes that had been planted many years before they arrived. They had tenderly cut them back, fertilized them, and nursed them to health. As a former hill-town resident, Luca remembered the terra-cotta urns planted with bright red and pink-accented geraniums and purple pansies and petunias that his mother had kept. Each summer she had carefully placed them on the steps leading up to their front door and on the balconies overhanging the street. By the middle of the summer the plants would be blooming profusely, cascading down the side of the old stone house, looking delightful against the ornate ironwork staircase. Now, during the height of the gardening season, Sophie and Luca were enchanted with how those small potted gardens looked, and wistfully thought how much easier their life would be without such a large garden.

Fencing the back of the garden was a long trellis of

grapevines. Behind that trellis were fifty-four more rows of vines; behind the fifty-four rows was a grove of olive trees; behind that grew vast fields of wheat. In the spring these fields were speckled with thousands of scarlet poppies.

"In England they're called Flanders poppies," Sophie told Luca. "They grow only where the earth has been rooted up after it has been lying dormant for a winter. The Flanders battlefield of the Western Front was so churned by war that, in the spring, millions of waiting poppy seeds germinated and bloomed, outlining the dead and rotting bodies."

Over the years there were horrendous rainstorms, hail the size of marbles, snow that was wet and heavy or light and fluffy, all falling upon their garden. But the worst catastrophe was the frenzied battle with the *cinghiale*, a wild boar.

It was late summer, a sultry evening with a full and glorious moon. Before going to bed Sophie stood at the second-floor window and looked across the fields to the towering village of Montefollonico. Fluttering up and down the hills were swaths of red, green, and gold-leafed vineyards, reminding her of the flags of African territories.

There was such heat over the valley that it was suffocating the fresh air. Luca and Sophie were lying in bed reading, trying to stay cool, and occasionally watching the darting fireflies through the wide-open windows. They could hear the swallows whooshing in and out of their nests under the eaves, along with the waiflike hoots of owls. All of a sudden they heard a loud grunting and snorting, a most unusual sound.

"*Cazzo!* It's a *cinghiale*," Luca said, and leapt out of bed and rushed down the stairs. Before Sophie could put on her robe, she heard him clanging a pan with a metal spoon as he flung his body through the door. "Get out, get out!" he shrieked, over and over.

"Luca, be careful!" she screamed from the upstairs window.

Sophie saw the boar, provoked by the clanging, furiously spin and paw the earth. Although she had seen its telltale hoof prints, spoor, and areas where it rooted, she had never seen such a creature, such an ugly animal. It looked like a huge domestic pig that had grown tusks and sprouted chaotic stiff hair.

Luca's cacophonic frenzy finally drove it away. But, unable to let well enough alone, he continued to chase it, banging on the pan, screaming, and looking hilarious, certainly more naked than the boar.

Once everything calmed down, they surveyed the garden. The wreckage the boar wrought was awful. Some of the rosebushes, lilacs, and lavender were stomped to shreds; whole areas of tomatoes and eggplant and zucchini were destroyed. The only pleasant result was the incredible potpourri of aromas filling the garden.

But most devastated were Sophie's paintings for the November exhibition in London. Only the day before, she had placed them outside on planks, loosely tacking them down. She had wanted to see them in natural light; she was looking for areas where she might have missed a daub of paint, a line that needed connecting, perhaps underpainting that was showing through and was not supposed to.

Sophie lost fourteen paintings, trodden upon and ripped, impossible to repair. She worried about making new paintings in only two months' time. The idea of exactly replicating them felt fraudulent. To uphold the integrity of the work, each one would have to be approached from a slightly different perspective. Fortunately, she had loosely rendered oil sketches to work from.

That night they made love, both longing to overcome their problems, seeking comfort, struggling to keep everything together. "Oh, Luca, I do love you so," she said. "I'm trying."

"I know you are Sophie, and so am I. But sometimes I'm so overwhelmed with our problems that I—"

"That you what?" she asked.

"Oh, it's nothing, nothing. Let's go to sleep."

The next morning Sophie talked to Luca while they were raking the dead plants into a pile. "I've got to go back to the studio. I'll work until the last possible moment and take them myself to London. I'm sorry, Luca—"

"It's all right. I'll finish here." And she heard the flat tone of his voice.

"Time's going by too quickly. I'm going to cancel," Sophie said.

"No, no, Sophie, you must finish. You can do it," Luca insisted.

For days she did not change her clothes, smoked too many cigarettes, drank too much coffee, slept in her studio chair. Luca conceded: "You should cancel, Sophie, this is too much."

"No, no, Luca, I can do it." And she did not want to admit that she was having a great time. Being completely absorbed in the work was an extravagance, almost like the days when she was alone in Paris.

Eight weeks after the calamity, Sophie left for London and Luca was alone.

If Luca had not had an exhibition in Rome, he would have gone to Paris. The change would have been good. It made him happy to be traveling. On the other hand, loving Sophie made him happy to come home again. In Paris, he had wedged himself into a tight corner with his gallery and was not convinced he knew how to handle the situation. But he loved the lazy hours in cafés watching people, especially women. Dreaming. Not working. Oh, well, soon enough.

He went to Sophie's studio and saw that she had cleaned it, leaving it ready for her return. There were three primed canvases tacked to the painting wall. But something was missing. Luca looked around and looked again. He realized that she had taken the portrait of André. She was finally taking him home.

There came a time when the risk to remain tight in the bud was more painful than the risk it took to blossom.

—ANAÏS NIN

Sophie arrived at Victoria Station overwhelmed by the sounds of her native language, the cars driving on the other side of the street, the smell in the air of boiling meat, the dimness of winter in London, the fog making the world look as if she had forgotten to focus her camera. But she was home.

After delivering the paintings to Leland's gallery, Sophie took a train to the Midlands. The terrain was much fuller than she remembered. The trees were larger, the farms bigger and more elaborate. There were new factories along the railroad line, new homes being built, even in the midst of winter. The canals and the brightly painted narrow boats were the same as always. Occasionally she saw the reminders of war: a bombed-out relic of a house, a rusted army truck at the side of a road. But nature prevailed. The fields were a quilt of assorted winter-wheat-green velvets, looking like patches from cut-up children's Christmas dresses. Sophie was surprised by the tidiness of everything. Not that Italy was untidy. But in comparison, Italy's countryside had a kind of intrinsic wildness, more spontaneous and individual.

For more than four hundred years, the Trentham Arms Hotel had dominated the High Street with its half-timbered façade and crooked red-tiled roof. Walking through the front door reminded Sophie of entering the England of her childhood; the smell of old tea, cigars, a vague odor of mildew. She rang a small brass bell.

"One moment, please," sang a lyrical voice from behind a wall and then, "Gracious, it's you, Sophie!"

And there was Sophie's old school friend, Anne Vernons.

"Anne, what are you doing here? The last time I saw you—Paris and—"

"You mean," Anne asked with humor, "what do my parents think?" And she came around the corner to embrace Sophie.

Sophie was taken aback. Anne had become a full-bodied woman with a bohemian look about her. Her blond hair was pulled back into a bun with unruly wisps coming unpinned here and there. Dressed in a loose black dress, she was wearing dripping silver earrings and an odd assortment of necklaces that sat upon her ample bosom.

"You look wonderful, darling," Anne said. "Come, let's have a pot of tea and catch up with each other."

After finishing school, Anne had been expected to marry; women from her class were not encouraged to go on to university. Her parents had a number of socially acceptable men in mind. She was bored with all of them. Sending Anne to Paris had been a tactical error. Even though she tried to please her parents, there was always a part of Anne that was rebellious. So she married down.

Her husband was Peter Sutton, a jazz piano player who traveled about England and the Continent playing in clubs. Anne and Peter decided to buy the old Trentham Arms, duly horrifying her parents.

"Oh, darling Sophie," she said while pouring the tea, "what a cock-up we created. You can just imagine, I'm sure. I wish Peter were here to meet you, but he's off playing in Scotland."

And, quickly changing the subject, as apparently was her style, Anne said, "And oh, how well I remember your grandparents. Especially Claire. I thought her so absolutely smashing that I wanted to imitate her and become a poet. And I even tried my hand at writing. But I was hopeless, simply hopeless. Poppycock I wrote, ridiculous nonsense."

While listening to Anne, Sophie was overwhelmed with memories. She remembered Anne as a timid and quiet girl. And even when they had met in Paris, Anne had still retained much of that demeanor. Now she had burst forth in a most remarkable fashion. Sophie was amazed at how calm Anne was about her husband's travels and wished she herself could be without her deep-rooted distrust. Sophie liked Anne. She liked her ebullience, her curiosity, her courage.

The next morning, dressed in trousers and practical shoes, armed with André's portrait, Sophie hired a car to take her to the property. It was cold, and a glistening frost blanketed the region. Sophie expected the road leading to the property to be deeply rutted, but it was no longer so. Now it was smooth, topped with crushed stone, and since there was no dust, most likely frozen. But she was not certain where she was.

"Are you sure you know the way?" she inquired of the driver.

"Dead cert, ma'am. Here you be." And he stopped the car by the side of the road.

Sophie was perplexed. It did not feel like her property. But then she saw the funny curve up ahead and knew the driver was right. She asked him to come back in an hour.

"You mean, go all the way back to the village and come back again?" he said.

"Yes, please. I'll pay you, of course."

And then she was alone.

Leaning against a crumbling brick wall, Sophie tried to get her bearings. Yes, there was the crater where the house had been. And there was the apple tree, although now it was almost full grown. That old tree's more rooted to the world than I am, Sophie thought.

*

A funeral was necessary. André's portrait had looked uncomfortable, foreign, on Sophie's Italian wall. He did not belong in Italy. She needed to put him to rest, bury him in his birthplace for all time. Peeling the protective piece of canvas from the front of the painting, she was struck by the contrast: she had unconsciously painted the portrait using the colors of Italy, not of England.

Sophie returned to the apple tree. The ground was crowded with nature's debris: limbs broken by storms, years of accumulated leaves, all turning to compost and making a soft and fertile ground for the future. Closing her eyes, she tried to remember where she had buried the paintings. Yes. On the far side of the tiny remnant of the apple tree. Sophie began to dig with her hands and a flat stone.

Although the earth was frozen, the top layer of dirt was easily loosened and she quickly glimpsed the edge of a painting. Sophie carefully pulled the paintings from the earth. She peeled back part of the canvas cover and disclosed the self-portrait of the soldier. Scraping away a bit of wax, she saw that it had kept most of the natural elements from eating away at the canvas. Even through the wax, Sophie could see that the soldier's violent dark surface had transformed into the luminescence of a peacock's feather. On the face of the canvas, a small insect had burrowed its way through the paint, leaving a living zigzag trail.

Her painting of the soldier came next. She was moved by a peculiar combination of feelings: elation and deep sadness. The change in colors was similar to that in Major Roderick's painting. But this one, having more light areas, was clearly a pleasing indicator of what was going to happen to André's portrait. An astonishing metamorphosis had transformed the painting's colors. Light, although dappled from all the trees, was illuminating the canvas as if it had been made in another world. As Sophie looked closer, an ancient moonlight appeared to be caught behind a veil of intaglio glaze, shimmering, trying to escape, like a moth behind an old lace curtain.

Before covering him with wax in her studio, Sophie had been moved at how tiny André appeared—so out of place, as if he had been away on a long journey and time had stood still for him, but not for the rest of the world. Sophie decided to trust that nature would be good to André, and she buried him with the major.

The sorrow of burying André's painting had unearthed questions and anxieties. Sophie could clearly see that the situation with Luca was gloomy, and she had an insight that nearly sent her into a panic. If she loved Luca too much, the pain of losing him would be unbearable. Without a doubt, she felt, she had not done a very good job of loving anyone.

Leaning against a tree, Sophie thought about how difficult she had been: how stubborn, how unyielding, how self-involved. She understood that she had to make some changes and began to think tenderly of seeing Luca soon. But it was too cold to dream.

"Ready for off, ma'am?" the driver asked as he opened the door for Sophie. "Pardon me for saying this, but you look like you've been rakin' up a graveyard."

Luca met Sophie at the station in Florence. "I'm so disappointed," she told him. "Indeed, I feel ashamed." The opening of her exhibition had been tepid; no paintings had yet sold. The critics were lukewarm. Sophie was far from content, and anxious to be home.

"I don't understand," Luca said, "how you can be ashamed. Every artist has awful exhibitions now and then. You've been spoiled. Anyway, what does shame have to do with it? Disappointment, yes, shame, no. You've not been disgraced, Sophie," he said, and he reached for her hand. "Don't let the establishment get you down."

"But the 'establishment,'" Sophie said, "pays our bills. What if this is the end of my career? What will we do?"

"Sophie, for Christ's sake, your exhibition will be up another four weeks. Let Leland do his job. You have to trust that he'll sell paintings."

"Well, you can be cavalier," Sophie bit back. "You're selling all over the place. Anyway, I really don't care that much about my career—it's not important."

Luca was seething.

"Goddamn it, Sophie—stop being such a martyr. You're always saying this—and you're lying. And it's really unbecoming."

They drove through a silent Tuscan winter countryside. Coming around corners, they saw fields that looked as if they were tiles made of pristine snow outlined in black. Some fields were planted with row upon row of bare, dark grapevines, looking like loosely drawn Japanese *sumie* paintings, as if an ink-filled brush had begun at the top of the vine, as the thinnest black line, and then the line squiggled down, getting fatter and broader as it met the earth. Edging the white fields and vineyards were startling rows of tall brownish and winter-green cypress trees. It felt as if everything were asleep. The beauty and the quiet soothed Sophie's distress.

It was late September of the following year and the dusty rows of grapes were swollen with their juices. Sophie and Luca's land was part of a consortium of five small vineyards. Each year there was one collective harvest. Sophie was expected to join the women to cook for the men, but she preferred the manual labor. It was the only time of year when she felt comfortable being seen in public in trousers. She was wearing an old pair of Luca's trousers, already colored with a history of grapes and paint.

She loved being under the hot sun, a kerchief rolled and tied around her forehead and an overlarge, brown, sweat-stained fedora pulled down low to shade her eyes. They began to harvest early in the morning, when the sun was just appearing over the hills and there was still a touch of dew on the vines. With shears to cut the bunches from the vines and tiny scissors to remove the rotten grapes, they moved along the rows. As it became warmer, the smell of the grapes grew stronger; their hands, arms, and clothing became sticky with must—which in turn attracted menacing wasps, bees, and flies. But the aroma of the warm, voluptuous fruit, mixed with the sunshine soaking the land, was mouthwatering.

After the last day of work, Sophie was sitting at the kitchen table while Luca started a fire in the wood-burning stove. He left the doors open so they could see the flames. Their hands were wrapped around bowls of strong coffee with hot milk.

"You look lovely, Sophie," Luca said. "Hard work suits you. The sun has turned you the burnished reddish-brown of my early rosewood sculptures."

Sophie had to admit that she felt well, even comely. Out of the blue, she realized that she must be pregnant. "Wait a minute," she said to Luca, and went to her studio to check the calendar.

"Oh, my god!" Sophie said. "I'm pregnant!"

"It's a gift, Sophie," and all Luca could do was smile and take her in his arms. For one of the few times in their relationship, Luca lost words.

"I feel like painting," Sophie said. "I'd like to do your portrait. It's a good time, don't you think?"

"Are you going to bury me?" Luca laughed.

"We'll see how you behave," she joked back.

It was a special day; they had their first killing frost. Having taken its last deep breath, the world was silent. Sophie sat Luca on a yellow-painted rush-seated chair in front of the window in her studio. There he could look out onto the garden. With so much to look at, it would take him a while to be bored. Luca's profile resembled Signorelli's portrait of Virgil. She had once bought a postcard showing Virgil sitting at a table, writing in a thick notebook. His right hand held a quill pen, which he rested gently upon the paper. The left hand was poised above the book as if it were trying to avoid the wet ink. Virgil was looking up and his face had an irritated expression, as if he had been rudely interrupted. Alongside that postcard Sophie had tacked a photograph of Luca in an almost identical pose, glancing up at her while writing a letter, looking irritated. Luca had the same elongated, bony face with the arched nose and the deep crease on either side of his mouth. After Sophie's first sketch, she asked Luca to remove his glasses.

It took six sittings to get the portrait roughly down on canvas. Then Sophie began to work on the details, patiently waiting for each day's work to dry. She was extra careful; she knew that with the slightest skewed stroke of her brush, she could demolish his smile. The portrait was different from the others in that she meticulously painted his hair strand by strand, with a 4/0 brush; the brush was not much more than a single hair itself. Sophie enjoyed the meditative quality of the detail painting; it gave her a chance to dream.

Even though Anne was coming for a week's visit, Sophie would not rush the painting. It was important to her to get it right. Almost as if she could be judged about her capacity to paint love.

There were three visual stories in the background, designed to complement the contours of the landscape. The first was of Luca and Sophie sitting on a bench, perched on top of a medieval-style pastoral hill. They were holding a baby between them. The choice of the color green was so important to the composition that Sophie threw caution to the winds and decided to use vert emeraude to paint the hill. She knew it was highly poisonous, but could not resist.

The second story was of Luca standing in the center of a vineyard and holding a luscious bunch of deep mars-violet grapes. One hand was holding the bunch up in the air, as if he were taking the lowest-hanging one into his mouth to eat. The other hand was resting on his hip, relaxed and sassy.

The final story was in the lower left-hand corner. She had painted Luca standing on the bottom edge of the portrait, in a wry way imitating the Signorelli self-portrait in the lower left-hand corner of his fresco in Orvieto. Placed in the same position, Luca, rather than standing and looking at his work, was holding a mallet in his right hand, a chisel in his left, as he chipped away at a wood sculpture of himself.

But there was something missing. It finally came to her when she cut her finger opening a tin can. Blood. Burgundy-red blood. Sophie sucked on her finger and went back to the studio. She painted the mallet that Luca was holding a toned-down scarlet and the entire image sprang to life.

Sophie mulled over the destiny of the painting. Her inclination was to hide it from Luca, to keep it locked away. It could become a talisman, a piece of hope, perhaps good luck. But eventually her painter's curiosity, and her need to share it with Luca, decided her.

"What do you think?" she warily asked.

"It's very beautiful. When our son is born, perhaps you could do one of him facing in the other direction. And then, when we hang them together, we'll be facing each other."

"But what if it's a girl?"

Luca dismissed the idea with a flick of his hand.

That made her cross and she turned to walk out of the room. "Sophie," he called. "Wait, I'm sorry. Of course it doesn't matter."

But he had ruined the moment. "Sophie, tell me you're angry," he persisted, following her. "Yell at me, stamp your feet; please don't be silent. You're trying to make me lose my temper!"

"Oh, do shut up, Luca, you're being childish. Let it go."

Sophie wanted the peevish moment to be over. She was determined that nothing was going to ruin that time of her life. She did not yell, nor did she stamp her feet. She swallowed her anger, dreading more conflict.

Sophie decided to plant the painting. "I can't bear *not* to see what the earth is going to tell it," she explained to Luca later. "Anyway, I'm not burying it; I'm planting it like a flower seed."

Luca took up knitting. "It's because of the baby," he explained. "I can't keep still. I have to be making something."

A neighbor had given him a simple pattern for a baby blanket and a large ball of blue wool. Much to Sophie's amusement, Luca was a good knitter. The better he got, the more adventurous he became. Before he was halfway through the blue blanket, he decided to experiment. Since everyone they knew unraveled old sweaters and rolled the wool into balls to be used again, Luca asked around. He collected a number of colors and proceeded to knit a red, pink, orange, purple, and blue baby blanket. It made Sophie smile each time she saw him knitting. She thought the colors and Luca were beautiful.

Anne arrived, alone. Peter was home tending the hotel, sobering up. "He's been drinking too much," she told Sophie and Luca. "For the first month he was home, I watched him like a hawk. And I didn't touch a drop either. But then I took to taking nips in the hotel's kitchen, swearing the cook to allegiance, and then chewing mouthfuls of mints. 'You're not fooling me,' Peter finally said. 'I know what you're doing.' So I stopped altogether.

"Now, darling," she laughed, "how about that glass of wine?"

Over a week's time, Sophie gave her a tour of their niche of Umbria. But later, all Anne would remember was the delicious red wine, the food, and Lippi's sublime, beatific *Madonna and Child* at the Uffizi in Florence.

"You, my darling," Anne said to Sophie, while pointing at the painting—"you are a mirror image of this Madonna. I've never seen you look as beautiful as now."

In the middle of a night, Sophie lost the baby. She was forty-one years old and already into her fifth month. It was not an easy miscarriage. Not only was there no time for a doctor, there was no doctor nearby. The contractions were coming too hard—too fast—

"Oh, Luca, no," she cried out. "No." She tried to push the baby back in with her hands. She tried to breathe slowly. For the first time in her life she prayed. But she knew it was hopeless.

Luca had never seen a birth, and had never seen her look like she did. Contorted face. Mouth gaping with pain. Sweat. Unearthly sounds. Blood. He had to trust her instructions. His hands were on her throughout the delivery. He held her. He put wet, cool towels on her forehead. He massaged her belly. He spoke to her. He soothed her. He cleaned up after her.

It was a girl.

She was dead.

When it was over, Sophie lay still for a long time.

André had gone up in flames. This child would be treated more gently. Luca wrapped her in the blanket he had knitted and got into bed with Sophie. Stunned, they held her and wept.

Later, Luca carried the baby to his studio and gently placed her on a pillow. He constructed a tiny, simple wooden coffin. When he returned to the house, the coffin was already firmly sealed.

Holding Sophie by the arm, with the coffin under his other arm, he left the house and walked up the road. In a daze of grief, they buried her beside one of the cerulean blue-painted apricot trees.

In bed that evening Sophie said, "Yet another burial. Oh, Luca, you're all I have. You're all I'll ever have. All I do is bury the people I love. It petrifies me to think that something will happen to you.

"Why," Sophie pleaded, "why have I been so battered by misfortune? I feel as if I'm being punished for having done something atrocious to someone in the world. And I don't know why—and oh, Luca, I've so disappointed you."

"Look, Sophie." Luca was trying to keep a pleasant tone in his voice. "I'm so sorry for both of us."

Two days later they drove to Siena to see the doctor. He was coolly precise. No more pregnancies. And Sophie's intuition told her that he was correct.

"But why?" Luca asked. "I don't understand. My mother had me when she was in her late thirties. Signora Brunelli had a baby when she was fifty-one. And—"

Patiently the doctor and Sophie listened to Luca. Finally the doctor had to interrupt. "I'm sorry, Signore Bondi, but all women are different, and Sophie has the misfortune of being one of the unlucky ones."

Luca's disappointment was palpable. He felt betrayed by unknown forces. Sophie did not know how to talk to him. They were both silent.

Before, their house had felt full. Every space seemed used. They had both marveled that even Giglio, their cat, was pregnant. But now, her growing fatter by the day was not enough to fill the void. Luca was in his own realm of bereavement. He reminded Sophie of a pacing lion. He could not sit still. He could not concentrate. He was sharp-tongued, then sorry, then sharp-tongued again. Two days later, the kittens were born in Sophie's studio on her old Paris chair. Neither of them could watch.

Sophie and Luca were living in a cocoon of friendship. But she was lonely. So was Luca. Money was no longer a problem. They were both having exhibitions throughout Europe. He was often in Paris meeting with collectors and museum directors. People were asking to write about both of them, to visit. It made Sophie uncomfortable and relieved at the same time.

For Luca it was terrific. He loved the attention, and was most happy when people were in the studio talking about his work. Luca's sculptures were becoming larger, more powerful, and had a disturbingly brutal edge to them. They were no longer recognizable human beings, but abstractions of people who were distorted, twisted away from their human forms.

"I understand that you're not working in wood any longer," an admirer once said. "But why don't you work in marble, it being a natural resource?"

"It would make more sense," Luca said, "but I'm too impetuous for marble. I don't have the patience to chip slowly away at a form that I may not like in the end. And I understand marble too well. I know that if I hit the stone in the wrong place, it could break apart. Steel is more forgiving, and far more flexible."

Sometimes Sophie thought Luca pretentious in his conversation and he embarrassed her. She often hid in her studio when art visitors arrived. She liked the people, but did not know what to say. A book, she could speak about. About music, she could try. But painting was difficult. Its language asked her to go too far into her unconscious—and she was loath to expose herself. Outbursts had become common again. Sophie was seeing Luca in a different light. Sometimes she was irritated if his hair was greasy, upset if he was unshaven, bothered if he was wearing a dirty shirt, peeved if he left one too many cupboard doors ajar. She could see that the days of not feeling kind, of not feeling warmly connected, were beginning to accumulate. Those feelings frightened her. When she had told Luca the truth about her past, Sophie thought she had given up most of her ancient sorrow. Now she recognized how naïve she had been.

Two years passed. A letter from a publisher in Paris arrived for Sophie. It asked permission to bring out a book of poems by her grandmother. These were the same poems that had appeared before the war in *The Potteries Poetry Review*.

"I knew there was interest in Claire's work," she told Luca, "but I didn't realize it was so serious. And this publisher is one of the best in France. They want me to go to Paris to negotiate a contract."

"It sounds interesting, Sophie. Wouldn't it be satisfying for you to see her work recognized?"

"Claire really didn't care if she was published," Sophie said. "When she happened to be published, and she was on occasion, it was in obscure literary journals. My grandfather, on the other hand, was bitter that he never showed in a serious gallery. He'd be filled with rancor when an artist he thought mediocre was given a major show."

"I can understand that!" Luca laughed. "In a way, I wish I had your grandmother's attitude. It would certainly make my life simpler. Really, you're like she was, Sophie. Sometimes I think you don't care about what happens to your work once it's finished. And if it weren't for Leland, I don't think you would even bother to have your paintings photographed for your archives."

Luca was preparing for another exhibition in Paris. He was still represented by a sculpture gallery on the right bank. Because his work was so large, a truck had been hired.

"I'll be gone for almost two months," he told Sophie, "between the assembling, then the interviews, and finally the opening."

"It always seems so long, though," Sophie said. "Perhaps I'll try to come to the opening."

Luca shrugged.

To make it easier to drive across Europe, Luca transported his sculptures in pieces. When all the parts were bolted together, they would be transformed into a group of fifteen totem-like figures that ranged from ten to fifteen feet high. There was a sense of their communicating among themselves, even though the pinnacles of the gesturing arabesques were turned away and facing up at the sky. An atmosphere was created by the figures that made one want to walk in, sit down, and be quiet.

Sophie was proud of him. She thought his work sensational.

The flatbed truck and driver arrived. With pulleys, he and Luca and a couple of hired hands from the village loaded all the pieces and tied them down with chains and heavy ropes.

Early the next morning, Luca teased, "You know, we can call each other on the telephone. It's not such a difficult thing to do." It always made Sophie apprehensive when it rang. She did not understand the science of speaking into the atmosphere, always feeling that she was interrupting because she could not see the caller's face.

"I'll try, Luca. Really I will. But don't be surprised if I arrive on your doorstep."

"Well, if you decide to come, Sophie, please don't surprise me. I would like to plan for your stay, to make it special."

They left, rattling down the dirt road. Sophie could hear the truck for a long time, until finally they drove onto the paved road, and then their sounds disappeared with the wind.

Sophie decided to go to Paris. Ignoring Luca's request, she wanted to surprise him; she felt the need for some excitement in their lives. Maybe they could stay in a nice hotel. Take walks in their old neighborhood. Drink wine in their favorite cafés. Even rekindle the shared passion that they had allowed to disappear into a dreary routine.

Paris was cleansed of the griminess of the war. There was a mood of innocence in the air. Now, even though it was winter, there was color everywhere. The shop windows displayed new calligraphy in elaborate gold, framed by fresh white starched lace curtains; pots of flowers were blooming as if it were summer; flashing and vibrant colors on billboards were shouting; chic clothing reflected the new prosperity.

After Sophie's meeting with the publisher, she hailed a taxi and drove to the gallery on the rue de Bièvre. The entire front of the exhibition space was glass and she could see men working inside. It was a beautiful site for Luca's work. He must have been pleased. She pushed open the door and set her suitcase down just inside. The space was enormous, with unusually high ceilings. Everything was painted a glossy white, including the floor. His sculpture could not have looked better.

"Monsieur Bondi?" Sophie asked, and one of the men tossed his head toward the back of the gallery.

Sophie walked through an echoing exhibition space and followed the hall to an office with an open door. Inside she saw a woman sitting at a desk, and assumed she was the gallery owner. She was certainly more attractive than Luca had described—blonde, with lovely ivory skin and nice features, and quite thin. Much younger than Sophie.

"May I help you?" she asked.

Sophie stepped into the office and saw Luca. He was lounging in a Moroccan red leather chair with a squirmy, ivory-skinned little boy on his lap. The child was the mirror image of Luca.

Luca was visibly stunned. "What are you doing here? I didn't know you were coming. I—"

At first Sophie could not make sense of what she was seeing. Within a few tense moments, it was apparent.

Sick to her stomach, fearful of fainting, she had to escape. She spun around. Out of the office. She ran across the gallery space. Behind her, she heard footsteps.

"Wait, Sophie! Wait. I can explain."

Sophie grabbed her suitcase and rushed out the door, down the street, across the quai de la Tournelle, and smack up against the stone wall that bordered the Seine.

Luca seized her arm.

"Stop, Sophie, right now! You have to listen to me. *You must!*" he shouted, and everyone stopped to look at them.

She punched him in the chest with her fist and he wrenched back and scrambled to get his balance. People were gathering.

"Ma'am, do you need help?" a man asked, thinking she was being accosted.

Sophie picked up her suitcase and, with all the force she could muster, slammed it against the wall and let out the astonishing howl of a wounded wild animal.

Her belongings flew in different directions: clothes, books, toiletries, everything. The crowd drew back, not sure what was going on.

"Sophie, please," Luca implored.

"It's a lovers' quarrel," someone in the crowd said, hearing Luca use her name. "Leave them alone." And they slowly dispersed.

Sophie was leaning with her hands on the wall, struggling to get her breath. "Here, let me help you," Luca said. But she shoved him away and sat on the bench with her head between her legs. He let her be, picking up her belongings and packing them again.

She snatched her suitcase out of his hand and got into a taxi. But Luca, who was quick, grabbed the door and got in with her.

"Get away from me. How dare you? Gare de Lyon," Sophie told the driver.

"Please let me explain," he pleaded. "Then you'll understand." And he proceeded, speaking loudly over the noise of the taxi, to justify his behavior to nearly deaf ears.

"When I started showing in Adele's gallery, I could tell that she was attracted to me. It made me feel good. But I kept the flirtation at a distance. I didn't succumb. But once we lost the baby, I sensed that nothing was happening with you and me. We weren't going to have children. That was obvious."

Sophie put her hands over her ears.

"Listen, Sophie, listen." Now he was yelling. "Instead, it seemed to me, we'd spend the rest of our lives as friends, rather than lovers. I was lonely. After the baby died, you burrowed deeper and deeper into your work. Of course, it never occurred to me to leave you."

She opened the window to let in more noise.

"I love you." Now Luca was shouting. "I love the way you think; you still intrigue me. I feel as if we're inextricably woven together by our history and time. But I was lonely, not for anything substantial, simply for sex. My art doesn't satisfy this longing, as it seems to do for you. So there was Adele, who isn't married and seemed perfect for an affair. For the first few years it was simply sex and companionship while I was in Paris. Then when you lost the baby it changed. I was desperate, feeling constant agitation. So one night I decided, the hell with it, I want a child—and she conceived."

Sophie felt sick. This affair had been going on for years! How could she have been so stupid? They reached the train station. Sophie paid the driver, got out, and headed for the entrance. Luca was rushing behind, intent upon keeping up. The next train for Rome was not for another two hours, and she was almost hysterical. With Luca looming beside her, Sophie bought a ticket for London.

"Sophie, please talk to me. What are you going to do? Where are you going? We can work this out."

"No," she barked in his face, "we can't 'work this out.' It's over."

"I'll leave the gallery. I promise. I won't continue the relationship with Adele."

"For Christ's sake, Luca, what about your child? Are you insane? Adele isn't someone simply to be erased. It's clear that she's special, not just a prostitute you've picked up on the street. She owns and runs one of the most prestigious galleries in Paris! You've got what you wanted. Now leave me alone."

For the next half hour Luca sat beside Sophie without saying a word. Their twenty-two-year bond was loosening its ties to the earth, to Italy, to Monterosa, to their home, their studios, the garden, the vineyards, the olive trees, to their hearts.

Finally, Luca said in a weary voice, "You know, Sophie, I tried to be what you once called your own private country. Your safe home. But I felt I was suffocating. I couldn't be everything to you. I'm sorry."

The train arrived and Luca carried her bag to the steps. Sophie reached down; he handed it up. The train left quietly, as if it knew that she was in desperate need of silence. At the next stop, she got off, changed her ticket, and went back the way she had come.

The pain passes but the beauty remains.

—Pierre-Auguste Renoir

It was April and Sophie thought she should be blooming rather than wilting. She locked her studio on a day with a thin and starving sun, understanding she was leaving forever. The realization was stunning. She had become a ghostly presence in a foreign land. The movements of Giglio as she settled down in the chair, the clock's hands rounding the bend at midnight, even the teapot's steam—all were observed from a vague, faraway place. The rooms of their house were dead. She was returning to the Midlands.

Luca's portrait was wrapped in paper and put in the bottom of her suitcase. Carlo telephoned. She needed to go to Rome to sign papers. Luca was putting a portion of the house in her name. Ah, guilt, Sophie thought. But it was fair. The next morning she took the train. She was early, and decided to walk along the Tiber, taking the long way to the office. It was colder in Rome than in the countryside; the cobbled streets were slippery with ice. She had to be careful, to pay attention.

Sophie was anxious about seeing Carlo. She knew he would try to talk her out of her decision. She steeled herself for the confrontation.

She rang the entry bell at his office and was ushered in.

"What is—what—Luca, what are you doing here? Goddamn it, what's going on here? Carlo? You, you tricked me. How dare you! How—" she said, and she turned to flee.

"No, no, Sophie, it's a mistake. Pardon, please pardon me!"

Carlo was short and Sophie was tall. She shoved him out of the way; he did not have a chance to stand his ground.

"Stop, no! Stop. There's an explanation," Luca yelled.

"It's my fault," Carlo insisted.

"No, it's my fault," Luca said. "I wanted to see you again, so I asked him not to tell you I was coming."

Chagall's *Painter to the Moon*—that was where Sophie wanted to be, floating in the universe with pastel poise and finality. She was an adult woman, yet seeing Luca made her feel like a young girl ready to swoon with love. Rather than swooning, Sophie sat and lit a cigarette, turning away so they would not see her trembling hand.

"All right, Luca, now you've seen me. Let's sign the papers and get this over with. Where, Carlo, do I sign?"

"Sophie," Luca pleaded, "do you think we could go have a coffee before we do this?"

"Yes, yes," Carlo encouraged. "Right around the corner's a bar. Please take your time."

"No."

"Yes."

"No."

"Please, yes."

And Sophie could not resist. They walked to the bar, side by side, each making a concentrated effort not to brush against the other. Such politeness, such coolness. How would a human being, supposedly welded to the heart of another, break those ancient bonds?

But Sophie was seething. "What are we doing here?"

"We're trying to have an adult conversation," Luca responded with a tint of sarcasm in his voice.

"I'm not an adult!" she screamed into his face. "For years you've betrayed me! How can I be calm?"

Rather than hitting him, she was out the door and racing for the train station, Luca in frantic pursuit. "I'm sorry, I'm sorry," she heard over and over again. "Please, Sophie, please stop."

She wanted to stop. She wanted to end the scene in a better way—quietly, gracefully. But it was impossible. Sophie turned on him, planning to push him away, beat him with fists of betrayal, slay him with hatred. All she saw was a sad face with tears making ugly tracks down cheeks dirtied by sweat. And her anger crashed, leaving debris that would take years to clean. Luca took her in his arms and they both wept.

Sophie faced her destination on the red-velvet train seat. It was a private compartment, built of dark wood and brass, waxed and polished over the years like a family heirloom. The motion of the train helped calm her, rocked her in a bewildered state of weariness.

Reaching into her pocket for a cigarette, she pulled out a small package wrapped in mauve paper, tied with a deep-sky-blue ribbon. *Sophie* was written in blue ink on the top. It was Luca's handwriting. Inside, wrapped in cotton, was the ruby that Luca had carried with him during the war. There was no note.

Rage, rage against the dying of the light.

—DYLAN THOMAS

S oon to be dark. Yeats's "trembling blue-green of the sky"
had become feathered with a deeper blue, almost cobalt.
Then suddenly the sky went ablaze with striations of
translucent yellowish pinks, then bluish grays, then slivers of
sea green, and finally a startling array of luminous purple and
orange, tinged with red. And night fell upon the Midlands.

Sophie knew she was near the Trentham Arms when she saw
the almost-full moon reflected upon the canals; then she recognized the sweet shop and the two thatched-roof houses on
either side. It was cold and late, the night a tincture of blue and
black brushed upon the shadows. There was a night clerk at
the desk.

All she wanted to do was to go to bed. She fell asleep and
dreamt about a shiny grey steel box. Crouched inside, she was
uncomfortable—wedged in, unable to move. It was dark and
silent. Suddenly, she heard a loud scream and tried to stand,
tried to get her fingers into a slot to open the top of the box—
panicked—

She left the hotel without seeing Anne. "Gratwich, please.
There's a village nearby named Gratwich, isn't there?"

"Right you are, Ma'am. It's out near the old sanitarium."

The driver let Sophie down on the High Street in Gratwich,
in front of Abbott's Newspaper & Tobacco Shop. She had no
idea why she remembered Gratwich. The name must have

been stored in her memory, a precious oasis in the middle of vast sands. She needed Nurse Watson. No one else would understand, not even Anne.

"Mornin,' Miss," the proprietor welcomed her. "Can I help you?"

"I'm looking for a Mrs. Watson. I remember she said she lived here."

"Watson? There be a handful of Watsons living around here."

"She's a nurse, in her late seventies. Tall and a bit on the stout side, and—"

"Right you are, Miss. Nurse Watson lives straight over there." And he pointed across the road. "The house with the black shutters, can't miss it."

Without hesitating, longing for Nurse Watson's comfort, she crossed over to the front door and knocked.

The door was opened by a gnarled old man. He had wisps of white hair standing straight up here and there, obviously left to finger-combing rather than a brush. Wearing an old gray cardigan with blue trousers and claret-colored carpet slippers worn down at the heels, he looked like a pensioner from a bank, or perhaps a schoolteacher.

"I'm sorry to disturb you, but I'm looking for Nurse Watson."

"Sorry, my dear," he replied in a rickety but clear voice. "My wife isn't practicing any longer. I can recommend someone else who lives just over the road."

"But I must see Nurse Watson, please; she knows me from long ago."

"But," he started to explain, and then looked at Sophie warily. "Come in, my dear. Come this way."

They walked down a shadowy passageway with faded green-and-white aspidistra-patterned wallpaper to the parlor. It was jammed with dark furniture, mementos, curios, mirrors, and cuckoo clocks—and doilies on every surface. It was hard to see straight.

"Here's my wife." And Sophie turned to where he was pointing. "She won't know you any longer."

Nurse Watson was now an old woman, shriveled as an apple doll; her face was scored with wrinkles. Her hair, obviously cut around the mold of a bowl, was short, with a baby-pink scalp showing through. A fringe covered her eyebrows and made her nose quite prominent. And she had whiskers, stiff white hairs poking straight out from her chin. Nurse Watson had changed from a vivacious, muscular woman to a frail, thin, almost transparent one. Her hands, quivering lightly on her lap, could easily have been branches on an old and barren tree. Both Mr. and Mrs. Watson and their house had the fusty smell of old people. The cuckoo clocks went off and they looked at each other and smiled.

But Nurse Watson looked back at Sophie with bare eyes. "Please, Nurse Watson, please help me," Sophie said. But Sophie saw her words sliding through Nurse Watson's head and sprinkling upon the ground.

"She doesn't understand you." Mr. Watson spoke loudly over the clocks' noise. "Please don't turn her up. Sometimes she gets into a dither and it's hard to calm her down."

Sophie returned to London only long enough to deliver the painting of Luca to Leland.

"Oh, lovely!" he said, "what a great painting. May I put it in your next exhibition? May I use it as a publicity photo? May I—"

"No, you can't sell it, nor use it in any way. As a friend, I'm entrusting it into your hands to store for me."

Sophie was relieved to be with Leland. He made her laugh. Always keeping up with the latest fashions, Leland was wearing aviator-shaped glasses, a psychedelic T-shirt, blue bell-bottom trousers, a leather-bound amulet around his neck, and an Afro that was obviously a perm.

"Are you painting?" Leland asked.

"No, I've nothing to say," Sophie confessed. And he looked at her as if she were truly mad.

The fisherman knows the sea is dangerous and the storms terrible, but he has never found these dangers sufficient reason for staying ashore.

—Vincent Van Gogh

Twenty-eight years after sailing across the sea, far away from Luca, Sophie walked to the edge of a road and stepped off into the desert. On either side were vast open fields rolling toward the mountains. It was a high desert valley, where she could see what the weather was going to do many hours before it reached her house. On that particular day there were dark, obese clouds, with white-brushed edges, rolling the rain into her valley. Not prepared for a downpour, she continued on more quickly, past the scattered piñon trees with their dark, scraggy bark and prickly pine needles and the small gray-green chamisas that sent a whisper of sweet perfume into the air as she grazed them with her foot. At the fork in the trail, she passed the lonely mountain mahogany, gnarled as her own old finger, but still attracting butterflies, fluttering against the increasing wind.

The army-issue knapsack, which Sophie had bought in Paris a half-century before, was heavier than when she began the day. Along with her sketch pad, charcoal sticks, and colored pencils, she had collected smooth, pearly-grey granite pieces, weather-worn wood, and the prize of the day, a coral-pink fossilized seashell the size of the tip of her little finger, which had been waiting on the floor of that once-upon-a-time sea.

Sophie began to climb. The trail had been beaten into the brush by generations of coyotes, and probably deer and antelope before they had been hunted out of existence. In the distance, she could see that the late-afternoon sun was leaning against her house, making it look as if it were wrapped in a glowing, rose-colored gauze. Flinging themselves out the window, the curtains waved to her in faded colors.

Half hidden behind the kitchen, in the shade of the cottonwood tree, there was an unfamiliar blue pickup truck. Oh damn, she thought. The day before, when she was in town, the proprietor of the art-supply store had told her that a young man was asking after her. Sophie's anxiety spun her in another direction. She turned and headed back down the road, taking the rut off to the right that led along the arroyo to her studio. The arroyo was one of the reasons she had chosen that particular site. From June through August, the rains could be so heavy that often the arroyo filled with raging waters. Standing on the porch, Sophie would watch the enormous, oceanlike waves tumble down the mountain toward the river, on their way to the Gulf of Mexico.

But that afternoon, late in Sophie's seventy-eighth year, there was no time for reflection. Although she wanted to get away from uninvited visitors, her feet were moored to the floor, her floor, a floor she had built in that sanctuary of her imagination, that studio of her longing. Since the end of Sophie's dreams in Italy, running away had been her solution—a twenty-eight-year pilgrimage of forgetting.

It is what we fear that happens to us.

—OSCAR WILDE

S ophie did not like meddling strangers. Her house was isolated at the end of a long and twisting road. A few years before, she had seen a strange dark-green car drive up and park. She waited, and soon heard footsteps, then a knock at the door.

"Hello. Is anyone home? Miss Marks, are you there?"

Sophie had tiptoed to the back door and let herself out, going down the path to her studio. From that window she could see the area in front of the house. The young, dark-haired woman, dressed in a red sleeveless shirt and blue jeans, had sat down beneath the cottonwood tree and begun to read. She took forever to go. Finally, at dusk, Sophie heard the car backing out, turning, and starting down the road.

Two years later, the same young woman appeared and Sophie went out the back door. But this time, the woman did not wait more than five minutes. Sophie found, propped against her front door, a large manila envelope, and on the envelope was written a note.

Dear Sophie Marks,

I came here once before, but sadly missed you, and then I tried to call but discovered that your number is unlisted. I've always admired your work, indeed did my university dissertation on your Paris paintings. Since then I've been writing for art journals and reviewing for various newspapers in London. I would like to make an appointment to interview you with an eye to writing your biography. Is this possible? I've included the piece I wrote about you in The Guardian. *I hope that if you like it, you will ring me and we can plan a time to talk. I'm staying with a friend and can be reached at 983.8394. Sincerely yours, Jane Simon.*

MYSTERIOUS ABSENCE by Jane Simon
January 15, 1990

Twenty-one years after leaving Europe, the reclusive Sophie Marks has reappeared in all her splendor. Her much anticipated retrospective, *Sophie Marks: 1946 to 1990*, opened a week ago at the Museum of Modern Art in New York, and, although the lines are long, the wait is worth it.

The portraits fill four large galleries, representing the four geographical areas where she has lived and worked: the Midlands, Paris, Italy, and an enigmatic desert. Even a wall of the rare, dazzling, early Italian buried paintings are here. The paintings are all in row, winding through the galleries like a rope of shimmering opals. Although this exhibition design can be quite repetitive, one doesn't become bored at all. Each portrait is uniquely Ms. Marks's subject forever. There are no faces to recognize, no celebrities; there are simply people she has embraced forever on small canvases. Encased in simple goldleaf frames, her work continues to be small in scale, and enormous in content.

Each painting glows with the sense that she has had an intense visit with the soul of each person. The visitations must have been long because these paintings are meticulous in detail while giving the illusion of being painted with a tiny palette knife. Like Jan van Eyck, even Bonnard, she has painted her subjects from the inside out. Steeped in personal history, each image begs to be contemplated in reverence—almost like an isolated icon perched on an altar.

Unlike the average thirty seconds that a viewer gives a painting, an entire morning or afternoon, I suggest, is needed to honor her work. Ms. Marks's world takes time.

————

Although Sophie Marks is so sublimely present in the galleries, she has disappeared in real life. Marks, whose work has been exhibited broadly in the past four decades, has no address. A couple of years ago I decided to find her. When I interviewed Leland Ross, her agent of many years, he simply smiled a sweet smile.

"I've heard she's living in the desert," I said. "But which desert? Which country?"

"Let her be," he said. "She wants her work to speak for itself."

But I was too curious. I couldn't leave the question alone. Through interviews with her collectors, various curators, and a reluctant childhood friend in the Midlands, I discovered some of the answers. But the one person, other than Sophie Marks, I wanted most to interview was her longtime lover, the sculptor Luca Bondi. He adamantly refused.

Her newest work gave me more clues. In direct contrast to the milky-white skins of people living in the Midlands (always indoors, because it was always raining), the desert paintings illustrate wind-battered faces, eyes squinting against the unforgiving light. Making an educated guess, I found my way to a desert a day's drive from the Mexican border.

In the town, I spoke to the local museum director, who was at first friendly, then taciturn, then silent. The stony-faced glare of the proprietor of the art-supply store made it clear that he was also protecting Marks. Then I got lucky. I was in a café and overheard someone at the next table whisper, "There's Sophie Marks."

And there she was, dressed in blue overalls and a white cotton T-shirt, wearing old brown leather work boots spattered with paint. She is about five feet nine inches tall, and, although already seventy-four years old, she stands straight as a young sapling and has a walk that is assured. Her face, elongated like one in a Modigliani painting, has large, piercing dark eyes. Her nose is a little too long to be fashionable and her lips are a mite too thin. But, overall, she is a handsome woman with a youthful vigor.

I followed her old car at a comfortable distance until she turned left onto an obscure dirt road. I kept going and then turned around farther on. The next afternoon I drove to her house. I knocked on her door. She ignored me. I knew that she was inside and had chosen not to let me in. I waited all day under a cottonwood tree. No luck. Sophie Marks will remain an enigma—but her work is a pure delight.

Dawn begins at midnight.
—HENRI MATISSE

After leaving Luca, Sophie might have slipped from the memory of the art world. The work simply did not come. Like the desert where she was living, she was dried up, brittle. However, interest in her painting grew, almost as if she had died. For a long time, none of this mattered to Sophie. She wandered, made friends, read. Primarily she waited for time to slip by, waited for the pain of losing Luca to fade away.

Then, little by little, she began to work again. Drawings of the landscape. A portrait of a neighbor. She needed to practice. As a musician friend said, she had to exercise her chops; she thought this image very American, and hilarious.

The unseen, the hidden in nature had always given her hope. Moving from the shadows into the clear desert light was deeply pleasing. She had brought her treasured microscope to the desert. All her portraits were influenced by what she saw through that lens—magnifying the incredible natural secrets that were not apparent to the human eye. She visually translated them. An idea for a glaze that she saw in a piece of mica, luminous with pearly grays and faded robin's-egg blues; the texture of a face revealed in a stone with the fossilized remnants of an ancient fire; leaves, burnt maroon by the first frost; more leaves freshened by a spring rain; skins of snakes, burnished even smoother; flowers from the inside out, the veins reminding her of her old hands. The list was endless; decades of searching was a very long time.

*

It was almost ten years before she had an exhibition of new work. Portraits—still portraits of the people around her. But these portraits were more jewel-like, easily held in the hand. Sophie was convinced that she painted smaller because the desert around her was so vast. She needed to focus closely to keep herself tethered to the earth.

The strange blue pickup truck was bothering her. She was not in the mood for visitors. Noiselessly, she entered the studio and sat in the old studio chair, brought from Paris, then from Italy. True, the colors of the covering had changed, as had the patterns. Once the chair had been a sea of old-fashioned tawny-yellow roses against a background of indigo blue. Another time she had draped it with a piece of blood-red velvet. Now it was covered with a red, yellow, and turquoise-blue Mexican blanket, with a wide orange stripe down the center, reminding Sophie of her old orange tabby cat, whose fur rose down her spine when she announced her preparation for battle. Although she had bought the blanket in Mexico only two years earlier, it had already been attacked by desert moths, famous for their voracious passion for wool.

But Sophie knew she had to contend with the stranger lingering around the edges of her house. What did he want? She did not sense he was dangerous. Escape? No, that was too strong an action. Anyway, she was too old to take off on foot across the valley, and her car was parked near his. She decided to wait.

As the light began to lower itself over the next mountain, and the spring rain clouds came closer, she sat quietly and looked out the window. The rain finally arrived after announcing itself with a dramatic array of flashing lights. It beat down upon the tin roof. The noise became a harmony, the harmony became a symphony. Now Sophie was in the world of herself.

Comfortable for the moment, she watched the storm release its burden.

Like most desert storms, it passed quickly and Sophie could see the rain turning a corner and heading southeast. It was funny, but, after living in the desert for a few years, Sophie realized that she actually missed the closeness of that almost suffocating nature of the Midlands. The vastness of the desert had begun to make her feel exposed and vulnerable. There was no place to hide, no place to contemplate the rest of her life. The clear, arid, startling blue atmosphere had made her feel deprived of sensation. She had felt dried up, like one of the tumbleweeds that rolled down her road with the wind.

Ever since Sophie left Luca, she had been serving time in the desert, honoring tradition. Moses told the Israelites that he would lead them for forty years in the wilderness because it would take them that long to understand everything they needed to know. She did not have another forty years, but her enduring curiosity made up for the time.

The dependency upon Luca as her symbol for home had finally cracked. Granted, it took a while, but she began to understand that "home" was only within herself—her own anchor that could be pulled up, moved, and lowered again. Now she knew that she was up against a decision. Either she had to settle in and wither away in that alien land, or take hold of a branch and pull herself into life for a while longer.

She had decided to go home. Home to England. How strange. She worried that she was too old for such a change. Yet she had been contemplating it, fretting it, twisting it, turning it around, looking at it from all angles. The idea offered ancient memories and unsolved problems. But once she had come to the decision, she felt an almost physical sense of solace. It was as if her body had reversed and was growing young again.

The American desert had been kind to her. When Sophie had arrived all those years ago, the area reminded her of Italy, and, of course, Luca. Most of the streets were still dirt; only the main ones were paved. The roughness of the terrain was pleasing. It looked exactly like the pictures she had seen as a child. For many years, the openness, the expanse of the valley, surprised her with its intimacy. Sophie felt private, blessedly alone.

But now she wanted change. She longed for the adventure of uprooting herself, for taking chances with the unknown. *Exiles,* Aeschylus wrote, *subsist on hope*—this was tacked on her kitchen window frame. She had not been able to live without regret. Luca's betrayal was merely one blade of tragedy in a row of knives. Her betrayal of him was far worse; she had emotionally sliced herself away, while pretending she was open, vulnerable, close to him. Sophie sometimes wondered why he had put up with her as long as he did. But up to now she had organized her life; indeed, in cowboy fashion, she had corralled it, and closed the gate.

Sophie could not get comfortable in the chair. Her inclination was to sit cross-legged; the seat was wide enough. But it no longer worked. She was simply too stiff for yogic acrobatics. Now she had to be content to sit like a lady and look out upon the land she had cherished for so long.

The window was open and she could smell the aroma of damp piñon and chamisa, hear the symphony of crickets. Some days they sounded sweet, some days bored; other times they were a cacophonic intrusion that made her jittery. That day, the day of the stranger, she welcomed them as their sounds moved into the dusty corners of her studio.

Creaking out of her chair, Sophie began to pace the room. It was drizzling; a remnant of the storm had appeared and she paused to look out a rear window. All she could see was her own reflection. Who in the world is this woman staring back at me, she asked herself. She did not look like Sophie Marks. It was quite peculiar. That woman must be old because her hair was white. But as Sophie leaned closer to see if that were true, her breath fogged the window and her image disappeared.

Because of the rain, Sophie wondered if the driver of the blue truck had made himself comfortable in the house. He was probably brewing a cup of tea, building a fire, perhaps even reading with his feet up on her sofa. So why was she so nervous about turning on a light? It was ridiculous. Sophie reached up and switched on the light.

All of a sudden, the studio door was flung open and there was the stranger—rainwater dripping from the rim of his battered cowboy hat, boots caked with mud. After all her bravado, she was petrified. She could feel her heart pounding against her ribs and tried to quiet it with her hands. No words came out of her mouth.

"It's all right," the man said, "I'm not going to hurt you. I'm sorry about the banging door, but the wind blew it out of my hand." He smiled broadly.

Sophie knew him, but could not remember from where.

"You don't recognize me?" he asked.

She shook her head "no," still too rattled to speak.

"I'm Luca Bondi's son. My father sent me for the ruby."

Sophie was stunned. Now she could see why he looked familiar. Only having seen his mother once, she could not identify that resemblance, but he was definitely Luca's son. Tall and lean with almost-black hair, he had the same deep creases on either side of his mouth.

"You look like a photograph of a cowboy," she said.

"And you look just as my father described, only with different-colored hair," he politely offered.

"Come in," Sophie invited, "and I'll make a pot of tea." Unsteadily, she rose from her chair and went to the rear of the studio. She reached for her familiar touchstones: the lapis-blue-and-white teapot with the bent-over shepherd and his two pure-white lambs; the tea ball to be filled with loose tea leaves; the shiny red honey jar with the crack in its lid. Sophie put on the kettle, fussing about, trying to gather her wits.

"Seeing you makes me feel old," Sophie said, trying to be humorous. "Would you feel more comfortable speaking French? Have a seat."

"English is fine with me," he said, and she was a trifle disappointed.

Well, Sophie thought, he certainly caught me napping, he did! She quietly scrutinized him. Scrunching his neck into his shoulders, he even sat in the chair like Luca. He was about the same age Luca was when they first met; no wonder Sophie found him so attractive. It was a cavalcade of time, just like those old sepia newsreels she used to see at the cinema.

While trying to gather her thoughts, she was aware of the sounds of her studio: the settling of a floorboard; the quivering noises of branches hitting the tin roof; the water dripping off the rain gutters into the barrel.

"My father said you were very quiet and I shouldn't take it as a sign that you wanted me to leave."

"That does sound like Luca. I'm sorry. You've unnerved me," Sophie said, and the teapot's whistle blew.

"Here, let me help you," he offered, and stood by her side while she poured the boiling water into the teapot.

"Are you taller than Luca?" Sophie asked, looking up at him.

"Yes, now I am. He's shrunk a little."

"I must be shrinking as well," she said, shaking her head.

He carried the tray to the table and set it down. "Here, let me pour," he offered.

"No, I can manage just fine," Sophie replied, a bit testily. "I don't understand; how did you know where to find me?"

"Oh, Sophie," he exclaimed, her first name rolling off his tongue. He took the cup of tea from her, balancing it on the saucer as if he were in an English sitting room. "It wasn't so hard. You're a famous artist and famous artists are easy to find. On top of which, my father has kept track of you. He spoke about you so often that I feel as if I've always known you."

"What do you mean 'spoke'? Is he all right? Are you here because something's happened? Oh, dear, I don't want to hear. This is all too much." With her hand trembling, she set down the cup.

"Oh, sorry. Yes, he's well, thank you. He can't run up and down the scaffolding around his sculptures as fast as he used to, but he's certainly well."

Sophie felt relief, a cool breeze blowing past her face on a warm summer's day.

"By the way," he said, politely standing, "my name's Niccolò, but everyone calls me Nico." And they shook hands.

He had the same endearing ease as Luca. If Sophie had been younger, or he had been older, she could have become interested in romance again.

It had been a tragedy—Adele, Nico's mother, was too young when she had died the year before. Her gallery had become one of the most successful in Europe. She was a glamorous and well-known figure in the world of art. Besides Luca, she represented many artists, a number of whom she had discovered and transformed into celebrities. Luca was her first success and she wanted to make her artist son, Nico, her last. But, now that she was gone, Nico was not certain whether he had lost his best advocate or his sternest critic.

After her death, Nico had been ill at ease and in a wandering mood. For the past six months he had been in New York.

Living in a corner of a closet-sized studio, he was painting and trying to find a gallery. He wanted no favors from his father; he felt that he would never be able to satisfy Luca anyway. And he certainly did not want anyone to know who his mother was. He needed to find his own way—to put both geographical and artistic distance between himself and Europe.

But he had rich ground to build on. When Nico was a little boy, Luca had been a good teacher. He was patient and firm in his belief that Nico had to work hard, that being an artist meant assuming a responsibility. Ever since Nico could lift a hammer, Luca had him making things. There was an area of Luca's studio where he kept crates filled with found objects: pieces of wood, scraps of metal, lengths of wire, seashells, rocks, even old, dried snail casings from the garden. He encouraged Nico to make a sculpture that sounded like their nightingale in Italy; challenged Nico to invent a tool that could be used to button his sweater if it was on backward; inspired him to make a bas-relief about the color purple, without using the color purple.

"May I," Nico asked Sophie, "have another cup of tea, please?"

"I never expected this, never ever imagined meeting you," Sophie told him while waiting for the water to boil again. "When I left London, I erased my European life. I had to. I'm so sorry about your mother. I didn't know."

"I'm surprised; it was in all the art magazines both in Europe and here. She left behind an amazing legacy. The artists called her *La Grande Mère*. She took great satisfaction in managing their careers, and sometimes," he said wryly, "sometimes even their lives."

Adele had kept a journal of all the things she had never been able to say aloud. How much she loved Luca. How she felt he was never entirely hers. How Luca had been created to be a father. What a struggle it had been to be maternal.

Before she died, she gave Nico permission to read the journal, telling him that nothing had been so burdensome to her as the secrets she kept. She had fallen in love with Luca and knew the only way to win him was to have a child. She was obsessed with her love for him. (That he had been living with Sophie for so many years, she wrote with a flip of her pen, did not count.) It took time for their love to build. Nico lived during the school year with his parents in Paris, where Luca had a studio. But each summer, as soon as Nico was out of school, he and his father returned to Monterosa. The house made Adele uncomfortable. She stayed in Paris.

"But," Sophie said, "I don't understand why they stayed together—"

"Why, they really loved each other!" Nico answered. "No matter how odd it sounds."

"The light of the truth is glaring."

"What did you say?" Nico asked. "You're mumbling."

"Oh, sorry, dear, I was just remembering something. It's nothing."

"Tell me," Nico insisted. "I'm interested."

"Drink your tea before it gets cold," she said.

"Yes, Ma'am," he teased.

"I'm thinking," Sophie said, "about the days before I left the house in Monterosa. After all these years I don't remember many details, but I do recall some things. One was that I looked out our bedroom window for the last time and was crushed with such overwhelming jealousy that I haven't forgotten it; it was deeply humiliating. Since I'd always prided myself on my ability to be alone, realizing that I loved Luca as much as I did came as a surprise. And now you tell me all this. I wonder what I was thinking—

"Nico." Sophie looked straight at him. "You realize that I've had an entirely different story written in my head?"

"Let's go up to the house," Sophie proposed. "I'll make us some dinner."

"Oh, good," Nico said with enthusiasm. "I've heard you're a terrific cook."

"Listen, Nico," she said, stopping short. "Your knowing so much about me is making me very nervous. Perhaps I should just arrange for you to fetch the ruby?" And then Sophie felt bad for being rude. "I'm sorry—"

"No, no, it's all right. Really it is. I imagine I must have overwhelmed you. It's I who should be apologizing. I'll go for the night and come back in the morning."

"Don't be silly," Sophie said. "Of course, I want you to stay. Come, I'll make us dinner, an Italian one. I have a feeling that you have a wolf in your stomach."

"You're correct, Ma'am; I always do!"

Sophie's house was a lovely, low-slung, hacienda-style adobe. It was built of mud-and-straw bricks, plastered with reddish-ochre mud, blending into the landscape. There was a courtyard in the center and a number of rooms running around the perimeter. The hallways were decorated with Sophie's painted rugs, leading guests from one space to another. The main room included a kitchen, with a porch that looked west over the valley.

The courtyard contained plants that were native to England and Italy; there were no cacti or piñon trees in sight. Except for the linden tree, whose blossoms she harvested and dried for tea, everything else—roses, lavender, lilacs, even a grapevine—was planted in enormous terra-cotta pots. She loved sitting under the tree, daydreaming among the captured perfumes and listening to the desert silence.

*

Her studio was separate. Sophie had been afraid that if she did not force herself away from making art, she would work only to fill her loneliness. But, even with all her comfort and success, the nights were forlorn, reminding Sophie of the intimacy of love. She too often woke with such an ache that she would hold her silky damask feather-filled quilt, scrunched up, close to her body, pretending it was a warm embrace.

Over the years there had been a few lovers, mainly artists she had met through her work. Although Sophie did enjoy the momentary feelings of connection, once the initial passion was over, she could never convince herself to keep the affairs going.

When Sophie was approaching seventy, a young and fine-looking man, also a painter, arrived to do some work for her. At first she was taken with him, and they became engaged in an affair. Perhaps, she thought, perhaps this would be good for me. But it was hard for her to disregard her worn and wrinkled body next to his smooth youth. She would close her eyes and pretend she was young again. For a few months it was lovely.

However, his self-aggrandizing manner soon began to grate on her. Finally, he took a step too deep into her privacy when he suggested he become her full-time assistant and move onto the property. Sophie told him to leave.

In the end, none of the men came close to tempting her toward love. As she got even older, every so often, one of them would stop in to check on her, have a cup of tea, repair something she could not handle. They did not come to court her, that was certain. Rather than looking for romance and sexual adventure, she had grown to cherish her sensuous memories. Between her painting, her friends, her gardening, and her reading, Sophie thought she had buried her bodily desire.

But with Nico standing beside her at the stove, peeling garlic and blithely chatting away, Sophie was flooded with the excitement of visiting her past. She felt herself straightening her back, lifting her chin. She wished she had combed her hair differently; taken it out of the perpetual braid traveling down her back; worn her new dark-green skirt; camouflaged her aging belly with a longer, more elegant shirt. Instead, she was dressed in her usual blue denim overalls with a red jersey and a red-and-black plaid shirt over it all. And to her distress, she realized that she was not wearing a brassiere. Now be calm, Sophie told herself, don't be in a kerfuffle, as her grandparents used to say.

"Sit beside me," Sophie invited, patting the other chair, "so we can both see out across the valley."

They sat side by side, elbows resting on the pine table. Nico poured them each a glass of red wine.

As they watched, the great flood of the western sky was being dammed off by the lowering light. It was magnificent, but Sophie's eyes were elsewhere. She was intrigued with the idea of passion and Nico. Her imagination was running rampant. Sophie saw herself in bed with him, but she had a young body. Bloody hell, she thought, what are you thinking! And she felt her cheeks flushing.

Trying not to interfere with Nico enjoying the sunset, Sophie barely turned her head to watch him.

But he caught her eye.

And grinned.

She knew that he knew what she was thinking.

It was a bright desert morning. The tall field grasses, the new leaves on the cottonwood tree—everything was greener and more brilliant as a result of the heavy rain. Sophie thought she had better check the road; she worried that the arroyo might have flooded and washed some of it away yet again. Then she heard footsteps on the wooden porch and remembered Nico.

"Morning, Sophie," he called out, not wanting to startle her.

And Sophie's entire world, in one inescapable moment, was wrapped in a rubescence of warmth.

In a most natural way, they traveled back over the years. He appeared to know her. And she, intuitively, knew him too. There was a familiar sensibility that had no hard edges, no shadows.

She offered a long walk; she wanted to show him her land and tell him its stories. The weather was cool, there were no clouds, and the sun was warm on their faces. They walked for more than an hour, speaking in the easy, direct manner that people engage in when they are comfortable with each other.

Nico leaned down to pick up a colorful rock. "Ouch!" he exclaimed, and grabbed his hand. "Ouch," he said again, even louder, more chagrined than hurt.

"Here, let me see," Sophie soothed. "It's only a prickle from a cactus. Hold still." And with the swiftness of experience she plucked it out of his finger. "Come," she suggested, "let's climb up to the top of that bluff and sit for a while."

"It's a long way. You must be tired," Nico said.

She looked at him as if to say, come, come, I'm much less tired than you are! And he laughed.

In a few minutes, they were seated and looking across the southern part of the valley. "Amazing, Sophie, we can almost see the curve of the earth."

She leaned against a convenient boulder. "How limber you are," Nico noticed.

"Yes, especially for my age," she said, and smiled at him.

For a long time they sat in a comradely silence. "What are you thinking?" he asked.

"About time. I often think about the passage of time; how there's no end to the beginning. We travel through time in constant movement. Even now, when we're sitting still, the universe is moving; the earth is moving; the blood in our bodies, the oxygen in our molecules, our minds—all are moving. Nothing is ever truly still. And in a more mundane way, I'm moving back home."

"You are! When? This is so exciting. Italy!"

"Ah, dear Nico, I wish I could. No, I'm going back to England—to my original home. I've found a young couple to buy this property.

"I've taken a chance and had a house and studio built to my specifications—although, I must admit, I'm nervous about it all. But I used an architect and builder who were recommended by my friend Anne in Trentham."

"But you could still change your mind and go to Italy. My father would be thrilled to have you there again."

"Oh, Nico, we're too old for that. It's been too long. No, I need to go back to where I came from. It's an animal instinct, I presume. When it's time to die, I can't imagine dying on this land. After all these years, I'm still a visitor. My love for this part of the world isn't in my bones, it's in my imagination. No, I have to die in my own woods, beside my son and grandparents. I may not have left children behind as a legacy, but I can certainly add these old bones to the loamy soil of England. And, anyway, I've left the history of my life there. It all needs to be dug back up and be given a proper burial."

"You mean the buried paintings?" Nico asked.

"Ah, you even know about those," she mused.

"Of course I do," he said, as if surprised that she should even ask.

"Nico," Sophie said with iron in her voice, "your arriving on my doorstep is clearly not about the ruby. Why, precisely, are you here?"

"I've told you," Nico said. "My father said you would fill in the blanks . . . No, I have to admit, that isn't entirely true. Sorry, Sophie, for being so vague. The truth is that I've been following your career since I decided to consider the arts. I saw a number of your exhibitions, many with my father. We even flew to New York to see your retrospective."

Sophie was confused. "Luca flew to New York? But why?"

"He told me you were contemporary art's classic example of how passion and art can be wedded on a two-dimensional surface."

"Your father," Sophie said, nodding, "always romanticized my work."

"Well, Sophie, you have to understand that every summer, when my father and I were in Monterosa, you were a part of my life. Your studio, left as it was, the rugs painted on the floors, your garden—you are everywhere."

"And then this year my father told me about how he had abandoned you."

"No, no, Nico! Your father didn't do that to me," she said, and there was a long pause.

"Come on," Sophie said, "let's walk back, it's getting late."

Nico had been silenced and Sophie felt awful about being so abrupt.

"The real horrors happened before we met," she continued as the path opened up to allow them to walk alongside each other.

"Your father suffered the result of my earlier torment, and I've forever been grateful to him for putting up with me as long as he did. It's true, at first, I felt as if I had been pushed off the mountainside. But, after floundering and flailing about, I found I could manage on my own. For this, in retrospect, I'm grateful."

"Can you tell me what happened during the war?" Nico asked.

"No, Nico, I can't. I need to let it rest."

"You're just like my father," Nico said tersely. "He won't tell me anything either."

"I'm sorry, Nico, but it's best to leave it alone."

"I was at least hoping you'd explain about the buried paintings," Nico pushed, with a hint of whine in his voice. Oh, he's not perfect, Sophie said to herself. What a relief.

"All I know," he continued, "is that there are paintings of men you have loved, and that they're buried under an old apple tree."

"Not under," she corrected, "beside it. I'll tell you what, Nico. Why don't I paint your portrait and when I return I'll bury it along with the others? Then some day, when you come to visit, I'll show them all to you and tell their stories."

That evening Sophie asked if she could see Nico's work. "I don't have any of the canvases," he said, "but I do have slides."

"Then let's go out to the studio and use the light box," Sophie said.

As he placed the slides on the light box, Sophie could see that his work was static, without character. He worked with tired abstract forms, somewhat gloomy and chunky, reminiscent of Cubism—without the lyricism. What to say?

Nico was nervous. He knew he had a lot to learn but he wanted Sophie to like his work. He was yearning for a teacher—someone other than his father.

"Nico, my honest response depends on what you're here for."

"I want to learn," he replied, "and there is no one better than you to tell me the truth. I love your work."

"All right, Nico, sit down, here it goes. You are not a painter. You are more likely a sculptor. Your forms are architectural—they are masses looking for the right surface to settle upon. They don't belong on a two-dimensional plane—they need air around them—to come alive they must be seen from a variety of angles.

"I'm sorry. Does this upset you?"

"I don't want to make work like my father," Nico replied in a flat voice.

"There's no reason why you would make the same work. You're a different generation; you have a different sensibility. I can assure you that you'll find your own voice. Anyway, look, you've come halfway around the world, searching for real meaning. This takes courage, you know."

"So, what do you suggest?" he asked.

"I suggest you take the back bedroom, which is the largest and has the most light, and begin by drawing three-dimensional forms. Then take paper and cut and fold to make those same forms. Watch them at different times of day and try to distinguish how the light changes on their surfaces."

The next day Sophie tacked a canvas to the painting wall. "I want you to sit here," she said, placing a straight-backed chair facing out the window. "Like your father, you need to be looking out upon the world." Nico simply smiled.

"You're always being compared to Lucien Freud," Nico told her when he took his place for the pose. "Are you aware of this?"

"I hope not," she protested. "His work is so despairing."

"But, Sophie, he's an icon. It's probably good for your career that critics make the comparison."

"Please, Nico," Sophie said, "I can't bear to hear this. You shouldn't be so concerned about fame, it doesn't become you."

Sophie switched on the radio and Bach filled the studio.

"I don't know if I can sit still," Nico said, concern in his voice.

"Simply listen to the music," she offered. "It will soothe you."

The sun streamed in through the open door. Sophie began to rough in the portrait—the first she had painted in this style since leaving Italy. It was as if she had been practicing in her imagination. The form came easily; the likeness was not debatable. Even in the black charcoal of a sketch, his inquisitive personality popped out at the viewer.

Nico sat for two hours in the mornings; then he would walk back to the house and make lunch. After the first hour of the first meal, he caught on that she was not going to engage in conversation. Sophie was lost to the portrait. He let her be and read and then went to his own room to work. But in the evenings they ate, drank wine, and listened to Sophie's favorite symphonies and Beethoven's string quartets. And they talked about art. Nico told her about his love of the contemporary Italian artists—the contemplative still-life painter Giorgio Morandi; the abstract painter Alberto Burri; the Futurist Lucio Fontana. They had good-natured debates and pulled art books from the shelves to support their claims.

Occasionally, in the evenings, they would go to Sophie's studio so she could show him techniques for brushstrokes, stretching canvases, mixing colors. "Just because you may be making three-dimensional forms doesn't mean you shouldn't know how to use paints.

"Watch," she said. "In oil painting, when two or more pigments of different colors are combined, 'broken colors' occur. Here, for example, is viridian," she said, and she squeezed a bead onto the palette. "See, it's a bright, pure tone of emerald green. Now, I can create a fake viridian by mixing a blue with a yellow. See? It looks close, doesn't it? But the difference is that it won't reflect the red light wave that make viridian so fresh. You have to remember that, to keep colors luminous and vibrant, it's important not to muddy your palette."

Sophie varied her traditional style. She painted Nico's face turned slightly, not in the usual abrupt profile. Also, she painted his hand in trompe l'oeil, resting on the painted frame around the painting. While she waited for it to dry each day, she began to work on sketches for the narratives. Again, she decided, there would be three stories. The one at the top was of a young Nico, sitting between Adele and Luca, being read to. Luca was dressed in a field worker's clothes, just as he was in the portrait she had painted of him many years before. Nico was wearing blue denim overalls and had a red scarf jauntily tied around his neck. His head came to just below Luca's chin and he was holding his mother's hand. In the background was a French chateau, perched on an Italian Renaissance-style green hill, with a road spiraling, climbing to the top. Capturing Adele's likeness was problematic.

"Do you have a photograph of your mother?" Sophie asked at dinner.

And Nico, without saying a word, took a creased one out of his wallet. Sophie put it in her shirt pocket, needing to study Adele's face while alone.

Once in her room, she took out the photograph, put on her reading glasses, and looked at it under the desk light. When the picture was taken, Adele must have been in her forties. She was sitting on a bench, under a tree, with her ankles crossed and her hand raised as if to say hello, or perhaps good-bye. Although it was difficult to see the details of her face, there was no doubt that she was beautiful.

I'm still envious, Sophie realized. Even at this age, and with Adele being dead, she still felt the stab of betrayal inflicted by the two of them. Oh, how she wished it would go away and let her be.

The second story on the canvas was of a smiling teenaged Nico standing on top of a plinth. He was dressed as a Renaissance nobleman, decked out in a white shirt with a richly embroidered red tunic over puffy black breeches and ecru hose. His arms were raised in the air in triumph, one hand holding a hoe and the other a large and long-handled paintbrush. The brush was tipped with a clear cerulean that trickled down, splattering the nearby rust-colored sculpture.

The last scene was of Nico and Sophie sitting at the table and looking out at the western mountains. Nico was dressed like a cowboy with slant-heeled brown leather boots, tight blue denims, a red checkered shirt, and his beloved battered cowboy hat, with its silver Hopi buckle, pulled down rakishly over one eye. He was sitting backward on the yellow chair, with his arms wrapped around its back and his hands resting on the table.

The hardest part of the picture was to paint her portrait. She had not painted herself since the portrait of Luca more than twenty-five years before. Using a mirror, she was able to get the body right. It was her face and the gray hair that did her in. She moved the mirror closer, but was so thrown by the clarity of age that she found herself frozen with indecision. Finally, she realized it was no use. Sophie could not bear painting her face. She ended up painting herself turning away, the emblematic silver braid dangling down her back. She sat in the same style of chair as Nico; her legs were crossed at the ankles and her hands were resting on the table. Draped over the back of the chair was an intricately woven Afghani cloth, dusty red, black, and deep ochre. In the middle of the table was a damson-red ceramic bowl of oranges and apples. And on the table in front of the bowl, between her hands, she painted the ruby, larger than life.

October, 1993. It was time to leave. Sophie had been postponing the event, engaging herself with Nico, saying good-bye to her friends. Now she was on a piece of taut string. The new owners were taking possession soon.

"What's the matter, Sophie?" Nico asked. "You seem nervous this morning."

"I need to ask you a favor," she said, turning from the sink, "but the time never seems right. I'm nervous about asking you—"

"You're making *me* nervous!"

"Would you—could you—help me with this move? I'll pay you, of course. I was going to hire someone from town, but I'd rather you."

"Naturally I'll help. Forget paying me. My father and mother were rich; consequently, so am I."

"But Luca never had a lot of money," she protested.

"I know, but now he does. He's made his fortune as an artist. You really don't know what's going on, do you?"

Sophie had to laugh. "No, I only get the local newspaper and that usually ends up under a can of paint before I've read it. I'm not very good at keeping up with the world. Anyway, as they say in England, today's news is tomorrow's—"

"May I," he interrupted, "may I ask you something personal?" And he forged ahead. "Don't forget you promised that when we get to England, you would show me my father's portrait, buried beside your apple tree."

"I didn't bury it."

"But—"

Sophie shrugged. "We'll talk about it later," she promised.

Movers were scheduled. Nico made crates. Once the first bookshelf was cleared, the entire house began to unravel. Now all the past years became more vague and insignificant.

But leaving was not easy. While packing, Sophie would catch herself emotionally spiraling downward, and then have to remind herself that it was she who had made this decision, no one else. On the packing went. She moved from room to room, throwing unwanted items onto a pile. Nico drove it all to the county's dump in his blue truck.

"You have to slow down," Nico warned. "You need to rest. We haven't even made our airline reservations yet."

"We're not going to fly, Nico. I'm afraid. We'll sail on the Queen Elizabeth 2. After all, being met by Mother England on a dock in America will better prepare me for the shock of going home after all these years."

Sophie could see the surprise on his face, the rosy flush of his cheeks. It had probably never occurred to him to go by boat, she realized. Even if she was not afraid, she would want to take her time. She needed the slow transition.

"What a strange idea," he finally said. "I've never gone anywhere by boat. Actually, to be honest, I rather like the idea. How do we get to New York from the middle of this desert?" He looked at her and smiled. "Of course, the train. I'm so spoiled by fast travel that I've forgotten about the other ways. How do we plan for it?"

"I'll sort it out. Don't worry," she said.

Sophie was driven to finish the packing. But at night she would quickly fall asleep, sometimes with her glasses on and a book in her hand. And she was repeating the same dream, feeling as if someone was trying to tell her something that she could not hear. The dream was of canvases painted with silver and gold that she found hidden in the dark stone corners of a black maze. An unknown source of radiance would catch one of the metallic edges, reflecting a glittering light into her eyes. Raising her hand to shield her face, she would exclaim, "Wait for me, the hall is deep!" And then wake up in a fright.

Sophie told the dream to Nico. "I'm not good at interpreting dreams," he said, "but my father is."

It was then she realized how dangerous her situation with Nico was. She had become too close. Indeed, ever since Nico had arrived, she had felt she was on an emotional precipice. Her memories of Luca were more vivid than ever. She was seeing his nude body, having whiffs of his smell, remembering his roving hands—hearing him through Nico's voice.

"Nico, I have to make myself clear. No matter how fond I am of you, indeed, how important you are to me, it doesn't mean I can have Luca in my life again. I hope you understand."

"But, Sophie, that's so hard, so unforgiving. It would do you good to see him."

"That's enough, Nico! Please, never suggest it again. My friendship with you must be kept apart. Once we get to England, you have to take the ruby and leave. Go back to your life. Hanging about with an old lady isn't healthy for you."

That evening was spent quietly among the chaos of the crates. Neither Nico nor Sophie had much to say. They were exhausted by the work, and emotionally spent with worrying about what lay ahead.

"Sophie, are you up?" Nico called out over the noise of water, while filling the teakettle.

"Sophie.

"Sophie," she heard him say as he tapped on her door, "may I come in? Oh, God! Sophie. What happened?"

She had not even prepared for sleep; she was still stretched out on top of the red cover. Her left arm was stiffly down by her side; her eyes were alive; her mouth was silent. She used the handkerchief in her right hand to wipe the trickle of saliva from her mouth. The room smelled like an old person, not Sophie's normal house aroma of roses and lavender.

"Sophie, can you talk?"

"My feet—are cold. I—need—to go—home."

He called for an ambulance.

Nico wrapped her warmly in a blanket, sitting by her and speaking softly; he encouraged her to stay awake.

It was a stroke. Not a catastrophic one. The doctor recommended a nursing home. Sophie spat the "no" into his face. He backed off.

It was a week before Sophie was able to leave the hospital. The main problem was her left side, her painting side. She could walk, dragging her left leg, but could barely hold a paintbrush.

"It'll take time," the doctor told her. "You'll have to be patient, and determined too. If you follow these exercises, you should have full use of your left hand and leg within a few months." And then he warned Sophie. "You must stop smoking. You really don't have a choice. Remember that the elderly can still have something new to look forward to. But you have to work toward it. It's no longer automatic."

"Oh, God, Nico, I'm dying for a cigarette," Sophie said as they were driving back to her valley.

"Sorry, Sophie." Nico, like his father, was not a smoker. "And I'm not going to stop and buy any either."

"I'll have another stroke from my craving!" she threatened.

Nico made arrangements for the new owners of Sophie's property to take possession a month later than planned. They were accommodating, but Sophie was not. She did not know what to do with herself. Except for her emotional infirmities and a broken leg after André was born, she had never had more than the flu. Now there she was, dependent upon the son of a former lover.

The answer was to do nothing and everything, especially heal from the stroke. Between a strict regime of physical therapy and feebly helping Nico finish packing, she had time to consider her predicament.

Rational questions were asked. Questions concerning her ability to live alone and care for herself and still drive a car and remember if the gas was on and to close the door and bathe herself. It was all too much.

Just that morning, Nico had said, "Now that you aren't smoking, your face is beginning to gain color. You're looking so much better. Let me get a mirror and I'll show you."

"Oh, no, horrors!" Sophie protested. "Keep away from me!"

They sailed from New York Harbor on a Sunday afternoon. Although Sophie was steadier, she was nervous about being aboard a rolling ship. A challenge. That was the way she perceived it. She had to move about; she could not bear being infirm. Much to her chagrin, she had to ask Nico to find a cane.

Nico had been stalwart in insisting she do her exercises and not sneak a cigarette. And he could see that, without a cigarette, it was disagreeable for her to have a glass of wine or even a cup of coffee. He watched her eye other people's cigarettes. Once he saw her pick up a half-smoked cigarette butt from an ashtray. She looked up, as if she were a thief with her hand in a bag of diamonds, and caught his eye. He winked. She grimaced and put it back.

"I feel that you're perched on my shoulder, watching me," Sophie complained. "It's really none of your business whether I smoke or not," she snarled at him. "Leave me alone!"

And he would. And Sophie would later find him on the deck nonchalantly reading, or at least trying to appear to be. "Sorry, Nico; I have no right to speak to you in such a fashion. I'm trying, but it's hard."

The only good thing Sophie could see in worrying about the smoking issue was that it did not leave much time for grieving about leaving her home. It was not until later, when she was settled at Pottery Cottage, and there would be days of relentless rain and gloom, that she would miss the desert. It was then she felt that familiar ache of leaving home—the same ache she had experienced when she left England for France, France for Italy, Italy for America, and America for England, again. A full circle.

Sitting on the deck, facing her destination, Sophie looked at the open sea, so vast that it spilled over the horizon. It was so beautiful she could hardly bear to watch it. The earth looked as if it were going off into space, out of her world, into nothingness. Perhaps, Sophie thought, this is what it feels like to get ready to die.

*You are lost the instant
you know what the result is.*

—JUAN GRIS

Sophie and Nico floated across the sea, swaying and creaking to a buoyant rhythm. Blissfully, the yearning for a cigarette was beginning to fade; whole hours would go by without her thinking of smoking.

"Do you realize," she said to Nico as they were waiting to go through customs, "that it's been twenty-eight years since I've been in Europe? And to think that now I've entered my eightieth year of life—"

"But I thought you were seventy-eight."

"Oh, I forgot to tell you that my birthday was last week. I'm seventy-nine now."

"You're seventy-nine and still impossible," Nico responded, exasperated. "Why didn't you tell me so we could celebrate?"

"Sorry, Nico, but you keep forgetting that I live alone. And so I do sometimes forget."

"Well, happy birthday, Sophie."

They were met by Leland. Even though she had seen him in America less than a year earlier, Sophie hardly recognized him. He was almost sixty-three and had suddenly gone nearly bald. Wearing a sleek dove-gray Italian suit with a shiny purple bow tie and black glasses shaped like two extreme rectangles bridged in the middle, he was a rich and polished-looking man.

"Welcome home, Sophie," Leland said. "Who is this adorable young man?"

"Luca's son," she admonished. "Stop acting dumb, Leland."

"Sophie, I'd no idea. You're as private as a turtle on the moon!"

Leland was driving them in his elegant maroon Jaguar. Once they turned off the main motorway onto a country road, he sank farther into the plush black leather driver's seat and relaxed.

"What a beautiful car," Nico said admiringly.

Leland whispered, "Thanks to Sophie and her last exhibition!" and he winked, as if she could not see him.

"Since your belongings will take another week to go through customs," he said, looking at her in the rear-view mirror, "I've bought a couple of cots to tide you over. Also, linens, two chairs, a table, and a few other items. Nothing to make a song about, but enough to make do."

Sophie heard little of his chatter. Everything was so different. She could not find familiar landmarks, could not place herself on a familiar road.

"Where are we?" Sophie asked.

"We're almost to Trentham," Leland reported.

"I've never been in this part of England," Nico said. "It's truly beautiful. What a contrast to the desert."

"Yes," she said from the back seat. "It's like being in a large earthen bowl of green pea soup." And they drove on.

Finally, Leland turned onto the High Street in Trentham.

"Well, here we are," he announced, gliding to a stop.

"Oh, how lovely to see the Trentham Arms again," Sophie said. "The last time I saw Anne was three or four years ago. She came to me for a holiday and we traipsed all over the countryside."

A doorman with a blond ponytail, dressed in a blue uniform with gold epaulets, came out to help with the baggage.

The plan was to spend the first night in the hotel and then go to the new cottage in the morning.

Gone were the musty smells of ale, cigars, and cabbage. Gone too were the comfortable leather armchairs. Now there were white linen tablecloths, burnished gold-leaf chairs with rush seats covered with blue-and-white checkered cushions, blue and white candles, and sparkling wineglasses. Sadly missing was the real fire in the real fireplace. Instead there were ceramic logs radiating red heat from an electric fire, surrounded by blue-and-white painted tiles of birds and flowers.

But still there was lovely Anne. She was enthusiastic as ever, but now bent at a right angle. "Oh, my darling, darling Sophie," she said, while having to look up to Sophie's face with an awkward twist. "I am so glad you're finally home! Come, let's have a drink before supper."

Being in the Midlands made Sophie nervous. She had begun to understand how she would, for the rest of her life, be reminded of everything she had been trying to forget.

"Sophie, why are you so quiet?" Leland whispered while they were sitting in the bar.

"You don't have to whisper, Leland, I haven't committed a crime! I'm quiet because I'm remembering. I came here after I left Luca and was having what is called a 'nervous breakdown.'"

"Oh, of course. Sorry, Sophie. I didn't put the pieces together. But," and he laughed, "I do wonder what a 'nervous breakdown' really is."

Anne piped in. "I can certainly tell you, since my late husband, bless his heart, was an expert in them.

"It's when one's nervous system goes berserk," Anne said. "At least that's the way I visualize it: red, blue, green, yellow, and black plastic-covered copper wire, haywire, popping out of one's head like an exploded toaster."

*

Peter had died a few years earlier. He had first become ill while playing piano in a jazz club in London. Too much whiskey and too many cigarettes—that was his nature.

"What I didn't write you, Sophie, was that Peter came home from London to try to change things around. But it was too late. His last year was most unpleasant: rages; sanitariums; liver failure; hospital; nurses, doctors, caretakers. Finally Peter, poor man, decided: no more. He took to his bed. One morning I looked in on him and he was sweetly asleep, with his hands tucked under his cheek in a prayerful pose, and a smile on his face. It was not until another hour went by that I realized he was dead."

Sophie was happy to be in Anne's company again. The two elderly women made plans together for small jaunts. *We must stay well*, Anne had written to Sophie in America. *We have a lot of catching up to do.*

The next morning they drove down the evergreen-edged road to the new Pottery Cottage. It was too new: frightfully bright and clean, a scar on the land. While Nico and Leland were declaring how grand—how handsome—how practical—Sophie had to struggle to put on a good face. She would not get out of the car. Apprehension nagged and tugged at her. Everything felt disjointed, out of kilter. She was deeply weary, her body crackly, as if her muscles had turned into eggshells.

"Let's walk around the cottage and see the back," Leland suggested.

"I don't want to take a walk," she growled.

"Why not?" he said. "Don't you want to see the rest of the house?"

"Oh, I can't!" And her eyes filled with tears.

"What's the matter?" Nico asked, "I've never seen you cry before. Oh, Sophie, let us try to help. Tell us!"

"I can't walk on out there," Sophie said, and she flung her arms toward the outside. "I just can't. It's sacred ground. It's a bloody graveyard!"

"Come on, Sophie," Leland encouraged. The two of them helped her out of the car, each took one of her hands, and they set off. Nico and Leland were chattering on as they criss-crossed the land. Around the grave, down the road, through the forest, back around the grave again, and through the front door. "There," Nico said, "the curse is broken."

But the ritual was not enough. It was even disturbing indoors. The architects had not reckoned with Sophie's sensitivity to color. All the walls had been painted a cold and glaring white. "My god," she blurted, "this looks like a blooming gallery!"

After a restless sleep, as Sophie brought tea to the table, her new telephone rang for the first time.

"I'll get it," Nico said.

She poured the tea and listened.

"Yes, I understand, yes. Thank you. Good-bye."

"Who was it, Nico?"

"Oh, it was the reservation office about my ticket. Now, you were saying—?"

"We have to dig up the paintings. Perhaps seeing them will encourage me to begin to work again. I'm worried; I've no urge to paint portraits. It's almost as if I've said everything I need or want to say through other people. The portrait I did of you may be the last. Now the biggest obstacle to working again is trying to get out of my own way. I'm in such a muddle—"

"What do you mean, a muddle? You always appear to be so sure of yourself."

"Hah, if only that were true. It's not so easy as that. All my life, every time I've finished a painting, it feels like a part of me dies. And every time"—she interrupted herself to take a sip of tea—"every time I send off a body of work to an exhibition, it feels like a funeral. The paintings are finished, and I'm bereft. And then I remember, yet again, how much nothingness there is."

"I guess I'm in the opposite place," Nico said. "I'm looking forward to getting back to work. Making art gives me something to look forward to."

"You're so much like your father. You have all his nice qualities."

"Well, there are things about me that you wouldn't like, but I keep them from you, wanting to make a good impression. But thanks, anyway, Sophie, I appreciate that. My father had assured me that a trip to America would give me material to make art about, and it surely did! Thanks to you, I feel filled with ideas—oh, sorry, Sophie, I don't mean to make you feel bad."

"Don't be silly, dear. I was only remembering how I was at your age—and longing for your kind of enthusiasm again."

A few days after the arrival of Sophie's crates from America, she and Nico were contemplating the apple tree. Nico, claiming archeological experience, took the shovel. The sun was out. The sky was wiped clean of impending storms. It was a good day for an exhumation. The apple tree was more than sixty years old. Its trunk was gnarled, its branches lumpy with wooden barnacles, and because it had not been nurtured, there were few leaves, and no apples. The ground beneath the tree was covered with bits of branches and weeds and debris from the building site.

"Start there," she said, pointing. "But be careful, Nico, because I don't think I buried them deeply. Wait. Let me try to figure it out." Sophie got down on her hands and knees and began to scrape off the top layer of soil.

"Here, I can help you," Nico offered. "I'll do it."

And gently he uncovered layer after layer, year after year.

"Wait, I think I found one!"

"Go slowly, Nico. I'm not sure we can bring them up in one piece. If they've crumbled, I'd like to save what I can."

She watched while Nico slowly brushed dirt away from a piece of canvas.

"Careful."

Using his fingers as a soft brush, he worked around the edges. Then he ran his pocket knife around the corners and began to pry it loose.

"I can feel it giving way, Sophie, hold on—"

He lifted the paintings out of the earth. They were stuck together. "Put them in the sun, Nico. I'm hoping it's the wax that has glued them together. We'll be able to separate them safely this afternoon. Look, there's still not a cloud in the sky— sun in the Midlands always seems a gift."

Nico reached down to give her a hand. "I can get up by myself, thank you very much!" And Nico, not wanting to embarrass her, turned away, as she first had to get on her knees and then hold on to the tree.

After lunch Sophie placed the two bundles on Nico's outstretched arms. He carried the portraits as if they were the crown jewels and put them on the long table in the studio.

Sophie used a soft-edged palette knife and began to work. She looked up at Nico. "I just remembered that Luca made this palette knife to my design. Imagine, I haven't lost it and it's still useful. Here, they're coming apart." And slowly, tenderly, she separated the portrait she had painted of the soldier. Sophie could see that they were all in fine condition. Time and nature had continued to treat them well. Like the seashell that she had found on the desert floor, these paintings had fossilized, never to die.

"Oh, Sophie, they're astonishing."

And she laughed.

Indeed they were.

"It looks as if we've dug up pieces of Egyptian mummies." Sophie scraped away some of the wax with her fingernail. "The images are undamaged. I'm shocked. I never expected this."

"What did you think would happen?"

"I don't know," she said. "I guess I thought they would crumble into dust and we wouldn't be able to find them at all.

"Just look at them," she marveled. "They have such a remarkable patina. I've never seen anything like it. I'm reluctant to clean it off, but too curious to leave it on. This one is Major Hugh Roderick's self-portrait, left to me when he died."

"Is he the same man whose drawing was on your desk?"

"Ah, yes, you noticed. Yes, it's he. But this one is the one I painted of him. Isn't the surface fascinating?"

"It is, but I want to see the picture—"

"Here, I'll clean the wax away. Soon we'll be able to see how well the paint held up." Sophie poured a small amount of carbon tetrachloride onto a rag and began to wipe the surface.

And there was Major Roderick in all his splendor. The paint had delicately crackled and darkened. But the luminosity was astounding. He looked intriguingly aged, the earth having been kinder to him than the human beings who shot blazing gunpowder into his face. Now it appeared that all the stars in the universe had gathered together to light the image. Even Nico was silenced for a moment by what he was beholding.

Then he burst forth. "My God, Sophie, this is remarkable!"

The two of them stood there, slightly stunned by the discovery. "Can I help you do the rest?" Nico asked.

"No, I'll do them. It's my job."

"They remind me," Nico said, "of ancient alabaster figurines that have been buried for centuries. I wish I had invented this process. It's truly miraculous."

"Oh, you can have it Nico. It's yours."

There was a pause. "For a woman so old, you're remarkably naïve," Nico said as he shook his head and brushed off his pants. "You just don't give away a style of painting. It has to come from within the artist, not be handed to him on a platter."

"Sometimes," Sophie shot back, "you can be very rude, and a mite pompous as well."

Take hold of yourself, Sophie thought, this is ridiculous. "I'm sorry, Nico, really I am."

"Me too," he said, trying not to growl.

André rose from his grave. His portrait had become a complex web of crackled lines, looking as if it were being lit by a full moon in an indigo night.

"It's your son, André. He looks so much like you."

"Yes, he does. Did you know that Luca and I had a daughter who died?"

"Yes, my father told me. And when I expressed sadness he said, 'But just think of it this way: If we had had that baby, you wouldn't be here. So, you see, treasures can come out of tragedies.'"

"I'm going to lie down for a rest. It's been an emotional day."

But Sophie did not sleep; she had lied to Nico about being tired. She had to be alone. Seeing the portraits made her acknowledge how lonely she had been, how bereft of intimacy, how deserted by passion. She still longed to return to the eve of being in love, and laughed at her absurdity.

Sophie had to be more serious about her situation. She did not think it would work any longer to fill her empty heart by painting portraits of other people's dreams. She simply did not have the same curiosity; there was too much emotional work necessary for each portrait. The intimacy they demanded was wearing. And now, with Nico there, she realized that the nature of her isolation had changed.

"I'm going to replace the wax and rebury the paintings, including the one of you," she announced after her rest.

"Oh, Sophie, no! I was so hoping to take the one of me back to my father. I could buy it from you—"

"Don't be ridiculous," she said. "One day, I'll give it to you, don't worry."

"Well, I don't want to wait until you're dead." And Nico threw down the rake and walked off.

That evening, he apologized. "No," Sophie answered, "there's nothing to apologize for. I'm a difficult, cantankerous old woman, and I'm at a serious turn in the road and I have absolutely no idea what to do about it. It's I who should be begging your pardon."

"I do have to admit," Nico said, "that I'm worried about you. It seems to me that you moved to the desert because you were so deeply hurt by my father and needed to go far away. Now I can see that the grief's mainly gone. But then, and I really don't understand this, you turn around and come back to another part of your life that's even more painful. I wonder why you can't be kinder to yourself. When will you stop chasing your life's shadows?"

He was right. Youth looks forward and old age backward. The problem was that Sophie had only a small step forward still to live.

"I need time to figure all this out," she said, and she turned away.

"You don't have that kind of time, Sophie. Sorry to be so blunt. But I'm worried about leaving you. My sense is that you're in complete turmoil and are trying to hold it all together on my behalf. You don't have to. We can get someone to come in once a day and cook and clean for you, be certain you're faring well. We can work together to figure things out, you know."

"Listen, Nico, you're making me angry. You're trying to tell me that I can't take care of myself. Are you saying I should be in a home for old people? Why, we're not even related and you're telling me what's best for me! I'm going to work again and I'll be fine. Now stop being such a romantic; it will only hurt you in the end."

"You're impossible! You really don't get it, do you? You, Luca, and I are all any of us have, and—"

"What in the world are you saying? Luca and you and me? What is going on here? You can't make me a part of your family."

"Oh, yes, I can!" he shouted, standing and shoving back his chair. "And I have. Whether you like it or not," he growled at her, "you've accepted me as a son—or almost a son. And, without telling you, I have reported everything back to my father—who, by the way, still loves you."

"Leave me alone," she barely whispered. "I can't bear this." Sophie rose from the table, went to her room, and silently, slowly, shut the door.

An hour later, Nico was getting worried. He tapped at her door and she invited him in. "Don't worry, I haven't had another stroke," she said, embarrassed that he could see that she had been crying.

"I'm sorry, Sophie. I lost my temper." He leaned against the door jamb with his arms folded, reminding her once again of Luca. "I should never have spoken to you like that. It's only that you make me so frustrated." And she could sense his frustration rising again.

"No, I must apologize to you. You're right about most everything. But you have to try to understand that my desire for being alone is partly who I really am. I know I've allowed you to come close; perhaps I've made a grave mistake. I'm sorry. I never thought you would see me as family."

"That's a lie, Sophie," Nico said as he leaned toward her. "As soon as you set eyes on me, you sensed who I was."

Sophie was lost in a jumble of unspoken words. She saw a glimmer of truth, but then mislaid it again. Nico was right. She may have intuited that he was Luca's son. She bowed to his certainty.

"What a mess I've made," Sophie admitted. "I'm sorry. I should have told you to leave months ago. But when I saw you, when I realized who you were, I couldn't let you go. I don't really know what you want. And of course, I've never had the courage to ask. Come, sit there on the bed, you're making me nervous and hurting my neck, making me look up at you."

Nico did as directed, taking off his shoes and sitting cross-legged.

"Luca wants to see you," he blurted out.

"I know. And I've been afraid of this moment. It seems so, well, so useless. I've never seen anyone again who was dead to me. Oh, what am I saying! What a stupid statement, that's not true. What I mean is this: my grandparents, my son, were all so far away from me. I mourned Luca in the same way. It's all I know how to do. Then you arrived like a blazing orange accent in a painting and I couldn't tone you down. When I tried to wipe you out of the painting, your color was so strong that it had stained the canvas. There's no getting rid of you. Oh, dear, Nico." Sophie could not help but begin to cry. "I don't know what to do."

"Well, I do," he said. "I'm going to leave. You're going to get yourself settled here. Comfortable. Safe. And we'll come to visit in a month. That's what's going to happen."

"I can't do it, Nico, I just can't."

"You don't have a choice, Sophie. He has an exhibition in London and already has his ticket. There's no stopping him. Unless, of course, you run away again. But then you'll have to reckon with me."

Sophie felt a surge of love for the young man, and the thought of never seeing him again was unbearable. Nico was watching while she held her hands on her lap, knotting and unknotting them.

"There's nothing more to say tonight," he decided. "I'll get each of us a cognac."

It was a warm evening. Nico brought two chairs to the porch and put the bottle of cognac on the floor between them. They did not speak, they simply listened to the symphony of the night. And when the nightingale began its oratorio, they looked at each other and smiled.

Nico departed with the ruby in his pocket and a portrait Sophie had done of a Navajo Indian potter. He left his cowboy hat with the silver buckle hanging on a nail in her studio.

"We'll see each other in a month," they promised. And there was no doubt in either of their minds that they would.

Although Sophie's new house had a smell of innocence, it echoed with loneliness and misplaced dreams. The structure was a close replica of the original Pottery Cottage, except that the rooms were lighter and more spacious and on one level—gone were the dark nooks and crannies. She tried to look forward to painting the rugs on the floors and wondered if she could still find the old-fashioned boat paint—the kind her grandfather used. Sophie could afford to buy whatever she wanted, but she was comforted by her old furniture, chipped and scarred, looking shabby against the freshly painted walls.

No matter how hard she tried to calm down, it seemed as if everything in her life was going in opposite directions. She was stunned by the havoc she had brought down upon herself. Why have I done this? she asked herself time and time again. I must be round the twist.

For the first week after Nico left, Sophie padded around in slippers and a flowered housedress. One afternoon Anne came for tea.

"For goodness sake, darling, have you had a good look at yourself? You appear ten years older than you already are . . . and that's ancient!"

Anne, even though she was lopsided with arthritis, looked like a vibrant and aging hippy, intriguing in bright colors and silver bangles; Sophie looked like a forgotten and frumpy housewife.

"You really make me angry," Anne said. "Here you have a chance for love, a reconciliation, and all you do is mope around the house and feel sorry for yourself. I love you dearly, but sometimes you can be a pill!"

"But," Sophie protested, hurt by Anne's anger, "I'm too old for love."

Sophie exchanged slippers for real shoes and dug out her blue overalls, christened with years of paint. Determined not to loll about in the bog any longer (as Anne would say), Sophie infused herself with a sparkling energy of decision. She hammered nails into the pristine walls and hung paintings and drawings; she tacked postcards on the wall near the kitchen telephone; she posed seashells and rocks and fossils on the windowsills. And, lastly, Sophie hung the remnants of her life: the sketch of her soldier, Claire's recipe for fish pie, Eli's pottery shard. All were installed as one would hang ancestral portraits.

It was late summer. Mornings had the tawny perfume of rotting leaves. The Virginia creeper, growing along the road and up the trunks of trees, was beginning to turn blood red, announcing the approaching cold. But yellow celandine was still blooming along the bottoms of the hedges, reminding her of childhood. Sophie remembered Claire telling her that mother swallows, with the saffron juice from celandine flowers, bathed the eyes of their young to strengthen their sight.

Sophie was nesting; she kept busy putting things away, buying necessary items. She reinstated her house rituals. White daisies, with yellow centers, went in the Prussian blue ceramic jug on the kitchen table. The brown East Indian wooden bowl, mounded with fresh red and green apples, oranges, and a bright yellow lemon posed for aesthetic effect, sat on the sunny windowsill in the kitchen. Stacks of books were on the table in front of the living room's daybed. Her familiar pieces of fabric were thrown over and tucked around the frayed areas of the furniture. She had a new music system that Nico had installed before he left. It was so complicated that he had drawn a whimsical map showing her how to turn it on and off. On the bottom right side he had signed it as if it were a piece of art—*Nico Bondi, 1994.*

And so Sophie began to hear her music again. Gigli singing *Tosca*; Schubert's *Part Songs*; Bach, especially the Violin Concertos; Simoneau singing *La Traviata*. The music soothed her uprooted mood. She spent days in a flurry of household-settling activity, giving her a sense of accomplishment.

Ever since the emotionally explosive talk with Nico, Sophie had felt glimmers of peace, a slight rekindled hope for the future. She was reassured, considering that earlier she had been facing a thick and viscous wall of black despair, the same opaque color as a raven's feathers.

Luca's visit was inevitable. Sophie understood this. But so much time had gone by, so much had changed. Even though her heart ached again with familiar longing, she had to ask herself if she was still in love with him, or if it was merely an elderly fantasy.

When Sophie looked in the mirror, she saw an old woman. Not really white-haired, more like her grandmother, with enough black hair to confuse a person who was seeing her from behind. Her skin looked like ancient tissue paper left in a hot attic, not too wrinkled, but thin and transparent. When she brought her face close to the mirror, she could trace the lines of tiny veins beneath the skin. Sophie could watch herself be alive. But her eyes were still startling—still young, not yet foggy, as she remembered old Nurse Watson's. Neither her eyelashes nor her eyebrows had turned silver. And, although she could see that her nose had drooped a little, when she looked closer, it was not so bad as she had feared. It was her mouth that bothered her most. There were small bird's-foot wrinkles radiating down toward her chin. But, fortunately, she could crow, she had all her teeth.

Sophie had not worked since the stroke, and now she felt the urge to make things again. Although her left side was still slightly off kilter, the movement in her arm and hand was normal. But she was forced to acknowledge that she did not have the energy or strength to work in the old way.

Watercolors. Sophie had always scoffed at them. They frustrated her with their inflexibility. Once she put down a stroke of watercolor, she could not change it. If she did not like it, she had to throw out the expensive paper and begin again. The idea of working directly on a surface, and taking her chances, was frightening. But she felt she had to give it another try.

A bowl of fruit. A thick piece of 100% rag paper. New tubes of watercolor. She divided the paper into eight sections. In each section she painted the same bowl of fruit from a different perspective. Nothing felt right. Then she remembered some Caran d'Ache water-soluble pencils she had been carrying around for years, never using them, but not willing to give them away. She found them in her old red metal toolbox from Italy.

Roughly, she painted the still life, laying down the forms of the fruit with broad strokes of color. Then she went back into the painting with an ochre watercolor pencil and outlined each piece of fruit. Finally, she used clear water in a soft brush and gently feathered the water-soluble pencil lines. The result was a transparent painting with opaque areas. Right! Sophie could see the possibilities and her spirits soared. It was not until the light had changed that she looked up. It was going to take her a while to get down the technique, but it felt good. There was something right about it. Perhaps it was simply that she had found the confidence to use the new medium.

The next morning, when Sophie walked into the studio, she realized that still-life paintings of bowls of fruit and vases of flowers were not for her. She considered doing a series of self-portraits. Perhaps she could explore layers of living, organic flesh, as she had earlier explored layers of human nature. Looking at herself in the mirror, she began to draw. The reflection of her face began to move into anomalous shapes and spill off the edges of the paper. In her mind's eye, she saw the answer. She saw what needed to be painted, but was resistant.

She had to take off her clothes.

She had to paint herself nude.

Blinking fool. She could not bear the idea of painting her nude self while standing in front of a mirror. Sophie had an idea. She went to Stoke-on-Trent and bought a Polaroid camera, six boxes of film, a tripod, and an extra-long timing cable. She watched the sun move past the windows and calculated she had an hour between four and five to get the depth of field she wanted for the eventual paintings. Knowing she had to conserve energy, she set up the camera and rehearsed the poses, taking notes. Sophie, the artist, succeeded in disassociating herself from Sophie, the subject.

The next day she rested and read and waited until half past three, until the sun was barely leaning against the windows, casting a low and distinct shadow. She switched on an old tape:

Non, rien de rien, non, je ne regrette rien, and Edith Piaf's soulful voice infused her studio with reminiscences of another time. She had a glass of wine. She disrobed. Working quickly—so as not to lose the distinctive light and have to do it all over again—Sophie began to pose. Each time she clicked a picture and removed it from the camera, she placed it on the worktable and went on to the next. Since each pose had already been visually considered, she almost danced through the hour. Then she had to look at the prints, reminding herself that they were a reversal of her own gaze.

The first three or four were horrifying. Folds of skin, creases of time, the years fluttering against her old bones. But she quickly erased herself from herself and allowed her mind's eye to travel. Then she could see the photos as abstract figures of an old woman waiting to be painted.

She began to paint. Sophie was obsessed. She did not answer the telephone, and after a few bouts of its incessant ringing, disconnected it. She had to make herself cook, make herself eat, make herself rest. But she was having a wonderful time.

Moistening the paper with a sponge, and with a five-inch-wide brush, Sophie laid down large areas of color. As each area was almost dry, she would lay down another layer of transparent forms, each form bleeding into the others, each form representing an area of her body. Weaving back and forth between the layers were her squiggly pencil lines. The more she worked, the more confident she became, and the more beautiful were the pieces. By the end of the first week, she was working to the full size of the toothy paper. By the end of the second week she was working to the full scale of the human body on a number of heavyweight, extra-large pieces of watercolor paper. Fleshy forms danced to their own rhythm, from cyclamen to voluptuous rose to peony pink, with the pencil lines ranging from sepia to rusty red. Except for when she was a young student,

Sophie had never used such color. At first it was hard for her to stand back and look; it was too overwhelming. Then she became excited and warmed by the endeavor. The work was flowing out of her, having been dammed up far too long.

Tell me, can anything ever be truly finished?

—LEONARDO DA VINCI

A nd then the end began. On a quiet morning, while taking a tea break, Sophie heard a car approaching. It sounded like the postman, but not quite.

"Sophie, are you there?" a male voice rang through the house. "Sophie, I'm coming inside."

Before she could get out of the chair to greet him, Nico had bounded into the studio in a flurry of blue denim.

"Jesus, Sophie, you scared me! I've been calling and calling and I almost called the constable."

"It's so nice to see you, Nico," she replied.

"How can you be so calm? You've really upset me." And then Nico saw the walls. "Oh, Sophie, what's going on here? They take your breath away! Are they you? I can't tell. Now I understand—"

"Ahem." A throat was cleared in the other room. "May I come in?"

And there stood an elderly man framed by the doorway, with the sunlight silhouetting his tall, thin figure. Pure-white wavy hair matched a wiry moustache. Slightly stooped. A nose made larger by the thinness of his face. Deeply etched lines that traveled from the sides of his nose to the corners of his mouth. Glistening lenses of silver-wire glasses. Cheeks sharply cut away to make strong, fine shadows.

"Sophie, say hello to Luca."

"Is it really you?" she asked.

"Yes, in all my ancient splendor," Luca said, laughing and trying to stand tall.

"Oh, my dear Luca," came out of Sophie's mouth, without thinking. "My dear Luca." And she struggled to stand to embrace him.

Her struggle made them laugh. "It's obviously been a long time," Sophie said, as Nico took hold of her hand and helped her out of the chair.

"Why Sophie," Nico whispered in her ear, "you're blushing." If she had had her cane, she would have hit him.

The next hour was agonizingly uncomfortable. They sat among shards of Sophie's old nude body hanging on the wall. Everything was fragmented. They could not complete a sentence. And since Sophie's French was rusty, there were pauses between words while she regenerated her vocabulary.

They tried to talk about the missing years. "No, that's not interesting," she would say. And, each time, Luca said, "What did you say?" in Italian.

Through their bumbling, Luca did not take his eyes off her. He knew he was making her self-conscious, but did not want her to see him study the nude watercolors, although he was very curious about it all. Of course, she had changed. Aged. It was natural. But there was something profoundly different. Her face was wide open, making her more comely than when she was young. He could see that the rest of her story was in her now unveiled eyes.

"My God," Nico exclaimed, "it's as if the two of you are idiots! Can't you even find a common language to converse in?"

"Nico, you're being rude," Luca admonished. "You sound like you're trying to force your parents to make up after an argument. Stop watching us like a petulant child. Please."

"All right. All right. Sorry, but I think I'm as nervous as the two of you. I'll get you each a glass of wine."

"That's a good idea, Nico," Luca said, "but bring the bottle."

Nico went into the kitchen, leaving them in the studio.

"Let me try again. This work is wonderful, Sophie," Luca said in their familiar French. "Is it all new? It's you, isn't it?"

And before she could answer, Nico returned with two glasses and a bottle of red wine and poured one for each of them. "See you later," he announced. "I'm going to the village to buy food for a commemorative dinner!"

They sipped their wine. "Is this your old studio chair from Paris?" Luca asked, trying to break the tension.

"Yes, it is. Oh, Luca, this is so uncomfortable—"

"Why don't you buy a new one then?" Luca asked.

"No, not the chair! This circumstance."

And they both laughed, and it sounded like the old days.

"I'm so fond of Nico. Actually, I love loving him," Sophie said. "But I'm afraid he's imagining some kind of movie scenario. And I know he's going to be disappointed."

"I wouldn't worry about Nico, Sophie, he's a strong man. A long time ago I realized that it would be hard to make him into a tragedy. No matter what, you've made a friend of him forever."

Luca was sitting in a stiff-backed chair and looked uncomfortable. "Why don't we go to the living room where it's more restful?" she suggested.

"No, I like it here. It feels familiar. You know, I expected to see an almost invisible Sophie. But, instead, you're as present as ever, although a bit thin. Doesn't it seem to you that every year we're alive makes more of us rather than less?"

"You mean," she corrected him, "less of us rather than more?"

"No." Luca laughed. "I mean what I said. There's much more of us, I suppose because we've been constructed out of seconds, of minutes, of hours, days, months, years, and now decades. And then add the weight of the emotional events of our lives—the tragedies, the happiness. You're right," he said, "this chair is uncomfortable. Let's bring in the one from the living room."

And just as in the old days, they tried to move a square through a rectangle using geometry and common sense. "It won't work," Luca pronounced.

"It will work," she encouraged him. "Just have patience." And after another attempt, she said, "We're going to have a heart attack doing this."

"Yes, but at least we'll die together!" Luca said.

"Oh, Luca, what are we doing?"

They gave up and Luca helped her back into the chair. "I'm not sure," he said, then sat in his chair facing her, their knees touching.

"I don't know how," he said, "but I'd like the chance to make everything right with you again. All these years, I've missed you terribly." And Luca began to cry. He slid off his chair and knelt on the floor with his head on Sophie's lap, holding her legs in an embrace. She caressed his head, running her fingers through his hair, until his crying slowed and then came to a stop. The late-afternoon light, almost orange in intensity, was flooding the studio, illuminating two old, creaking bodies. Now Luca sat straight, at eye level, and took her face in his hands. He kissed her deeply, just as in the old days.

"It still feels good," she marveled.

"Why! You're blushing!"

"And so are you, Luca."

They sat and quietly spoke about the past years. The birds announced the arrival of dusk.

"Do you know the Hans Christian Andersen fairytale about the nightingale?" Luca asked, and Sophie shook her head no.

"It's about a nightingale that lived in the gardens of the emperor of China. Every night, at this time, the bird sang its enchanted song. One day a stranger presented a large box to the emperor; it contained a jewel-encrusted sculpture of a nightingale. The emperor banished the real nightingale from his kingdom. But then, when the emperor was ancient, he realized that he was longing for the nightingale's song.

"This is my story, Sophie, except I'm not an emperor, but a weary old man who has been forever sorry for forcing you away."

Time flew through their reverie. Before they knew it, Nico was coming up the lane. Doors slammed. Heavy footsteps.

"You're still in the same place I left you," he exclaimed, looking like a stern father. "You need to walk around. Exercise. Get your blood moving—why do you both look so guilty? Why—?"

"*Basta*, Nico," his father admonished. "We are old enough to take care of ourselves."

They prepared the meal together. Luca made a pesto and black-olive sauce for the pasta; Nico's crostini was baked with mozzarella, tomato, capers, and parmesan; Sophie made a salad.

Nico served. "Just a little for me," Sophie said. "I can't eat as much as I used to."

"Me, either!" Luca exclaimed. "It's our age, you know?"

"No, you're not old," she reprimanded him. "After all, you're seven years younger than I."

"There isn't a big difference between the two of us any longer," Luca answered. "My being seventy-two isn't middle-aged, you know, dear. It's old! Here's to this wonderful dinner," Luca said, raising his glass of wine. "And here's to you, Sophie—"

268 · MICHELE ZACKHEIM

She was tongue-tied; she felt things she had never, in all the nooks and crannies of her imagination, foreseen. In the background she heard Luca say, "Sophie?"

"Oh, no, not another stroke!" Nico called out. And she raised her hand.

"No, I'm all right. Really, I am. This has all been a bit much excitement for me." And Sophie spread the napkin over her lap, smoothed it out, and said, "Let's eat our dinner and not talk about me. Yes?" Nico served. "I've missed your cooking, Nico," she said. "I ate much better when you were around."

"I know," Nico scolded. "There wasn't even fresh garlic or a decent bottle of olive oil in your larder!"

Nico and his father began to talk about exhibitions they had recently seen in Rome. Sophie listened in wonder. She had always seen herself as an informed artist, an artist who had spoken about the world through her work for the past sixty years. But listening to the men, Sophie realized how out of touch she had been.

Until her second glass of wine, she held herself aside, then slowly folded herself into their conversation. As the wine flowed, their hearts opened into the night. And a full circle of their friendship was finally accomplished with the merry sprinklings of "*ma chère*s," "*caro*s," and "luvs."

They were invigorated by the excitement and a little drunk as well. But when Nico got up to do the dishes, the thrill was finally calmed and weariness was painted in a range of grays across their faces.

"I must go to sleep," Sophie announced. "Nico, you know where the linens are." And the two men seemed to stop on a coin. "Oh, but I don't have an extra bed," she realized out loud. "How stupid of me. I have two empty bedrooms, but no mattresses. Well, Nico, you can sleep on the sofa here, and Luca can sleep on the studio bed."

"No, Sophie, it's fine," Luca said. "We're staying in a hotel in Stoke-on-Trent."

"But everyone has had so much to drink," she insisted. "You shouldn't be driving."

"I'm all right, Sophie," Nico said comfortingly. "Don't worry; we'll see you in the morning."

It was still dark. There was such a thundering of rain upon the roof that Sophie went into the studio to check on possible leaks from the skylights. Turning on the switch, she saw that all was safe and started back to the kitchen. But yesterday's drawing on the wall stopped her.

Sophie could not resist. Starting the fire in the stove, she began to work. When she had closed up the studio the day before, she had been trying to resolve a problem with the spatial quality of a drawing. That morning she picked up a Payne's gray water-soluble pencil and began to draw. Her lines quivered over the paper, looking for a place to stop and rest. When she finally stepped back to look, she could see that she had rounded a pleasing corner. Instead of leaving the delicate lines that she had feathered with a wet brush (mere whispers that they were), Sophie had gone back in and modeled the lines with another layer of the pencil.

Now, on that cloudy and rainy morning, Sophie saw that they were grisaille paintings, monochromatic in gradations of gray and flesh, as in a replica of a bas-relief . . . as in that morning's gray sky.

The phone rang in the kitchen and she rushed to answer it. "Yes?"

"You still don't like the phone, do you, Sophie?" she heard Luca ask with a laugh.

"Good morning, Luca. You're right. It still irritates me. I guess I'll never get used to it. Where are you? You sound far away."

"We're in London."

"But I thought you were coming here in the morning."

"I've the distinct feeling," he said, "that we overwhelmed you with our visit. I thought it wise to leave you alone for a while. So early this morning, we drove back to London."

"What time is it?" she asked. "It feels like the middle of the night."

"Sophie, it's ten in the morning!"

"Oh, for heaven's sake, the cottage appears to be cemented to an evening cloud, and I'm working under artificial lights. I didn't notice."

Luca laughed. "It's so refreshing to hear that you haven't changed. It was one of the most appealing and maddening things about you, you being swallowed by your work."

"Now, Luca," she chided him. "What do you mean by that?"

He changed the subject. "Would you like to come to London to my opening?"

"No. Thank you, but no. I've pretty much given up traveling, except in my head, of course. I'd rather be here working and using whatever energy I have left in this poor old body than spending it on travel. Sorry."

"It's all right. I understand. May I come to see you after the opening, before I return to Italy?"

"Of course, Luca. I'd like that."

"Oh, and Sophie, I didn't ask you last night. When I come to visit, may I see the buried portraits? I'd love to see the one of Nico. He's told me that they're more than beautiful. He said they looked otherworldly—'as if you had an exhibition in heaven and God was the gallery director!' Those were his exact words."

"Yes, yes," she laughed. "Perhaps, when you return."

"I have one more question," Luca asked after a fat pause. "Are you happy to see me? Am I welcome?"

"For goodness sakes, yes, Luca. Indeed, I'm wondering why we ever took so long!"

Later, Sophie realized she was feeling shaky. Perhaps, she said to herself, you need to take a rest. No, perhaps you need to take a walk. No, it's raining, you silly goose. Perhaps you need to tighten down the bolts in your head. No, perhaps, you old woman, you need to admit to yourself that you are still in love with Luca. That after all these years, you have been waiting to see him again; you decided to return to England to reconcile with him, even before Nico appeared. That Nico's much wiser than the two of you, and certainly braver.

So now, she asked herself, what are you going to do about it?

The next day, the phone rang. She ruefully recognized that her pirouetting heart was the same as that of a young woman in love. Trying to be calm, she answered.

"Sophie, I'm sorry to tell you this," Nico reported, "but Luca has fallen and broken some of the bones in his right hand. He's in surgery now and the doctors have assured me that he'll be fine.

"Sophie, are you there? Sophie?"

"I'm here, Nico. What can I do? Should I come? Oh, the poor dear man."

"Let's see how the surgery goes. He doesn't want you here right now. He told me to tell you not to worry. But, quite honestly, Sophie, I don't think he wants you to see him in this state. I think he's embarrassed."

Sophie could not work. She was angry at herself. Why had she been so stubborn? Look at all the wasted time. Now, just as hope arrived for the first time in so many, many years, Luca was in trouble.

Luca called. He told Sophie that he was resting comfortably, but was upset he could not use his right hand. He went on a bit and she finally offered, "Then use your left one, for heaven's sake! If Matisse could draw with a long stick on paper tacked above his head, you can learn to draw in a new way, too."

"You're right, Sophie, sorry. I'm feeling sorry for myself. I need to go home."

And within a couple of hours, Nico called to say that they were going back to Monterosa. "He's so anxious that I think it's better to take him back. Would you consider coming too?"

"You mean to Italy?" Sophie asked. "I can't go back there, Nico. I'm too old. What would I do? Watch Luca mend? Perhaps, maybe he could come here?"

"No, I presented that idea to him. He needs to go home. Once I get him settled, we can discuss any ideas the two of you have. But I have to admit, Sophie, I'm a bit weary of you both being so stubborn."

Six months after Luca's accident, his right hand was not functioning well, the broken bones accentuating the arthritis. But he was using his left hand, with pride.

"Please come," he pleaded with her on the now indispensable telephone. "Your old studio is empty, waiting for you."

"But I thought Nico was using my studio."

"No, no one has ever used it. You remember old Signore Pasquale? Well, when he died, I bought his farm for Nico. I thought you knew this."

"No, there are many things I still don't know, Luca. It's hard to keep up."

"Sophie, I realize this is long overdue. Can't we work out a way to be together? There's hardly a minute to waste."

"That's true," she had to admit. "I'm really old now, Luca. I've turned eighty—imagine!"

"You still sound like the young woman I knew all those

years ago. Some people sound their age, but you still have music in your voice."

For goodness sake, she thought, this blasted telephone has become an instrument of romance. She had come to depend on it, imagine that. Now, whenever they said good-bye, Sophie felt as if she had lost another chunk of time. And each time they spoke, Luca pushed for her to come. Finally, probably because Nico told his father to stop pestering, he did. But Sophie had made up her mind; once she finished the nude series, she would seriously consider a visit.

Sophie stoked the fire in the wood stove in the studio and drove to the village to fetch groceries. It was winter. January. A metal landscape of ice and stone. Occasionally, she could see a field, bright green with winter wheat. Hovering above those moist fields were clouds of fog. The hedgerows were bare, looking as if someone with an extra-fine gum eraser had removed the leaves. The pine trees were whiskered with ice. Old Mr. McDougal at the chemist's was forever reminding Sophie to watch her feet. "Now, you don't need to take no falls, Miss Marks. I worry that you're out there by yourself."

"You're so kind, Mr. McDougal, but not to worry. I'm very careful, I can assure you."

Sophie had forgotten to close the door of the stove.

Hot embers, reaching for air, flew away and landed on the floor, igniting a smoldering fire. Smoke was billowing. Out of fear came a burst of energy. Sophie knew what to do. Pulling the hose from around the lilac bushes, she turned on the water. So as not to create a wind to feed the fire, she opened the front door ever so slightly. Slithering into the house, she moved forward, spraying a wide path before her, saving the house from bursting into flames. It was a mess.

"Oh, bloody hell, the portraits," she said aloud, and rushed to the studio where they had been stored in racks. She found them intact and felt more relief than even saving the house from burning down. The new drawings were singed and water damaged and could not be saved.

Sophie was furious. Can you not see anymore? she berated herself. Bloody hell, she could not even remember to turn off the friggin' teakettle, or lock the door. A few days before, she had found one of her new yellow bathroom towels in the studio and did not remember taking it there. Too many queer things, too many queer things she had done lately. And now this. She was such an old woman that she had even tried to burn down the rest of her life.

It was impossible to stay. Sophie drove to her old stand-by, the Trentham Arms. "Another problem," Sophie said to Anne, and told her what happened.

Within a short time, Sophie was soaking in a tub of hot, sudsy water and Anne was bustling around gathering her clothes for laundering. Through the door, she was carrying on a one-way conversation. "I'll get you a dressing gown and slippers and the hotel's sponge bag. And I'll bring you up a pot of tea, and—are you hungry?" No answer. "Well, never mind." And she was gone.

Ah, such quiet bliss, and Sophie sank farther into the water. The phone rang and she ignored it; she was floating in hundreds of watery questions. They rolled against her and over her and around her in confusion. Sophie tried to separate the questions in her mind. Even though she could occasionally be vague, she knew she was still keen enough. She realized she would have to see if the cottage was livable. If it was, how long would it take to clean? Where would she stay while it was being cleaned? She supposed she could stay with Anne. Then, perhaps she could hire a crew and have the main room cleaned first and move her studio there. But when she thought about the time it would take to replace all the damaged things, and the mess and noise that would be inflicted upon her, her heart sank. She was not being realistic. It would be dreadfully noisy, too noisy to work, dusty and dirty. She was snookered in a corner, with few choices.

Sophie got herself dried off and into the dressing gown, and greeted Anne. But she did not make it to the chair; she slid to the floor like a piece of silk. "I'm all right, Anne. I'm all right. Just overcome. Overcome." And Sophie began to cry, heaped on the rose-patterned carpet like a pile of rags. She was an old woman with silver wisps of hair in her mouth. She felt such shame. It was all her fault. She had proven to herself what she had been trying so hard to deny; she was old and forgetful and careless. Her heart was pounding. She heard through the screeching in her ears, "I'll get the doctor, don't you move."

Sophie was looking at her reality through many veils. Now, for all time, was this the end? Had she taken her life as far as possible? A decision had to be made. She understood that right now she could loosen her grip and quite simply fade away. She could decide to die. Shrouded in a lovely lilac haze, she sensed that her physical body was balanced on the edge; it simply needed a slight nudge. Sophie felt peace. Fading into reverie, Sophie waited to answer herself.

Instead, she heard Anne's insistent voice and felt her warm breath close to her ear. "Now just a tick there, darling; you're not going to dip out on me here. You just get yourself back into this room. We're not done yet; and don't you ignore me, do you hear?"

Then Sophie felt much bustling around her body. The doctor was poking and prodding and saying, "Can you hear me, Miss Marks? Can you hear me, Miss Marks?" And Sophie did not want to hear.

"Her vital signs are normal," she heard him say. "I think

she's in shock. Let me call for the ambulance to take her to hospital."

It was Anne who intervened. "If you don't open your eyes, Sophie, they're going to cart you off to the old people's hospital. It's purgatory, darling; you'll hate it. Do you hear me?"

And knowing what that meant, Sophie pulled herself out of the chasm, hand over hand, until she opened her eyes. And what did she see but Anne's considerable bosom, draped with silver and amethyst beads, heaving, looming, over her face— and it made her smile.

"No hospital, please," Sophie begged the doctor, a hulking man, somewhat frightening, with an extremely small nose set square in the middle of an unusually large face. "All right," he said, as a bit of breakfast scone dangled off his moustache. "But you'll have to rest." Sophie was flabbergasted by his tiny voice, and had to lower her eyes so he would not see her amusement.

"Just help me get up and help me walk around. And please be so kind as to open the window. I need air."

By the time all the commotion died down, and the doctor had departed with Anne close behind, Sophie had made up her mind. Two enormously significant realities appeared to her in glorified, sparkling colors. The first was seeing Luca's face in her imagination and realizing that she wanted—no, that she longed—to see him again. Excited with the memory of the pleasure of his kiss, she wished to try to finish what they had begun all those years ago. The other was reminding herself of the deliciousness of the fear and excitement that she always experienced upon approaching a blank canvas. The challenge still thrilled her, still gave her hope.

Sophie fell asleep. Through the haze of a dream, she heard the telephone ring. She had no idea where she was. The phone's brassy sound was so beastly that she put the pillow over her head to drown it out. It persisted. Then she remembered. And she was stunned—sick to her stomach, lost in a tumultuous sea of regret and, yes, dread. And the phone kept ringing. What was she to do? And the phone kept ringing. How could she go on? And the phone kept ringing. Where would she go? And there was a knock at the door. The phone stopped ringing.

"Sophie? Are you awake?" she heard Anne ask, as the master key was inserted in the lock.

"Yes. Thank you," Sophie replied, trying awfully hard to look as if it were a normal morning in February, 1995.

The phone rang again.

Sophie picked up the phone. "Yes?"

"Oh, thank the holy heavens!" She heard Nico's voice.

"How in the world did you know where I was?"

"Hell, Sophie, you didn't answer and I got worried and asked the constable to go and check on you. Then I called Anne. Why didn't you let me know there was a fire in your house? Sophie, you make me so angry! Here's my father. Perhaps he can get you to think straight."

"Sophie? Sophie, dear, are you there?"

"I'm here, Luca. Why's Nico so turned up? You know, I didn't do this on purpose! Listen, I'm fed up with being pushed around by the two of you; I won't—"

She heard a clunk, and "She's impossible—talk to her please—"

"Sophie, it's Nico. Damn it, don't yell anymore."

She took a deep breath and tried to settle her roiling stomach by looking out the window at the continuing rain. "All right, Nico, I know you have a plan. What is it?"

"Well, you already know what I'm going to say," Nico grumbled.

"You mean to move back to Monterosa, don't you?"

"Yes, exactly. Listen, Sophie, I know this is difficult, but you have to be realistic. You have no one else who cares for you as we do. We're your family, like it or not!"

"I know you want to be, Nico. But what about Luca? He could always find a younger woman. He loves romance, you know."

Nico laughed. "You're both romantics, Sophie! And you're both too old to go carousing. Why don't you simply accept this and allow yourself the pleasure of coming home?"

"But I am home, Nico. I was born here. My son's buried here, and my grandparents, too. My roots are entangled in the apple tree, in the hedgerows, even in the foundation of the cottage. I've told the bank that I want to be buried here, as well. With André. It's in my will."

"Sophie, you can still be buried there. I'll see to it. I promise. But in the meantime, you have many good years ahead of you. Just think of all the work you can get done."

She thought that a compelling argument.

"My father hires a woman from the village who comes in every other day to clean the house. He doesn't want anyone to cook because he still enjoys it so much. I'm hoping that perhaps, between the two of you, you can remember to turn off the blasted burners."

"Why are you cursing so much, Nico?" Sophie asked with a laugh. "I've never heard this from you before."

"Oh, I'm sorry, Sophie. But you're both driving me crazy. It's hard for me to do my own work, between holding Luca's hand because he's mooning about missing you and holding yours about your indecision. You must make up your mind. I really mean it! Think about it, Sophie. I'll call you back in the morning."

"But, Nico, that's not enough time."

"That's all the time I'm giving you. You decide. Either you live alone for the rest of your life or you come here. I'm afraid it's down to those two choices. Good-bye, Sophie." And he hung up without waiting for a response.

Such a nasty mood.

A great flame follows a little spark.

—DANTE

W ell, Luca," Sophie said two days later, after he answered the telephone on the first ring, "I now understand that people start their lives at many different beginnings. If you still want me to come, I will."

"If we weren't separated by hundreds of miles, I would embrace you! This is wonderful news."

"Now, listen here, Luca, we must speak about what this all means—"

"You mean love?" Luca asked. "There's no doubt about that, I can assure you. And I think you know that already, don't you?"

"Yes, I suppose I do—but I must confess, I don't understand how you can love such an old woman." And she kept rambling on, not having the courage to hear his answer.

"Listen, Sophie, be still for a moment. You're not the only elderly person in this story.

"I know what's going on," he said. "This will be the first time since the bomb fell that you're making a wide-awake decision while staring straight on at gruesome memories. I know that. Before your decisions were wrapped in vague hopes, but cluttered with despair."

"I don't understand, Luca. What are you saying? That I don't know what I'm doing?"

"No, the opposite. You've always presumed that all I wanted was a child, that, because you had lost two children, you needed to get out of my way, to be gracious, generous. But, truth be told, I had hoped that you would fight for me." Luca laughed into an echo.

"All right, I can tell that I need to be more clear.

"All those years ago," he continued, "I had wished for you to offer up a startling solution, a creative arrangement. I supposed that if it were not for hope, the heart would break, so I kept hoping that something could be worked out. It embarrasses me now to admit my disappointment."

"Excuse *me*," Sophie said, "you were the one who had an affair, not I."

There was a long pause, and Sophie's stomach turned in another direction.

Obviously chagrined, Luca said, "What keeps going through my head, Sophie, is an old saying: If men will have no care for the future, they will soon have sorrow for the present. It seems to me, considering your age, that you must do everything possible to exonerate yourself from the guilt of the war. You've been feeling guilty all your life for having survived your family, particularly André. I feel you've spent much of your life searching for family on one hand, and trying to keep family away on the other."

"But—"

"No, let me finish. This is important. If you were younger, and the fire had happened, you would have found a reason to stay where you are. But now, well, I don't feel you have enough emotional or physical reserves to handle rebuilding alone. And I'm being selfish, I have to admit. I want you here, enjoying what we've rediscovered, not depleted by yet another tragedy. Now, what were you going to say before I so rudely interrupted?"

"I was simply going to say that you're right, Luca. I agree with you." And she could almost hear Luca smiling.

"You knew I would agree, didn't you?"

"I was certainly hoping," Luca admitted with a laugh. "And

Sophie, I forgot to tell you. Nico will be arriving tomorrow afternoon to help you. He's already in Paris."

"But—" and Sophie laughed at all the colors of his eagerness.

"You look awful," was the first thing Nico said when he met Sophie in the hotel's lobby.

"Oh, for God's sake, Nico, you could lie, you know."

"Well, Luca doesn't look so good either. And I told him so, too."

When they left the hotel, it was another overcast and mizzling day. All along the road, the firs stood against the gray backdrop like frozen brooms. Yet as they neared Pottery Cottage, the sun began to escape from behind a cloud and cast a hopeful sigh upon the landscape; everything glowed russet, ochre, and sweet green. As soon as they turned down the rutted road, the smell of the air changed. It smelled like death.

They carefully surveyed the cottage and studio. Besides the fire and water damage, the smoke had completed the predicament.

"If I were younger, I would send everything to be cleaned. But not now, Nico. It's too much. Never mind, I'm not so upset about losing my new drawings as I am about the loss of my books. This is most heartbreaking. I referred to them almost every day; I even remember some poems by heart." A bit proud of herself, standing amidst the shambles, Sophie recited a poem by Michelangelo about the Sistine ceiling. "*My beard toward Heaven, I feel the back of my brain, / Upon my neck, I grow the breast of a Harpy; / My brush, above my face continually, / Makes it a splendid floor by dripping down.*"

"That's impressive, I must say," Nico had to admit. "Perhaps you don't really need your books any longer; they're all in your head. Now, what do you want to do, Sophie? Do you want my opinion?"

Sophie laughed. "I know what it is, Nico. Close up the house and walk away?"

"Yes, exactly."

"Well, I've already agreed with your father to return to Monterosa. Didn't he tell you?"

"Yes, but I wanted to hear it for myself. My father accuses me of being impractical and never getting the facts right. But I think he's the one whose head's always in the clouds."

"Oh, and before I forget," Sophie said, "we're going to be married."

"You mean you'll actually marry my father? Oh, I can't wait to tell him!"

"Excuse me, dear, but I would like to tell him myself. I do believe it would be better coming from me, don't you?

"Now, help me gather what I absolutely must save." Nico followed Sophie as she made choices. In a cabinet she found her three copies of *The Potteries Poetry Review*. "Look, Nico, how wonderful. My grandmother's poems are all right. Oh, this makes me so happy," and she hugged them to her chest.

"Years ago, I found them in an old bookseller's stall in London. They're smelly from the smoke, but I don't care."

By the time they finished, the back seat of the car was filled. All the oil paintings were saved. The pictures behind glass were safe too. Once in Italy, she could put them all face-down in the direct sun. The dryness and the heat would naturally eliminate the burnt odor. But Nico's cowboy hat was beyond repair. She saved the silver buckle and threw the hat in the trash.

"Now, there is something I have to do," Sophie said, "and I have to do it alone."

From inside the house, Nico silently watched her take André's portrait and a shovel back to the apple tree. He knew not to interfere. Sophie cleared out the original hole. She must have decided to do this before, because the painting had been covered with wax, prepared for its burial. Balancing herself against the apple tree, she got on her knees and smoothed out André's grave and gently placed him inside. With no more than a moment's pause, Sophie buried André forever.

Later, keeping her eyes straight ahead, not for a moment daring to look at the faint ancient imprint of the bomb crater, they drove down the Marks family's road. As they passed the farthest copse of trees, she felt the wind shudder. How odd. She could feel in her body that she had reached the end of a plague of grief. It was the first time in her life that she wanted to say, "Amen."

In the evening they were sitting in the dining room with Anne, finishing dinner.

"Perhaps, since you have so little baggage," Nico suggested, "we could fly home?"

Out of the question, Sophie immediately said to herself. But out of her mouth came, "Of course, yes, let's do that."

"You will?" he asked, obviously surprised.

"I can't believe you, Sophie! You'll love flying. It will transport you into a kind of vagueness that you're familiar with—" and they all three laughed.

"Will you come to visit me, Anne?" Sophie asked. "I can't bear the idea of never seeing you again."

"Of course I will," she answered, and reached into her pocket. Before their very eyes, Anne lit a cigarette.

"What are you doing?" Sophie almost yelled.

"Having an after-dinner cigarette, darling."

"Anne, you're asking for terrible trouble."

Anne shrugged. "I promised myself that when I was seventy-two, I would start smoking again. But the years went by and I forgot!

"Then I found some cigarettes lying about and decided to give them a try. And I like it. And it doesn't matter. I'm so old and bent, few things please me. So don't give me grief, do you hear?"

"Couldn't you try chocolate, or something less harmful?" Sophie said.

"No, darling. I like a cigarette with a glass of whiskey. It doesn't taste good with chocolate."

The next morning was spent with Nico driving her around while she did business: with the assurance society, canceling the telephone, electricity, and gas, stopping the delivery of the newspaper, changing her address at the post office, arranging for the house pipes to be drained of water. Closing down the family home forever.

Sophie had deeded the house and property to *The Potteries Poetry Review*, after first offering it to Nico. He had raised his hands as if to ward off the devil. "Absolutely not," he told her. "Please don't burden me with such a legacy—disappointment and death, a terrible inheritance."

The next stop was the village green. "I want to show you something," Sophie said, and they walked to the middle where there was a large, dark-gray granite war memorial. Each side had an extensive list of engraved names from the Second World War. Sophie walked around to the north side and pointed toward the top.

ELIJAH JOSEPH MARKS 1858 ~ 1942
CLAIRE SIMONE MARKS 1856 ~ 1942
ANDRÉ ETHAN MARKS 1936 ~ 1942
JACOB S. SAMUELS 1898 ~ 1942
MIRIAM ROSE SAMUELS 1902 ~ 1942

The woman's work is exceptional.
Too bad she's not a man.
—ÉDOUARD MANET,
ON THE WORK OF BERTHE MORISOT

S ophie had one task to do before leaving England forever. She had to take the paintings of Major Hugh Roderick back to Cardine Manor.

Nico drove up to the intercom next to the gate and rang.

"Yes," answered a female voice. "May I help you?"

"I hope so," Nico shouted into the intercom. "I'm accompanying Sophie Marks."

"You don't have to shout," the phantom said. "I can hear you. One moment please." The gates opened as smoothly as a silk fan moving in a summer breeze.

Greeting them was a somewhat plump, middle-aged woman, smartly dressed in brown tweed trousers with an autumn-red sweater and sensible shoes. Her peppery hair was short and straight around her head in a cut that was as blunt as an old knife. The only softness was a wave in front that came down over her left eyebrow, accentuating her inquisitive eyes.

"I am Rose Spenser. My father was Hugh Roderick—and I had heard that you were home."

"Oh, I knew your father."

"Yes, I know. Come in."

Once they were settled with a cup of tea, Rose Spenser said, "I hardly remember my father. I was barely three when he died. But I've lived with him each day of my life. His paintings are everywhere in the house. As you can see."

Sophie saw traditional landscapes of the Midlands in the

romantic style of Turner, but more defined. Rolling pasture-land, painted at each season; a close of beechnut trees painted at different times of day; the canals, shimmering yellows of light, bordered with flowers and grasses representing different times of the year. No portraits at all.

"My father was born into too much money. When he was a young man, my grandparents sent him off to see the world. But my mother told me that, in reality, their money erased the need to rebel. He longed for adventures that would get him in trouble—that would force him to see the world in another way. But the troubles didn't happen. After a year, he returned home, married, and set up a studio."

"The paintings are very beautiful," Sophie said.

"Yes." Mrs. Spenser smiled, obviously pleased.

But Sophie was being polite. Although technically well done, the paintings were unimaginative, straight-on views of local landscapes. She was disappointed, having always imagined her soldier as a great and unknown artist, waiting to be discovered.

Now Sophie understood that he had not had the patience to live on and perhaps change his approach to painting. His foremost adventure in life was losing half of his handsome face and all of his hope. It was not until he was disfigured that he finally painted as he had always dreamed of doing. Angry, bitter, even dramatic; his response to the world poured out of his very being. But, by then, it was too late.

Mrs. Spenser took them upstairs to the music room. Next to another landscape, tucked into a corner, hanging beside the mirror-like ebony grand piano, was one of Eli's small portraits.

"Sophie, isn't that you?" Nico asked.

"No, it's my grandmother, painted by Eli."

It was a portrait of Claire, looking out the window while seated at the beloved rosewood writing table, with her old paisley shawl draped around her shoulders. Sophie remembered the shawl as coming from Russia, and that sometimes Claire threw it over the back of one of the chairs beside the fireplace. "To give the room a dab of color," she would say.

They all stood quietly in front of the painting.

"It's so beautiful," Sophie mused. "Her face has been painted with a secret."

Once they returned to the sitting room, where Nico had left the parcels, Sophie said, "Mrs. Spenser, I'd like you to have these." Nico unwrapped the first one: the painting she had done of the soldier.

"Oh, but that isn't one of my father's, is it?" Mrs. Spenser asked, sitting forward in her chair to see better.

"No, I did this when we were together in the sanitarium. I'm convinced that, when Major Roderick allowed me to paint him, he saved my life. And I've always felt horribly guilty for not being able to do the same for him."

"He was handsome, wasn't he?" Mrs. Spenser responded, stepping back to get a better view. "I've never before seen your work in this style. It must be quite valuable—I'd like to buy it from you."

"Absolutely not, Mrs. Spenser. This is a gift. Please don't say another word."

"But—"

"No *but*, Mrs. Spenser! And here's the other painting. This one was done by your father." Nico, whose busy tongue had gone on a holiday, unwrapped the second one; the dark, stormy oil with the cut-out hole where the eye used to be.

"Oh, please!" Mrs. Spenser said. "Are you sure he did this?"

"Absolutely sure," Sophie replied, "and here's the last piece." She unwrapped the cheerful and radiant pencil drawing she had kept for all those years.

"Nico, please hand me the painting. Now—watch. When he died," Sophie said, leaning toward Mrs. Spenser, "this drawing was taped on the back, showing through the hole. It was the way he wanted to be remembered."

"Oh, I so wish my mother were alive," Mrs. Spenser said. "If she could have seen this painting, especially the drawing, I think she would have been relieved. I've always felt that his act of suicide was his way of not burdening us. But, if a man can draw a likeness like that, only hours before he takes his own life, then—"

"Maybe if I had brought these paintings to you sooner, your mother's mind would have been made easier. I'm frightfully sorry for this—"

"Oh, but there's no reason for you to apologize. How in the world would you ever have known? I have to apologize to *you* for burdening you with my thoughts. No, Miss Marks," she continued earnestly, "it's better that my mother didn't see them. You see, years later, after the grief had faded and she had remarried, she told me that she had planned to go to the sanitarium to meet you and collect his belongings. But because of his letters she suspected there had been an affair between you and my father and she simply couldn't face knowing."

Sophie sensed Nico's head swivel toward her. She felt a hot-pink flush, beginning at the bottom of her neck and rising to her cheeks.

"Please have another cup of tea," Mrs. Spenser invited, obviously wanting to change the subject.

"Thank you, but no, we must go."

"Wait one moment," Mrs. Spenser said. "I won't be but a minute." And she hurried up the stairs.

She returned with Eli's painting under her arm. "You must take this, Miss Marks, as a gift from me. You've given me back part of my life; I want to do the same for you. Here, your son can carry it for you, it's a little heavy."

Neither of them corrected her.

The next morning, Leland drove down from London to take them all the way back to the airport. "I want to do this for you, Sophie. It's my pleasure," he declared.

Leland's glasses were no longer black-framed; now they were sleek, brushed silver, Italian. He was so fashion conscious you could make a timeline of contemporary European taste by noting his clothing and hairstyles, Sophie thought.

When they arrived at the airport, Sophie said, "Leland, did you bring the painting?"

"What painting?" Nico asked.

"Why, the one of your father," Sophie said.

Leland unwrapped Luca's portrait and handed it to Nico. Nico studied it for a long time. "Sophie, it's remarkable. And it's not been aged."

"For some reason I just couldn't bury him," Sophie said. "Since my family had been so violently entombed, it made sense to bury the paintings of people I loved. The world could not keep them safe, so maybe the earth could. But I do have to admit that Luca's painting was another issue. There must have been a part of me that was hoping for a better ending to our story."

*I hope with all my heart
that there will be painting in heaven.*
—Jean-Baptiste-Camille Corot

The word "yes" was spoken and Sophie landed in Rome. Clinging to Nico's hand, as if she were going to drown, she swore, "Good God, I never want to do this again."

"But only a few minutes ago," Nico reminded her, "you said you were having such a good time."

"Yes, as long as the plane's steady and I can calmly watch the clouds. Then I'm fine. But the bumps; and the taking off, and the landing? No, it's a once-in-a-lifetime event for me, thank you very much."

They walked through opaque glass doors into Italy. Sophie was looking for Luca. "Where is he?" she asked, becoming worried. Then she realized that she was searching for the face of the young Luca. Nico's voice raised an octave. "Sophie, he's right in front of you. Can't you see?" And they embraced while Nico looked on like a proud parent.

"No, I want to sit in the back with Sophie," Luca said as they were getting in the car at the airport. "Pretend you're a chauffeur, Nico."

"As you wish," he airily replied. "I've escorted Sophie halfway around the world. Another hundred and forty miles will be easy."

They drove over the mountains. Below, the velvety, tawny hills were visible through the fog. "Sophie," she heard through her daydreams, "we're almost there."

As they turned left onto a smaller road, she felt she was

traveling back in time. Everything looked the same. Through the fog, drifting with a slight breeze around the hills, she recognized the undulating green winter-wheat fields, the square-cut stone houses and their red-tile roofs, the bare, wintry grapevines, the pearly-gray olive trees, and the rows of cypresses pointing to the heavens. Her new world was poised before a brushstroke of misty magenta, announcing that the sun was going behind the day.

And then they approached the blue-painted apricot trees leading to the house. "Why, Luca," Sophie said, "they're still here! How lovely," and then she remembered that their baby was buried there.

"Oh, I had forgotten that part—"

She changed the subject. "But something's different, what is it?"

"We put in a track from my house, so I wouldn't have to make that complicated loop on the main road to get here," Nico said.

"I keep forgetting that you live in another house. I'm so used to your being around that I can't imagine your not being here."

"Oh, don't worry," he replied, amused. "I'm here more than not. Remember, it's Luca who's the great cook."

Sophie was nervous. She was going to be alone with Luca. Stone the crows, as Anne would say; what had she done?

At the end of the road, ethereal in the mist, was the house, as beautiful as ever. Rather than looking as if it was built on top of the land, it appeared to have sprouted from it. Its rosy and fawn-colored stones reflected the moistly tinted setting sun. There was a solemn loveliness about it. Nothing appeared to be very different. Terra-cotta pots were scattered here and there, waiting to be planted with herbs and geraniums in the spring. The wisteria had grown up the side of the kitchen and across the second-story eaves, looking as ancient and gnarled as a complicated ink-and-colored-chalk drawing from the sixteenth century. As the swallows were crying plaintively, a number of tabby cats, all resembling Giglio, scampered away from the car.

"Generations of Giglios," Luca smiled. "Since I don't have the heart to alter them, I haven't individually named them either. They all answer to Giglio."

They sat in the car while Nico unloaded the trunk. "Why are you still sitting there? Don't you want to go in?"

"Actually," Sophie said, "I don't know if I do."

"Look, you two," Nico said as he opened her door, "let's get on with it. You're acting like stubborn children!"

Reluctantly, the elderly couple, stiff from sitting for more than three hours, hobbled to the door. "See, that wasn't so bad, was it?" Nico teased.

It was Luca who brought the curious situation into the light as they were standing awkwardly in the kitchen entrance, not quite in and not quite out. "It's been twenty-eight years, Nico, since Sophie's been here. A very long time. I think it's a good idea if you go home and let us muddle through this alone."

"I think that's an incredibly good idea," Nico said, relieved. "I'll take her bags upstairs and then I'll be gone."

Which bedroom? What on earth was she doing there? She was feeling dizzy. Well, you silly old goat, she said to herself, you haven't eaten for hours. "I need to sit down," she said, and they both surged inside like a tide finding the shore.

"Are you all right?" Luca asked, helping her to a chair.

"Yes, but I realize that I'm starving—"

"Hell! I forgot to feed you," Nico said as he came back down the stairs—and they all laughed.

"Go home, Nico," said Luca.

He was out the door, with a dramatic "*Ciao, Papà! Ciao, Sophie!*"

"Don't worry, Sophie," Luca reassured her. "You'll sleep in our old room. I've moved my things to the spare room. No," he protested, raising his hands, anticipating her objection. "I want you to wake to the view you've always loved. I'm just as nervous as you are about the bedroom question.

"Oh, and you should know that all your painted rugs on the upstairs floors are still there but have grown very, very faint with time."

"How lovely. I thought you would get rid of them, Luca," she said, and he smiled and shook his head.

The kitchen was almost the same; the long wooden table and two benches were there, but the ancient stone sink had been replaced with a modern metal one. Sophie immediately noticed the glazed-blue Majorcan ceramic bowl. It was overflowing with light-green and white bulbs of fennel, zucchini, gray-green globe artichokes, smoky greengages, and deep-purple, almost black eggplants. "Have you always kept such a beautiful bowl of vegetables on the table? It's exquisite."

"Not really," he answered. "Just when I'm trying to impress. Now, how about a glass of wine made from our very own grapes?" And they both rested, snacking on bread sprinkled with olive oil, coarse salt, and chunks of pecorino cheese.

"I wonder," Sophie asked, "why Italian food tastes so much better here than in another country? I always use Italian ingredients and cook them as I did here, but it's never the same."

"It's not the food," Luca declared. "It's the 'gold air,' as Rossetti wrote."

Silence. Sophie took another sip of wine.

"For some reason, I feel irritable."

"I know. I can tell. I remember," Luca said with a tinge of humor, and sat back, leaning against the wall.

"I'm happy to be here, Luca. Really I am. But I'm still giving refuge to old resentments. They're so old that they're sepia-colored. I know it's nonsensical. I'm sorry. But they sit here," and she pointed between her breasts, "like a ball of hardened clay.

"It's so sad," she said. "All that lost time. I knew that I could have stayed with you, Luca. I knew you would have made arrangements to have Nico as much as possible and remain here with me. And I have to confess that I presumed you were unhappy with Adele. I thought your having to stay with her was your just punishment.

"I wanted revenge. No, that's not all true, dear," Sophie said, taking his hand as he moved to sit beside her. "I think at the beginning, I punished you because you were a symbol of my lost grandparents—and André—all the people who left me alone. You took the brunt of my sorrow.

"I hadn't counted on your loving Adele. When I under-stood this truth from Nico, I became even more confused. I'm sorry for being so difficult."

"Sophie, I understand. I do. I only hope that your being home for a while will smooth it all away. You know how much—"

"I know," she interrupted. "I do know. But knowing and feeling are sometimes difficult to reconcile. Dear Luca, I just can't seem to get over the habit of worrying."

Luca put his elbows on the table and leaned forward. "Sophie," he said kindly, "let us stop apologizing to each other for past wrongs."

Later, standing at the window, Sophie marveled at how the evening sky could be such a soft veil of blue, yet sprinkled with an almost garish glistening gold. I'll always be a stranger in this land, she thought. But being here is as close as I'll get to home.

Sophie was up early. She had tidied up from the evening meal and found herself irritated with Luca's messy ways. Drawers not quite shut. Dirty dishes left in the sink with old food swimming in disgusting water. Oh, Sophie, get yourself unknotted, she told herself. Life is but a parcel of moments. It will not hurt to close the drawers yourself, nor wash the dishes; it is not a competition for perfection.

Later, she sat with her bare feet up on a chair, drinking a cup of tea, sketching on a paper napkin with the stub of a pencil. She had not heard Luca; she was lost in reverie with a cat curled into her lap.

"Oh, Luca, you startled me, good morning."

"What's the matter?" he asked. "You look as if you've been crying."

"It's nothing to worry about," she assured him. "They're simply tears of relief. I had a dream last night that unhinged me—and at the same time, excited me.

"I dreamt about a raging river of grief. It made me sad. And I do know what the dream means," she said, and took a deep breath. "At first I had a strange response. I didn't want the river of tears to go away. It had become part of me. I watched the grief hurtle itself over rocks and broken tree branches. And there I stood—naked, exposed; the wind hurting my bare skin; the sunlight blinding me.

'When I woke, I was so clear-headed that I felt I could see across the rest of time."

"Stand up, dear, please," Luca said, "so I can embrace you."

"It will be a task," she laughed. "I've been afraid to move and disturb this sweet cat for well over an hour."

Luca lifted the warm and relaxed cat and helped Sophie up. They embraced. And it felt incredibly good. She could feel his body through the thin silk. He could feel her body still fitting against his. They both sensed not only old love, but a slightly pink brushstroke of passion.

"Here," Sophie said, moving away and closing the gaping gown over her breasts, "let me get you something to eat."

"No, no, Sophie, I'll do it. Just like the old days. You sit down and I'll prepare coffee. How about a *caffè corretto,* with this delicious grappa?"

She watched him move about the kitchen. He was still a handsome man. In some ways, aging had made him more so. Although he listed slightly to one side, his body appeared fit, not fragile. His face, now softer, even a bit jowly, was dramatic in its cragginess. Bridged by silver, untamed eyebrows, Luca's eyes retained the intensity of his youth. But when caught unaware, his eyes reflected the deep-pooled and complicated story that only age can create.

The morning's light was again obscured by fog. The world was quiet. After breakfast, her hand in his, they walked to his studio. "Everything's the same, but isn't," Sophie said in a whisper, honoring the silence. "I know that cherry tree, but it has grown so much taller. I know those grapevines," and she pointed between the house and the studio, "but their scribbles are now drawn with a big fat brush, rather than a thin one. Even standing here with you, everything feels like *déjà vu*, rather than a clear memory. What does it seem like to you?" she asked, turning to him.

"As if Sisyphus finally found a foothold and was able to roll the boulder to the top of the mountain." And they smiled at each other and walked on.

"It's so quiet."

"It's Sunday, dear," Luca reminded her.

"For goodness sakes! Of course. I hope I'm not losing my memory, just as I arrive in Italy."

"Keep asking all your interminably complicated questions, Sophie," he said, laughing. "It will exercise your brain."

Luca had quadrupled the size of his studio. There were chain hoists and blocks and tackle hanging from the steel beams that were at least twenty feet off the floor. Parked in the corner of the new addition was a large forklift, and next to it a crane. Two mammoth steel sculptures (obviously works-in-progress), at least fifteen feet high, were inside on the cement pad. There was another large sculpture installed in the field. Luca's work had changed considerably in one way, and very little in another. He still used raw steel, preferring to let the surface rust and corrode and be eaten by time. His abstract forms were larger than life. But instead of outsized, flat surfaces of rusted steel, patinated either by nature or by applied chemicals, now there were faint interruptions in the surfaces. Plates of steel, copper, and aluminum had been installed using grommets and welds. The plates were all sizes; however, none of them looked like a patch, nor did any of them look out of place. They were craftily integrated into the skin of the larger forms. When she got up close, she could see that each plate was delicately engraved with abstract, flowing lines.

"I'm stunned by the beauty of it all," Sophie declared honestly. "Tell me about the plates."

"It's simple," Luca explained. "I'm too old to be climbing around on these giants, yet I'm still enthralled with their forms and mass. I can't imagine making them smaller. And to be honest," he said, turning to her and throwing up his arms, "I'd like to make them even bigger.

"By accident, I came across the idea of the plates. I'd made a calculation error in a sculpture. But it wasn't until we were doing the installation that the error was discovered. After much mulling, I realized that if I added a steel plate at the junction of two of the pieces, like this," and he showed her by reaching up with the end of a broom and pointing to an engraved plate, "the entire structure would have the necessary mechanical integrity—and, I hoped, still be beautiful and speak for me.

"That error helped me see how I could carry on making art

into my old age, using assistants for the heavy work, of course. And see Sophie, look here." He showed her various plates on his workbench.

"I understand the mechanical reasoning, Luca, but not the philosophical one."

"The answer's simple. The plates, or links, as I refer to them, represent how we all search for ways to stay together as couples, as families, as communities, even if we are scattered emotionally, even geographically. My work has always been for groups of people—that's why it's primarily in public spaces."

While Luca was talking, he was also watching them in a mirror on the studio wall. It was remarkable, he thought, we really are shorter. Look at us in our old farm boots. If I was wearing an apron and a floppy Italian beret, and Sophie had on a straw hat, we would be mistaken for elderly farmers, visiting from down the road. And in a sense, he supposed, that is what we really are: harvesters of art.

"What's that noise?" Sophie asked, nodding toward the west.

"It's Nico, already at work. I wonder if he's unpacked. Probably not, I suspect. He tends to be even more untidy than I!" And Sophie had to grin at the similarity between father and son.

As they were leaving the studio, Sophie noticed his office in one corner. Along with a comfortable brown leather chair and ottoman, there was a poorly made-up old army cot with old and liverish-looking pillows. Under the window was a long wooden tabletop balanced on sawhorses; on the table were his black sketchbooks, tidily stacked with little pieces of paper sticking out here and there.

"My goodness, Luca," she exclaimed. "What are you planning to do with those?"

"Burn them!" he growled.

"Oh, but you can't do that."

"Oh, yes, I can. But first I have to go through every damn one of them and save the pages with my drawings. The project got started when I couldn't keep my mouth quiet and I told Nico what I was going to do. He had the same response as you."

Luca's voice raised another decibel. "I don't want people reading my whining—my inane ideas—my grappling with losing you—Adele's death—my spewing of bitterness toward the world—my searching for some meaning, my—"

"Never mind," Sophie said. "Sorry I asked."

"It's all right, Sophie. I just don't like having to go through them page by page. It's boring and upsetting at the same time. But I promised Nico, and I do understand that they may be valuable for my estate, which means for Nico and his imaginary family. But I have to force myself to sit down and work. I've only finished five books, with at least twenty more to do. At my age, I could topple over any day, and can just see myself moaning over what you and Nico would read, rather than enjoying the moment of death."

They walked down the old dirt path to the first row of grapevines. Sophie could see that before each row was a rosebush, each just beginning to form new leaves. "They can't be the same rosebushes, can they?"

"Actually, many of them are. Even some of your English tea roses have survived all these years. It proves how healthy this soil is. Ever since that 1950 heat wave, there's hardly ever been an unhealthy rosebush, and, consequently, no unhealthy grapes."

Although the ground was soaked, they waded unconcerned through the puddles. They skirted the grove to the left and continued on a path until they came to a stone wall.

"This is new, isn't it?" Sophie asked, seeing a newly built wall with a blue gate between two feathery yellow-grassed hills.

"Yes, come this way," Luca said.

Nico had built the wall four years earlier, during a summer of disquiet. At that time, Luca assumed that Nico wanted to be a painter. He had already deeded him Signore Pasquale's house to live in and the barn to use as a studio. But Nico was uncertain. Luca knew Nico was afraid of imitating him. His son was simply too young, and did not yet have the clarity to separate his own aesthetic from his father's. He needed time away from Italy. Away from Luca. It was not until he visited Sophie in America that he allowed to himself that he was an artist—and a sculptor at that.

But he had already built the wall, and without an opening. If Luca wanted to visit him, he had to climb over the wall or walk all the way around on the new track. Luca had to admit that it became tiresome to visit his son. As a result, he saw him less and less, understanding that that was what Nico had intended.

"Then one day last spring, I heard the sound of rocks being piled upon one another and walked out to see what was going on. Nico had made an opening in the wall. 'It's for you, *Papà*,' he said.

"By the end of the next day he'd installed a solid door, hinges and all. He painted it turquoise blue as he had seen in the desert, assuring me that the color would keep away the evil eye. 'I learned this from Sophie,' he told me. Now I understood that Nico was inviting me into his life again, more as a fellow artist and less as his overbearing father."

Sophie and Luca walked through the door. As they drew closer, they heard strains of Italian pop music. By the time they reached the studio, drums vibrated through the trunks of the olive trees; electric guitars sang off the ends of the branches.

"I'm up here," they heard Nico yell, and there he was, balancing on the branch of a tree.

"What are you doing?" Luca shouted above the music.

"Hold on," he hollered, and jumped down.

"I'm installing a bird feeder," and he disappeared to turn off the radio.

"My goodness, it's like the end of torture, isn't it?" Sophie marveled to Luca.

Sophie thought Nico handsome, sitting there in the barn that had been converted into his studio. He was thirty-one years old. He was not so thin as he had been in America. His face, although still craggy like his father's, had filled in just enough to age him well. Luca said that he had a bevy of girlfriends and Sophie could see why.

"—for instance," Nico said, breaking into her musing, "I began to pay more attention to natural things, like mountains. I learned that mountains get softer, rounder with age. The more jagged, the younger they are. All of this I find fascinating and—"

Oh, dear, Sophie thought. I have totally lost the gist of our conversation. "But what does that have to do with making art?" Luca asked.

"Primarily, it has to do with the idea of enduring," he answered. "Come look in the other room and I'll show you the work."

"I love how everything smells," Sophie said. "Old memories of cows, wood, sawdust. It's heavenly."

Nico's sculpture was like Luca's old work in one way, and, in another, entirely different. Luca had originally carved people from trees; now Nico used trees to construct nonobjective sculptures. The idea for his work came from a boyhood visit to Venice. Luca had taken him to one of the outlying islands to watch artisans constructing gondolas. Nico was more impressed with the ancient walnut pilings lying around outside the workshops. A craftsman explained to him that the wood was found at the far edge of the city, most likely from the foundations of crumbled buildings. The idea that untold thousands of pieces of wood were holding up the city of Venice never left him. When he was in the American desert, he was fascinated by the Petrified Forest. It reminded him of Venice, but in reverse.

Later, after he had returned home, he began to wonder about nature being able to preserve itself over eons of time. Could he make art that would explore the mystery of such timelessness?

At first Sophie was put off by the work. She found it awkward. What Nico had done was to take tree trunks, eight to ten feet tall by about four feet in diameter, and immerse them in old wooden wine vats filled with highly salted water, imitating Venice. At the bottom of each barrel was a coned piece of steel that put pressure in the center of the trunk, but allowed the area around it to be slightly suspended. Then he positioned heavy chunks of steel on top of the tree trunks. As the water was absorbed by the wood, the weight of the steel pieces forced the bottom of the trunks to splay. Of course, in Venice, enormous palaces of stone were constructed, balanced on wood pilings. Nico, understanding the premise, placed his weights asunder, purposely unbalanced.

"Once they've splayed," Nico explained, "I drain the water into an empty vat, take apart the original vat, and then let the trunk dry, still with the steel on top. Sometimes I install a steel band around the trunk if I think it will both look good and act as a stabilizer. Then I move the piece out into the sun. Come out back and I'll show you."

At the back of his studio was a hay barn. It had a red-tiled roof, five brick columns (one in the middle), and no walls, and it was sparsely filled with the sculptures. Now that Sophie could see them in a spacious setting, she was relieved to be able to reconsider her first impression. The bark had been carefully stripped from all the trees, leaving the exposed wood with the look of skin, worn by age. Nico had sanded and smoothed the wood, both on the surface and within the crevices. However, he had left all the traces of time: the footpaths of worms and insects; the knots and gnarls of former tree diseases; the empty spaces left by interior contracting or dying wood. All of these natural time-tracks were enhanced with a Vandyke brown stain, delicately rubbed in with whispers of burnt carmine here and there.

Sophie began to walk around one of the pieces, smoothing it with her hands, exploring it. And then, as if by fate, the sun appeared. All of a sudden she could see shadows: forms made by the want of light, and conversely, forms accentuated by the light. "What a thrilling body of work, Nico. Why, Nico, you're crying. What's wrong?"

"Oh, nothing's wrong at all, Sophie," he said, both crying and laughing. "It's just that I wanted so badly for you to be here and to see my work and to like it."

When she looked over at Luca, he was obviously moved as well. Now she understood that both she and Luca had just barely, imperceptibly, caught fleeing time by the tip of its tail. It was love. Her heart was beating like the wings of a butterfly; her body was tingling with millions of tiny lights. If she were to die now, it would be perfectly lovely.

They heard thunder and the sun became dimmer. "Come, I'll drive you back," Nico offered. "I think it's going to rain. And perhaps Luca will make us lunch."

"I'll do anything anyone asks," Luca said, laughing and taking out his blue handkerchief to wipe his eyes. "Here, Nico, this corner is clean," he offered.

Nico helped them into his battered green van with the bumper sticker that read **Make Art, Not War**. Off they drove in a wide and circular path, home.

"All right, you two, entertain yourselves," Luca instructed. "I'm going to cook us a feast."

"I'll be down in a minute, Nico. I need something upstairs." Sophie had to have a think. Concern was still gnawing at her and she was tired of it. Perhaps, if she could catch the wind of anger enough times, she could finally make it blow away and leave her in peace.

She leaned against the frame and looked out at the hills. There were many cranky predicaments to be resolved. The bedroom dilemma, meeting old friends, getting back to work, finding a new doctor; and then, and then. It was enough fretting; she scolded, it was enough.

"All right, I'm ready to see my studio," she announced to Nico. "Let's go."

He opened the familiar door that was now the same blue as his stone-wall gate. The tile floor was glistening clean. Nico and Luca had painted the studio a soft white, almost an alabaster. The frames of the windows were newly painted with the magical blue; the room smelled like a forgotten dream, and poked at Sophie's consciousness.

"Here's the surprise," and Nico yanked an army-green tarp off a chair. "It's not your favorite chair from Paris, I know. But Luca found it for you."

"I bet it's more comfortable," Sophie said with pleasure. "The other one had sunk so far toward the floor that I could hardly get out. It's a wonderful chair, Nico. The whole room's wonderful. Thank you. I have to sit down, dear."

Nico turned to help. "No, no, Nico, you must let me do everything on my own. Otherwise I'll begin to feel that I'm merely an ancient cloth doll being posed and moved around."

Spring waltzed into Umbria. The air was soft and inviting. All

Sophie wanted was to be outside. After an unproductive struggle in her studio, she chose to sit in blissful nostalgia on the stone bench in the sun and smell the memories. Around her the cats lazily bathed themselves, occasionally chasing bright-green lizards or imaginary shadows.

The old cypresses lining the road leading to the house had changed color. The bleak, shadowy crevices between the limbs no longer reminded her of Vincent van Gogh's painterly allusions to madness. And the memorable blood-red poppies, those same Flanders poppies, were sprinkled everywhere. But Sophie no longer saw them as puddles of blood, but as luscious brushstrokes of a miraculous Mother Nature. They were vividly scattered among the brilliant blue of cornflowers and the tall, almost dazzling green stalks of new wheat. The landscape positively shimmered with a painter's palette.

On the day it rained on Sophie's sun-warmed reveries, she returned to work. Between the blanket of water and the intimacy of her studio, she felt encapsulated, safe from everything but her resistant self. It was always such a battle to get started. She groused about. She would never do another portrait; she was no longer interested in seeing her life through her subjects. No. Now was the last chance to travel in her imagination. Listening to Strauss, she was stirred by its exquisiteness, by its facility to embody the waltzes of the human heart. Sophie consciously moved her hand across the paper, keeping time with the symphony. When the music stopped, she had drawn the melody; she had truly seen the music.

A letter arrived for Sophie. "It's from Stoke-on-Trent," Luca said. "It must be from Anne."

But as soon as Sophie saw the handwriting, she knew it was not Anne's.

Dear Miss Marks, it said in a scratchy blue script on a barrister's letterhead. *I'm sorry to inform you that your friend, Mrs. Anne Sutton, has passed away. She fell, and, although she didn't break anything, she was badly bruised and shaken. It was decided to hospitalize her. But the doctor told me that she simply had 'no will to thrive,' and she died within two days. She was buried at the church, alongside her husband and her parents. I know you were best of friends and I'm very sad for you. All the best, Mr. Jack Crawford.*

Sophie went to bed. She simply did not have the energy to continue with the day. Many friends had died in the past, but Anne was different. She was the last remaining link to the Midlands—to her grandparents—to her youth.

"Do you want a cup of tea?" Luca asked.

"No, you, Luca, I want you."

And Luca held her while she wept, his consolation causing her to cry even more.

"Everything's gone, Luca," she said when she had finally cried herself out. "Everything's gone except for what I have here. I am so very fortunate."

Sophie began to work in earnest on the music pieces. She imagined her pencils and brushes as a violin bow, a conductor's baton. Working on smaller sheets of paper, she used the same materials she had used for the nude self-portraits. But now she added colored inks, some transparent, some opaque. Rather than the landscape of her body, she was painting the ethereal nature of music.

Over the next few days, she visually scored Chopin's Concerto No. 1, Opus 10, by painting large and elaborate abstract forms of translucent, veiled Persian blues and mulberry purples. Over these layers came drawn lines: siennas, creamy whites, and unexpected metallic-golden colors, orchestrated by cello strings and ivory keys and silver flutes.

"May I come in?" Luca said. "I would like to see today's work."

"Of course, come in," she said, and they chatted a while about the work.

"You know," Luca said, "this work reminds me of something Miró said. 'I try to apply colors like words that shape poems, like notes that shape music.'"

Sophie worked on visual scores in a format of quartets and quintets, trying to create the illusion of depth by moving color toward the vanishing point. That point, being irresistible to the eye, took the viewer off the edge of the world into a musical universe.

Again, Sophie was completely involved in her work, and loving every moment. She was working at a mad pace and Luca was constantly warning her to slow down. "Don't worry, dear," she would say, laughing, "this work is emerging by magic—I'm hardly doing a thing!"

Leland was thrilled. Every two weeks, one of Luca's assistants would ship off another crate of Sophie's paintings. "These paintings," he said to her on the telephone, "are sending my gallery to the stars."

After she had worked on the music series for a little more than three months, Leland rang. "Are you sitting down, Sophie?" he asked.

"Oh, Leland," she replied, "stop being so dramatic."

"I'm serious, Sophie, sit down."

"Oh no, what happened?" Sophie said, now thinking he was ill or someone dear had died.

"Stop being such an old fuddy-duddy," he said. "We've just sold five pieces of the music series to a consortium of collectors. And they are donating the work to the Tate Modern for its permanent collection."

"Oh, Leland, I *am* glad I'm sitting down."

I'll tell you how the sun rose–
A Ribbon at a time–

—EMILY DICKINSON

S ophie went to bed early. Within a few minutes she dozed off sitting up, her blue plastic-rimmed reading glasses perched on her nose, the light on, a book on her lap.

She woke, having sensed someone at the side of the bed.

"I'm sorry, I was trying not to wake you," Luca, already in his dressing gown, said as he took off her glasses.

"You have such a sweet smile, Luca. Do you want to get married?" The words simply glided over her tongue and tumbled from her mouth.

For a moment, he was speechless. Then a grin was drawn across his face.

"Why, yes—oh, yes I do, indeed! Oh, my dearest Sophie, oh—"

Then there was a pregnant pause.

"Yes, you may," Sophie answered, and lifted the covers, inviting Luca in.

They lay together for a few minutes, nose to nose, smiling— at a loss for how to begin.

"May I take out your braid?"

"Oh, Luca, my hair's much thinner; I'll look like a witch."

"Ssh, dear. You're being silly. Here," he said, patting the bed. "Sit up and turn around." As Luca settled himself behind Sophie, he began.

Without talking, with Luca unbraiding her hair gently, they entered a floating and unfettered time. Each segment of the plait he unwound seemed to unchain another year they had lost. When Luca finished, he reached around, brushing against her breasts as he began to unbutton a complicated gown.

And Sophie—well, Sophie was flushed with such a surprising, almost aching, passion that, at last, time stood still.

She felt Luca's warm breath on her neck and heard him quietly say, "All these clothes. Remember how we used to sleep nude?"

"Yes," she purred with pleasure, "and how we would wear our nightclothes if we were angry at each other?"

"You're not angry now, are you?" he said, gently turning her around, her gown open, her breasts and belly exposed.

"No, and you aren't either, are you?" Sophie said, as she slowly unbuttoned his shirt and slipped it off his shoulders. Then, ever so gently, she reached down between the cloth and his stomach.

"It's not the same as it was," he whispered again. "It takes longer."

"I like that." And Sophie sighed. "We have all the time in the world."

ABOUT THE AUTHOR

Michele Zackheim is the author of the novel
Violette's Embrace, based on the life of the
writer Violette Leduc. *Einstein's Daughter: The
Search for Lieserl* is her non-fiction account of
the search for Einstein's missing daughter. She is
also a visual artist who has shown in numerous
museums and galleries in Europe and the
United States. She lives with her husband, the
sculptor Charles Ramsburg, in New York City.